THE
GIRL
WHO
WASN'T
THERE

ALSO BY VINCENT ZANDRI

The Remains

The Ashes

The Scream Catcher

When Shadows Come

Everything Burns

Orchard Grove

The Detonator

The Caretaker's Wife

Deadly is the Night

The Chase Baker Action Adventure Series

The Sam Savage Air Marshal Action Adventure Series

The Dick Moonlight PI Series

The Jack "Keeper" Marconi PI Series

The Steve Jobz PI Series

For more books, novellas, nonfiction titles,
short stories and more, go to www.vincentzandri.com

THE GIRL WHO WASN'T THERE

VINCENT ZANDRI

OCEANVIEW PUBLISHING
SARASOTA, FLORIDA

The author is represented by MacGregor Literary, Inc

ISBN 978-1-60809-396-0

Published in the United States of America by Oceanview Publishing

Sarasota, Florida

www.oceanviewpub.com

10 9 8 7 6 5 4 3 2 1

PRINTED IN THE UNITED STATES OF AMERICA

*"Dreams are true while they last,
and do we not live in dreams?"*
—ALFRED LORD TENNYSON

CHAPTER 1

Lake Placid, NY

It's good to be home again.

And I'm lucky to be alive, having survived a ten-year stint in an upstate New York maximum security prison bookended by the Hudson River on one side and a magnificent forest on the other. You know the kind, with the tall concrete walls, the razor wire barriers, the guard houses manned by corrections officers armed with M16s, and a curious metal banner mounted above the main entrance that reads "There but for the grace of God go I." As though God had anything to do with my being incarcerated for a quadruple homicide I did not commit.

But being home again is like a dream come true.

Truth be told, however, I'm not really sure I know what home is anymore. The house my wife, Penny, and I bought together in North Albany was sold off to help pay for my legal expenses. My belongings, what was left of them, were stuffed into boxes when she had no choice but to move into a one-bedroom apartment, which she shared with our daughter. Then, when she was forced to move into a studio apartment, my boxed belongings were transferred to a mobile storage unit on the south side of the city.

From what Penny tells me, she hasn't visited the storage unit in some time, but that we can go there as soon as we get back from our first weekend away together as a family in more than a decade.

Right now . . . right this very second . . . I have Penny and I have Chloe, and they are my home. My home-sweet-home. For the first time in ten years, I'm free, paroled for good if I keep my *nose clean*, as the rednecks like to say. I've got my girls back, and it's a beautiful day up in the Adirondacks. The lake is clean and cold, the sand white and soft underfoot, the air warm, and the sky bright. A beautiful summer day. Like I said, my new lease on life . . . it's a sweet dream come true.

I mean, what more could a wrongly imprisoned ex-con want?

*　　*　　*

The little beach that overlooks Mirror Lake, the smaller lake that adjoins the much larger Lake Placid to the north, is owned by the hotel we're staying at for a few days. We had to break the bank to afford it, but when you've been away from your family for ten years, you'll do anything for a little time away from it all. Anything short of breaking the law, that is.

Like the name suggests, the very still, very clear glass-like lake truly mimics a mirror. I stand in the cool shallow waters, only my feet submerged. I stare at the reflection of my face. A somewhat distorted reflection. But I can still make out the scruffy face, the short hair, the dark brown eyes masked by sunglasses. I see me, or someone who looks like me.

But the mirror reflects more than just my face.

It reflects the memories. The bad ones.

You know, the big black Suburban I drove to the house lived in by a Chinese family who owed my boss, Mickey Rabuffo, too much money. Money they could never hope to pay back in this lifetime or the next. I look into the water and see me, the driver. I see myself sitting behind the wheel of the SUV, while the two men the boss entrusted to collect the money head inside the house in the middle of the night. What could be more frightening than a home invasion in the middle of the night?

I see myself waiting behind the wheel, the 5.7 Liter V8 engine idling, heart pounding in my chest, knowing that at any moment a police cruiser could come around the corner.

Then came disaster—like my gut told me it would.

Muzzle flashes that lit up the windows like bolts of lightning, and I knew in my sinking heart that the Chinese family did not have the money. That they never had the damned money. That they never had a chance.

I was just the driver, but when that family died that night, my soul died along with them.

*   *   *

So we've come to Lake Placid. The lake of calm. The lake of peace and tranquility. It's our escape from Albany. Escape from our past.

Or perhaps I should put it another way. Because maybe Penny wants to escape ten years of loneliness. Of nights all alone, of empty bank accounts, of not knowing if her next paycheck is going to be enough. Not knowing if the man who knocks on the door will be informing her of the tragic death of her husband inside one of the most dangerous maximum security prisons in the country.

As for me, I needed the escape from the gangbangers, the killers, the rapists, the Aryans, the radical Muslims, the foul stench, the constant fear of looking over my shoulder knowing that, at any time, Rabuffo could send someone in after me. To silence me, once and forever.

I was the last man standing that horrible night.

The others—the assassins—had been two old high school pals by the names of Singh and Wemps. But I never recognized who they'd become as adults. Perhaps it was a blessing they'd been *killed by cops* when they reemerged from the house, their semi-automatics in hand, barrels smoking.

But it ended up being me who took the entire wrap for murders I did not commit. The hell of it is, I never revealed the truth. Not once. But then, that's not right, either. It doesn't mean I didn't say something I shouldn't have during the exhausting and punishing thirty-six hours of interviews with the Albany Police Department in the wake of the brutal Chen family murder, all four of them found dead in their beds, the victims of execution-style murders. Nine-millimeter rounds to the back of the skull, directly above the external occipital protuberance, to be specific.

It doesn't mean I didn't bring up the name Rabuffo on several occasions. Didn't bring up the names of my old pals, Wemps and Singh, the former a tall blond cokehead devil, and the latter, a stocky dark-haired weightlifting son of Satan.

Lack of sleep will do that to a man, especially during a prolonged police interrogation, when life becomes a living nightmare. My pre-med studies in Human Behavior—which I enjoyed far more than calculus or bio chem—defined the symptoms of sleep deprivation as disorientation, paranoia, difficulty concentrating, and even hallucinations. Symptoms also included impaired judgment, memory problems, and just good old-fashioned diarrhea of the mouth. It's this last bit the cops tried to take advantage of.

I repeat, I was the last man standing, and I never told anyone in law enforcement anything that would endanger the liberty of my fellow employees with the Rabuffo organization. Rather, never *purposely* spilled the beans. At least, I don't remember saying anything to anyone about who was behind the killing. About who reigned as the big boss behind the entire illegal Chinese smuggling operation in Albany, New York.

Rabuffo . . .

I never said a word to nobody, if you'll pardon the double negative.

That's what I keep telling myself. Been telling myself for more years than I care to count. Or let's put it another way, I didn't say a word to anyone acting in an official law enforcement capacity, until ten years later when I was offered the deal of the century. That's when I sang not like a bird—if you'll pardon the cliché— but instead, like Luciano Pavarotti, may God rest his soul.

* * *

The water looks so inviting I could just drink it all up.

But for now, I head back up onto the beach and sit in my beach chair, my sunglass-covered eyes focused on my eleven-year-old daughter while she wades in the lake, careful not to go in over her head, nor over her waist seeing as her iPod is stuffed in her bathing suit bottoms. She's wearing a teeny-weeny yellow polka dot bikini, just like the old song says. It's exactly how she put it to me in her singsong voice early this morning when she came out of the bathroom sporting the brand-new two-piece.

"Sooo, what do you think, Doc?" she said, one eye in the wall-mounted mirror, the other on me. I was lying in bed beside her mother. Something that was new to her. As new as having her father around, a mythical, almost storybook character who resided behind concrete castle walls, up until now.

"I love it," I said. But as a dad, even one just getting to know his daughter, I might have preferred something less revealing.

"There's even room for my iPod," she added, sliding the device into the bottoms.

"No iPod in the water, little lady," Penny warned. "That's our second iPod in two months already, and God knows I could not afford the first one. Which means, you destroy this one, there won't be another."

"Don't worry, Mom," Chloe said. "I'm taking good care of it. Unless you want to buy me an iPhone, which makes a lot more sense. That way you can call or text me whenever you want. It's for my safety. Right, Doc?"

"Your father is not *Doc*," Penny said, giving my hand a squeeze under the covers. "It's dad, silly. And no, you will *not* get an iPhone until high school. We've been over this before, young lady."

Penny looked at me over her shoulder, her neck-length brunette hair mussed, her smooth face healthy and radiant, her brown eyes hopeful, even after all she'd been through. My long absence. It was a strange feeling being physically beside her again when, for so many years, I could only imagine what it would feel like. I could only dream. I could only live in my dreams.

When you're doing twenty-five to life for a brutal multiple homicide, you begin to lose hope that you'll ever smell fresh air again, much less lie beside the one woman you love more than any other. You don't pinch yourself. You kick yourself again and again. You pound your head against the concrete block wall. You picture yourself holding her in your arms once more.

You ask yourself, *Is this real? Or am I dreaming it?*

For a hopelessly incarcerated man, dream reality can be as real as tangible reality.

I spot Penny walking toward me from the opposite side of the small beach. She's carrying two bottles of beer. One in each hand. When she arrives, she sets them down on the small white table set beside our beach chairs. The beers are Dos Equis and lime wedges are shoved into the bottlenecks. The beers are sweating in the hot midday sun. They look cold and refreshing, like heaven in a bottle.

"Wow, beer," I say, my mouth watering. "It's been too damned long."

"I brought you a cooler full," she says.

Just the simple act of Penny sitting down makes my heart beat faster, the blood flow through my veins and arteries more rapidly than God and nature intended. My lungs are robbed of oxygen. My skin tingles. Physiologically speaking, she is a study in the science of sexy.

She's wearing a simple black bikini.

It makes her shapely body look like it's been carved from the best Italian marble. Her maiden name is Fannuci, her family originating from Rome many generations ago, so the metaphor is not entirely an exaggeration.

She glances down at my lap. Reaching out, she quickly, but gently, runs her fingers over my midsection.

"Gee, Doc," she says, giggling, "you glad to see me or is that a banana in your swim trunks?"

My face must turn redder than a fire hydrant, the sudden adrenaline and oxygen rush in my system forcing all those little blood vessels to dilate. I glance over both shoulders to make sure no one is watching.

"Tempt me no more, evil harlot. But yeah, let's just say I'm so very happy."

Truth is, while I arrived home from prison five days ago, Penny and I have yet to find the alone time we need to consummate my prodigal return to the family fold. Chloe is ever present, especially when it comes to our sharing a studio apartment and now, a hotel room.

Penny picks up her beer, holds it like she's trying to make a toast.

"To my husband," she says, "and his triumphant return to the land of the living. To the family who loves him to death and beyond."

I grab hold of my beer bottle and clink her bottleneck. Pressing the lime wedge into the bottle with my thumb, I then take a generous swig while keeping my eyes on Penny's or else break the spell of the toast. Coming up for air, I wipe my mouth with the back of my hand.

"That might just be the best beer I have ever tasted in my life."

"Everything should taste better now, Doc," she says, smiling.

Doc—it's the nickname Penny bestowed upon me when we first met and I'd revealed my intention to head back to med school. An aspiration that had fallen by the wayside during my failed marriage to Lauren. In fact, I never made it past the second semester.

Memories come back to haunt me like bad dreams.

The dark night more than ten years ago. Me sitting behind the wheel of the Suburban, Wemps and Singh entering into the Albany bungalow under the cover of darkness. Then, that darkness shattered by the flash of gunshots. Police cruisers pulling up behind me and in front of me. Wemps and Singh shooting it out with them, falling to their deaths on the concrete walkaway leading out to the road . . .

"Maybe you shouldn't call me that anymore, Pen," I say, my eyes drifting back to the lake's edge and Chloe splashing around in the fresh water. She looks so damn happy it's almost painful to watch. I can only hope she doesn't ruin her iPod like her mom warned.

"You still have time, Doc," Penny says. But it's like she doesn't want to let go of the past. The past we had before the murders, that is. A past that, to me anyway, hasn't been tarnished, so much as trampled on, crushed, destroyed.

I place my hand on hers.

"Always the eternal optimist, Pen. I'm fifty years old now. But I love you for that."

"You're not lying just to make me feel good?"

"Hey, Pen, I never stopped loving you. Not even when it got hopeless."

For a moment we look into one another's eyes. Even if we don't pose them to one another, the questions loom large. Like a pack of whales that's suddenly surfaced on Mirror Lake. Questions about loneliness, about fidelity, about staying true to one's husband. How is it possible that a woman as beautiful and sweet as Penny could have managed to remain celibate for ten full years knowing that any hope of my parole was next to impossible? Is it fair for me to even ask the question?

Another gaze at the lake.

Chloe is now out of the water, playing with another girl about her own age in the sand. The girl's parents are seated close by, watching the two kids play. The kids are digging a big hole in the sand with plastic shovels. Their bodies are developing into little women, so it looks almost silly the way they're playing in the sand like preschoolers.

That's what happens when little girls are caught up in that hinterland between child and young adult. The body releases the hormones that stimulate the ovaries that create the estrogen. If only I'd been around to see the little girl. The toddler. The baby.

But just because I wasn't with Chloe or Penny for ten years didn't mean they weren't with me. In my head I was making plans for us. I knew that my getting out of prison one day was a complete long shot. The long shot of long shots. But that reality didn't prevent me from harboring hopes and dreams.

Here's how I lived in dreams: I saw me and my family walking hand in hand on a long stretch of beach so sun-soaked that it hurt our eyes. The water would be blue and crystal clear, the sky brilliant, the breeze cool, and even the natives would be friendly. A place like Cuba, maybe. Far away from America, but not too far. We'd start a new life there of fishing, swimming, playing, loving one another like a real family should. The love would be our bond, our impenetrable shield, the glue that would hold us together.

It was the sweet dream I would fall asleep to most nights.

My hand is still pressing against Penny's. I can feel her pulse throbbing against my skin. I look into her eyes. She's not speaking, but I sense she knows precisely what I'm thinking.

"Our room is on the ground floor," she reminds me in a soft voice. "It's only twenty feet away. We can come and go through the sliding glass doors off the terrace. No one will even know we're gone."

The grin on my face grows into a full-blown smile. I'm finding it hard to swallow. Heart is beating in my throat. What's the technical term for it? Palpitations.

"What are you suggesting, temptress?"

"Shall I spell it out for you, Doc?" she probes. Then, silently mouthing the letters, "S . . . E . . . X."

But something important occurs to me. Something wonderful. Something I've been planning ever since I got out. It was a matter of finding the right time. A time when Penny and I would be alone.

"Pen," I say, sitting up. "You really think we can steal a minute alone?"

"That's what I've been trying to tell you," she presses. "Chloe has a new friend. She's eleven now, Doc. It's okay to leave her alone with a friend for a few minutes." Drinking some of her beer, setting the bottle back down gently onto the table onto its own condensate ring. "If we go now, our beers won't even have the chance to lose their cool."

Together we focus on Chloe.

"I'm game if you're game," I say.

"Let me go tell Chloe we're going to the room to grab my other pair of sunglasses and that you need to use the bathroom."

"Sounds like a plan, Stan."

Penny stands, begins heading down the beach in the direction of the water. Maybe feeling a little self-conscious about playing in the sand like a girl half her age, Chloe smiles shyly when she notices her mother making her way toward her. She stands up straight, wipes the excess sand from her tummy and her yellow polka-dotted back end.

I try to listen to what's being said between mother and daughter, but it's impossible to hear from this distance. It makes me wonder about all the many conversations they've shared together that I've missed out on over the years. The many moments I've not been included in. The many events and holidays that eluded me. The Thanksgivings, the Christmases, the New Years, the Easters.

That's the real tragedy of incarceration.

Not iron bars or concrete walls, but separation from your loved ones. The missing out, the alienation, the way your imagination plays tricks on you. Human nature takes over. You develop a finely tuned imagination. You picture things in full high-def color. Like your wife lying in the arms of another man for example. It's what eats away at you, eats you alive. It's what poisons any semblance of hope you have left, like a metastasized cancer that ravages your brain, your heart, and your soul.

Penny starts back up the beach, looking lovely and sexy in her bikini, her dark hair blowing in the breeze. I stand. She takes me by the hand.

She says, "Let's make this quick, cowboy."

"What I have planned won't take but a minute, fair maiden," I say.

CHAPTER 2

WHEN PENNY AND I enter into the bedroom through the ground level sliding glass doors, closing the wall-length curtain behind us, we feel like teenagers who've snuck out of their respective houses to meet up on the sly. Two youngsters on a first date. At least, that's the way I feel.

But this isn't a first date. We aren't young anymore and Penny is already my wife, even if we haven't shared the same bed in years.

"So what's up that sleeve of yours, Doc?" she asks, standing tall and gorgeous in the room by the newly made bed.

I go to my suitcase, dig inside through the clothes until I feel the plain paper bag. I pull the bag out. Reaching into it, I pull out a metal ring I constructed inside the prison machine shop. It's made from a cheap metal and there's no diamond or stone embedded in it, but it means the world to me. I made it for Penny after she told me she had no choice but to sell her engagement diamond to help pay the bills. My legal bills included. That makes this ring priceless.

I lower myself onto one knee, take her hand in mine, slide the ring onto her marriage finger. Thank God it fits.

"Penny Fanucci," I declare. "Will you marry me again?"

She's smiling, but tears are falling down her smooth cheeks. Gentle tears. Happy tears? Maybe.

"Yes, Doc," she answers with a sniffle. "I . . . am . . . yours."

I stand, take her in my arms, kiss her gently on the mouth, hold her like I'm never letting go. Rather, like I don't want her to let go. Because if I let go, a big bad wind will come and blow me straight back to prison.

*   *   *

When we do finally separate, we find ourselves gazing at one another. It's like we're caught up in a trance. I find myself wanting to ravage Penny. But in truth, I'm not entirely sure how to go about touching her. In prison, if an inmate wants you, and he has enough size and strength, he can pull you into a dark corner and have you bent over in the time it takes you to spit out, *Help me!*

Me . . . I was one of the lucky ones.

I kept my head down, avoided unnecessary eye contact, and by sheer luck, never became the victim. But I'd seen plenty of poor souls who were. Believe me when I say they weren't the same man afterwards. Their souls were ripped out of them at the precise moment the rapist entered into them. It wasn't a pretty sight—the soft tissue lacerations alone can cause significant bleeding, not to mention the emotional scars.

The rapists and the gangbangers left me alone, but I'm not sure it had everything to do with luck. I was known as a killer, after all. It was a reputation I allowed to ferment inside the iron house. Not because I was proud of what I'd done to that family up in Albany—Christ, I was just the *driver* after all—but because it helped me survive.

Being known as a ruthless killer wasn't something I was honored with. But let me tell you something. It gave me hope.

"Come on, Doc," Penny whispers, as she reaches behind her back with both hands, unclasps the top on her bathing suit, allows it to drop to the carpeted floor. "Get in bed while we have a quiet moment alone."

For the record, I'm not so sure this is a good idea. Leaving Chloe alone like that, even if she has made a new friend, the parents of whom are watching over them.

But then I see Penny's pale, naked breasts, her erect nipples, and it's all I can do to catch a breath. I pull the bed cover back exposing fresh white sheets, and I sit myself down, my bathing trunks still on. Shifting myself so that I'm sitting upright in the bed, I watch Penny as she slowly removes her bottoms, allowing them to slip down her smooth legs.

"It's not going to work, Doc, if you keep your suit on," she says.

I don't know why it's happening. The hesitation. Physically speaking, I'm more excited than I've been in my entire life. Hyper hormonal teenage years included. In terms of Penny, it's mission accomplished. Seeing her undress has sent significant chemical messaging to the blood vessels in my penis. The blood's been allowed in and it ain't getting out until the corpora cavernosa flushes it back out. What it wants, in other words, is to get laid.

But I'm hesitating.

I'm afraid and I don't know why. That's not entirely right. I know why. As I tentatively pull off my trunks, the questions once more plague me. What if I can't perform? What if I go too quickly? What if I go too slow? What if I don't satisfy her? What if she's been with someone far better than me? What if she doesn't really love me anymore?

Okay, I'm sporting an erection that just won't quit. For now, anyway. But it doesn't help that we're strapped for time. The pressure is not something I expected to wrestle with during our first time back in the saddle.

Penny comes to me, on all fours, like a sleek lioness. She buries her face into the nape of my neck. It's all I can do to restrain myself from tossing her onto her back violently and consuming her entirely. This isn't prison, I remind myself. This is heaven. A little slice of heaven in the form of a mid-range-priced hotel room located lakeside in the six-million-acre Adirondack Park.

She kisses me.

I shift my head slowly so that my lips meet hers. Our tongues play, our teeth gently biting our lips. I roll her over onto her back and stare into her wide eyes. I feel myself close to entering her even before I intend the physical act to begin. It is the strangest sensation to have lived alone for so many years and now giving one's self over entirely to this woman. It is a matter of trust. Of letting go of the wheel, of flying blind, but somehow feeling entirely safe at the same time.

Using her hand, she guides me, and when I am finally inside her, I feel reduced to tears. My entire body moves with hers. The cheap bed is banging against the wall, and if this were many years ago, we would both have a quick laugh over it. But for now, we ignore everything that is happening all around us. There is no world outside our combined skin and flesh. There is only our world. There is only our love. And when the time comes for me to release, she once more presses her face into my neck, whispers, "Let it go . . . Let it go, Sidney. Let it all out." I'm not sure where it comes from, but I shout while releasing a profound breath. Then, I roll over onto my back, and I begin to cry.

She steals a quiet moment to catch her breath before rolling onto her side. She wipes the tears from my eyes with her fingers.

"It's okay," she consoles. "It's okay, I'm here."

The tears stream down my face. I taste the salt on my lips and tongue. I am filled with battling emotions. Embarrassment and relief. Or, technically speaking, it's a rush of oxytocin inside the brain. But should I be crying in front of the one woman who wants me to be strong for her? For Chloe?

Or maybe she doesn't mind the tears. Maybe by revealing weakness, I am also proving my humanity. The fact that prison didn't rob me entirely of my humanness.

*   *   *

. . . He sneaks up on me from behind. Not directly behind me but off to the side, so that I catch him out the corner of my eye. That's his fatal mistake. I've got both hands loaded up with dirty laundry, which I'm stuffing into the machine. He's got something in his hands. More than likely, a plastic shiv made from a sharpened toothbrush.

"Rabuffo appreciates your silence," he spits, as he goes to thrust the shiv into my side.

But I drop the laundry, spin around, catch his wrist at the last possible second before blade meets flesh. Spinning him around, I twist his wrist in a way God never intended and plant the shiv into his liver.

He drops like a stone.

I then cover him with a pile of laundry.

Slowly, unassumingly, I start making my way around the long row of metal washing machines toward the laundry facility exit. But before making my way completely around, I turn, steal one last glance at the dark blood soaking into the cairn constructed of white linens. Continuing on around the machines and across the facility floor, I nod politely to the bored-out-of-his-skull screw manning the exit.

"Have a nice day," I say, before pushing the doors open.

*   *   *

The faucet of tears is turned off as fast as it was turned on.

Get ahold of yourself, Sid. Buck up . . .

"Sorry about that, Pen. It's just been . . . well, it's been a long time, you know."

"Hey, Doc," she says, not without a giggle. "It's usually me who enjoys a good cry after sex. Hormones."

Me, once more picturing her in the arms of another. Don't go there, I tell myself. Do *not* go there. I bite my bottom lip, hard, every time I want to pose the question. Pretty soon I'll be drawing blood.

"Well, maybe you *should* be crying," I say. "Took me what? Less than a minute? I can only assume you aren't entirely . . . how shall I put this . . . satisfied."

"Hey, we've got lots of time to get back into the swing." She gives me a love tap with her bare knuckles. "Whoa nelly, where'd you get them muscles, Arnold?"

"Lots of time to lift weights on the yard," I point out. "That and read. That's pretty much how I spent my days. Lifting, reading, working, thinking about you two. Dreaming that . . ."

"Dreaming what, Doc?"

"Dreaming I'd get you both back one day."

I glance down at her fingers touching my bicep. It's peaked even though I'm not flexing. There's a heart tattooed to the bicep. The heart is not red since there was no red ink to be found on the inside. But instead, black, from the black ink you find in a common Bic pen. Even that had to be smuggled in since a pen makes one hell of a weapon. The heart is crying tears. Two tears, one for each of the loves I was forever missing.

"And this heart," Penny goes on. "I'm still trying to get used to it, Doc. It's very well done, but it's also . . . what's the word I'm looking for here?"

I'm saying the word for her in my head even before she utters it.

"Sad," she whispers. Then, her fingers still strumming the tight skin that covers my muscle. "The tears. What do they mean?" She exhales. "I once heard that tears represent the men you've killed inside prison walls. One for each man. Is that true, Doc?"

I shake my head, bring my lips to the top of her head. I can tell she's worried. That she's been worried since I got home and first took off my shirt, revealing the crying heart tattoo. She waited to ask the question. I'll give her credit for that. She didn't want to go on the attack right away.

"The tears are you and Chloe," I explain. It's not entirely a lie.

She looks into my eyes.

"But why?" she asks. "We're still here. We're alive."

"It broke my heart that I could not be with you. I was preparing myself for a life behind concrete walls and iron bars. Without you. Without Chloe."

"But it didn't turn out that way, did it?"

"No. Thank God."

She falls into a sea of thought.

"Can I ask you a frank question, Doc?" she says. "A hard question. And can you promise not to get mad at me for asking it?"

Pulse speeds up a little.

"Ask away," I say. Because what choice do I have?

"Did you kill anyone in prison, Doc?"

* * *

In my head, the shiv sliding into his liver . . . how easily it slipped inside. Not two months after that, another man, a heavy Chinese goon, cornering me in the shower. The shiv he'd constructed out of a piece of wood chair back and a disposable razor cut his neck almost to the bone after I'd snatched it out of his hand. His dark arterial blood was circling the drain as I dried off, and slipped back into gen pop, no one the wiser.

One week later, I had a crying heart tattoo planted on my arm with two teardrops falling from it . . .

"No, babe," I say, hoping to God she can't see through the lie. "I kept my head down. Did as I was told. Stayed out of the way. Stayed alive."

Outside the sliding glass doors, I can make out the sound of people enjoying themselves. Vacationers. People taking it easy. Kids and adults, mucking it up on the beach. I see Chloe in her polka-dot bikini. See her in my head.

"It must have been so hard," Penny says. "I don't know how you did it. Especially knowing you might never get out. How did you stay sane, Doc?"

"I thought of you. You and Chloe, all the time. You were both in my head when I went to sleep at night and when I woke up in the mornings."

"We visited. We were true."

"I would have died if you hadn't. You were my Penny from heaven, especially when I was locked up in hell."

She falls quiet one more time, and I know there is another question coming.

"Doc," she says, "tell me something. How did you get out so early? What changed?"

Pulse picks up more speed.

"You know what happened, Pen. Joel kept demanding new appeals. Eventually, we won out. We owe it all to him. And to you. To the letters you got people to write for me on my behalf."

The Joel I'm referring to is Joel Harwood. My lawyer. The guy who fought for me when I had no fight left in my system.

"So you didn't tell on anyone," she says, like a question.

"What are you trying to say?" I ask.

"You didn't, you know, mention anyone by name. Anyone in particular who might be responsible for the Chen family killings. Other than those two guys who did the actual shooting."

"You mean, did I call my boss out by name?" I say, feeling a burning sensation that starts in my toes and runs up and down my spine.

"That's not what I said, honey."

"But it's what you mean."

I feel the skin around my bicep grow tighter, tauter. All my muscles go tight. Ten years of frustration feels like it's culminating right here, right now, in this bed. And there's not a goddamned thing I can do about it.

"Listen, Doc," she says, slipping out of the bed and putting her bathing suit back on. "You got screwed. You took the rap for those two abhorrent assholes who shot that poor family to death. When they died from their wounds, there was no one else to blame but you, the driver. Joel fought for you, and even though it took a while, he made the court realize their errors, and they released you. That's all that counts now."

"I guess you're right, Pen. That's all that counts."

But I know she's *not* right. Some truths, however, are better left unspoken.

"You know, Doc," she goes on, "you never would utter the name of your boss after they arrested you. The man who you owed so much to. The man you felt so indebted to that you were willing to break the law for him. But, of course, I always knew his identity. How could I *not* know?"

. . . Rabuffo . . . Of course, she knew . . .

"It's better that we didn't mention his name while I was in prison. It was safer that way. So let's not talk about it anymore."

"You always say that," she says. "You've been saying the same thing for ten years."

"It was the smart play."

"The smart play?"

"It's how I stayed a step ahead of my enemies for ten years. And that's the way it's going to stay now."

She puts her top back on, smiles for me. But I can't help sensing something in her voice and in her tone that is untrusting or, at the very least, guarded. Maybe that's because I'm not telling her the whole truth and nothing but the truth, and she knows it.

"Oh my God, look at what time it is," she says, staring at the clock set on the bedside table. "Chloe will think we abandoned her." She heads into the bathroom.

"I agree. We need to go, Pen."

Now that Penny is out of the room, I grab hold of the television remote, flick the TV on. After ten years of incarceration, I can see that television is a still a mind suck—I never watched much of our limited channel selection in gen pop—even though there's more channel choices than ever before. There's a cooking show taking place at a roadside diner. The host has crazy blond hair. I switch to a bowling tournament on a sports channel. I catch an infomercial for a special pillow that conforms to your head when you rest your skull on it. Something I definitely could have used in prison.

And here's a shocker for you. When I switch to the local twenty-four-hour news channel, I see myself.

"I knew it," I whisper aloud. "Speaking of the devil."

In all disclosure, my lawyer warned me immediately upon my parole that I would make the news. Perhaps even national news. So while I'm somewhat shocked at seeing my face broadcast on my hotel room flat screen, I'm not blown away by any means.

The woman reading the teleprompter informs her audience that Sidney O'Keefe, arrested back in 2007 on multiple counts of murder in the tragic deaths of four undocumented Chinese aliens down in Albany, has been granted parole after a court reduced his initial sentence of homicide in the first degree to manslaughter.

The shot shifts to my lawyer, Joel, standing at a podium, a microphone before his face.

"Justice has been served in the case of my client, Mr. O'Keefe. While the courts knew all along he never shot anyone in that house, and in fact, never left the vehicle which was parked outside the murder scene, they still pinned the murders on him. And that's just plain wrong in both the eyes of God and the law. I consider this a great victory for all men and women serving out sentences in maximum security prisons on behalf of Class A felonies they did not commit."

Back to the live studio and my mug shot, which is broadcast above the news anchor's shoulder. My sad, tired-looking, stubble-covered face.

"O'Keefe is said to be residing with his wife of twelve years and their eleven-year-old daughter in an apartment in North Albany. He has refused comment with News Channel 9 despite repeated attempts to contact him. In other news . . ."

"What attempted contact?" I find myself saying out loud.

"Did you say something, Doc?"

"Nothing," I say, shaking my head. "Just something I saw on the news that caught my eye."

"We need to head back outside before the cops come," Penny says, not without a chuckle. "Yikes. We're such evil parents, you and me."

I aim the clicker at the TV to kill the broadcast. But then comes yet a second, far more electric shock when I see a face I haven't seen up close and personal in over ten years.

It's Rabuffo.

Mickey Rabuffo standing in the center of a clothing store. He's got a tape measure in his hands and he's taking the measurements on a man who is standing on a small pedestal in front of a tall mirror. There's a song playing in the background. "Rabuffo's Custom Clothiers . . . That's as good as it gets." The style of the music is old big band, the tune lifted from an old Sinatra tune, "Day and Night," the voice belting out the lyrics in imitation of Old Blue Eyes himself. Or is it a Cole Porter song?

Rabuffo's Custom Clothiers . . . Just one of the many legal cover operations for his massive illegal drug and human trafficking operations.

I look into Rabuffo's blue eyes and I feel like he's looking right at me through the flat-screened TV. In my imagination, I see him taking a couple of steps toward the camera.

"You fucking threw me under the bus, didn't you, Sid?" he says in his raspy smoker's voice. "You sold me and my operations out in exchange for your freedom. It took you a while, I'll give you that. But in the end, you sold me out. You were like a son to me. I trusted you with my life, my money, my home. Now you're going to pay the price, my friend."

"Rabuffo's Custom Clothier," Penny sings, mimicking the tune precisely. "That's as good as it gets." She follows up with a hearty laugh. "I just love that commercial. Catchy little tune for a crook like Mickey."

Rabuffo's put on weight. His face is rounder than I remember it, the hair line more receded. But he's still the same guy. No doubt he's being hounded by the FBI as this commercial airs. No doubt he's feeling the heat for his smuggling operations from ICE and even Homeland Security. He's a target now, thanks to me.

It's only a matter of time until he pays me a visit. Or one of his goons anyway. Someone like Wemps or Singh. Two men genetically predisposed to violent murder. In other words, natural born killers.

I turn the TV off, toss the clicker back onto the bed.

"You look like you've just seen a ghost," Penny comments. The way her eyes bore holes into me tells me she knows precisely how much Rabuffo can still shake me up. Shake *us* up.

"Nothing's wrong," I lie. "Come on. Chloe will be worried."

Penny goes to the curtain, pulls it open. She slides open the glass door, steps out.

"Rabuffo's Custom Clothier," she sings under her breath, "that's as good as it gets."

CHAPTER 3

THE BEACH IS crowded at midday. The bright sun is hot, but the cool Adirondack breeze more than compensates. I focus my gaze on the water's edge, where Chloe was digging a deep trench in the sand with her new friend. Chloe is nowhere to be found, at least upon initial glance.

I feel a slight jolt in my heart.

I'm not good when it comes to lack of control. But it's quickly becoming apparent that I'm especially not good when it comes to not knowing where my own kid is. What's that? Another double negative? But then, there's nothing very positive about this situation. Maybe I haven't spent much time with my daughter, but that doesn't mean my instincts aren't finely tuned. And right now, my instinct is to call out for her.

"Chloe?!" I shout. So loud I startle Penny and cause just about every head on every man, woman, and child located within a fifty-foot radius to suddenly turn and stare at me.

"Take it easy, Doc," Penny whispers forcefully.

I look at her. Her face has turned beet red, as if she's embarrassed by what I've just done. By the attention we're getting from my shout.

"What do you mean take it easy, Pen?" I say. "I don't see Chloe anywhere."

"Relax," she presses. "You're just not used to being a parent." She takes hold of my hand. "Chloe is here. I'm sure she's just taking a walk, or maybe she went around front to grab a snack or something." Squeezing my hand. "Just take a breath, big fella."

Breathing in and out, I feel myself calming down somewhat. Maybe Penny is right. Maybe I'm flying off the handle because I'm not used to all this. Being a parent and all. I'm more used to taking care of myself. Of making sure I don't become a victim. That kind of thinking has to stop now. The world no longer revolves around me, nor the men who wish to silence me. It also includes my wife and my daughter.

Penny releases my hand.

"Let's go talk to the parents of the girl Chloe was playing with before we went inside."

"Proactive medicine," I say. "By far the best approach."

But what wasn't a good approach, I now realize, was our decision to head back to our room to be alone in the first place. This is my fault.

*   *   *

We head back down the beach, the faces and eyes of the vacationers still staring, but quickly turning away when I stare back at them. I'm not sure if I look like I've just gotten out of prison, but they sure can feel it when I dig my eyes into them. Rather, they feel the desperation and rawness that oozes off of me. I can bench press almost twice my own weight. I can squat three times my weight, and I can do twenty-five bicep curls without breaking a sweat. You can leave the prison yard, but like a jagged purple scar, it takes one hell of a long time for it to leave you. Trust me on that.

When we come to the spot where Chloe and her new friend have dug a big hole in the sand, we stop. Penny assumes her best polite parent smile. Since the little girl is still busy digging, Penny doesn't bother her, but instead, holds out her hand for the mother.

"Hello," she says. "I'm Penny O'Keefe and this is my husband, Sidney. We're Chloe's parents . . . the little girl who was playing with your daughter just a few moments ago."

"Oh, what a sweet girl," the woman says, sitting up in her beach chair. She's got short brunette hair and a pleasant face. A little on the heavier side, just like her husband, or the guy who I assume is her husband, who's portly in the gut and bald. They're both wearing sunglasses. They also have matching sterling silver crosses hanging from their necks by thin silver chains. Good Catholics maybe. Christians anyway. I can't remember the last time I prayed.

"Thank you," Penny says. "I can see you're blessed, too."

"Thanks," the man interjects. "Susan is our pride and joy. We could only have one child, so we spoil her. Don't we, dolly?"

"Daaaad," Susan says, looking up and taking a breather from her digging. "You *don't* spoil me. Or else I'd have an iPhone by now." She giggles, her hair thick and wavy. There's some sand in it. There's something about her eyes. They're glassy. Like she just woke up from a long nap in the hot sun.

"No iPhones yet, young lady," her mother insists. "High school will be time enough."

The conversation resounds inside my brain. It's nearly identical to the argument Chloe and Penny were having this morning inside our hotel room.

"It would be safer if I had one now, Mom," Susan argues. "That way you'd know where I am at all times."

"We know where you are at all times because we keep a constant eye on you, sweetie," the father chimes in. "Isn't that right, dear?"

"You never can be too careful, now can you?" the mother says looking into both Penny's and my eyes.

The guilt washes over me like a bucket of tainted blood. Bad decisions . . . They will be the death of me, which, in some ways, is fine. So long as they aren't the death of someone else. Someone I love very much.

"Oh, I know what you mean, Mrs. . . . ." Penny allows the *Missus* to dangle.

"Mrs. Stevens," she says. "Claudia Stevens, and this is Burt."

He reaches out with his meaty hand. I take it in mine, shake and release.

"Pleasure to meet you, Burt."

"Jeeze, where'd you get that grip, pal?" he inquires.

"My husband spends a lot of time in the weight room," Penny interrupts.

"He looks like quite the tough guy," Burt says. "Every man on the beach is probably intimidated." Patting his belly. "Guess I should get back to the gym one of these days."

"Keep dreaming, Burt," Claudia comments.

Now I'm not only worried about Chloe, I'm genuinely embarrassed. Has prison turned me into a physical monster?

Then, Penny, breaking in. "If you don't mind my asking, Claudia and Burt, have you seen our daughter?"

As if taking a cue from a script, the two turn and gaze into one another's eyes, then refocus their gaze on us.

"You mean you don't *know* where she is?" Claudia asks.

Penny issues a nervous laugh.

"Oh, well, we know she's around here somewhere," she insists. "Just like you and your daughter, we're always keeping our eye on her. But we had to go back to the room together for a minute. You'll recall I spoke to Chloe before we went back to the room. I instructed her not to leave this spot for any reason."

Burt turns to Claudia.

"That so," he says. "I must have been taking a catnap because I don't remember seeing you." He laughs. "But that doesn't mean anything. I enjoy my naps. I enjoy my daydreams." He leans forward in his chair so that his beer gut presses against his white thighs. "If you don't mind my saying," he says a bit under his breath, "I bet you snuck in a little quality time alone." He gives us both a wink. "Tough to get alone time on vacay."

"Dad," Susan says, from her sand trench, "don't make me want to throw up."

Claudia waves her hand at her husband like, *don't pay any attention to him.*

"The girls were playing nicely," she goes on. "I'm sure she didn't go far." She stands. "I can help you look for her if you want. Shall I call the hotel house detective? They have one, you know. I've seen her."

I lock eyes with Penny, shake my head slowly. She knows what I'm thinking. I'm newly paroled. I'm a headline on the local hourly news reports. Last thing we need right now is getting any kind of organized law enforcement involved in something that could be a great big nothing burger.

"It's okay," Penny says. "Really, it's fine. You've been very helpful."

I'm looking over one shoulder then the other. Seeing nothing. Only beach on one side, scattered beachgoers, and behind that, the long four-story hotel. On the other side, nothing but open water, and beyond that, the wooded, residential area of Lake Placid.

I bite down on my lip again. Harder than normal. I taste the blood in my mouth.

. . . Go easy, Sid. Don't say anything stupid. Don't do anything stupid. Like Penny says, Chloe just drifted off like a lot of pre-teens will. She's probably got her earbuds in and listening to some loud music and wandering around the downtown . . .

"Is something wrong with Chloe?"

The voice of the little girl playing in the sand. Susan.

"No," I say, staring into her dreamy blue eyes. "We can't find her right now, Susan. Do you know where she might be?"

Claudia steps in front of me, takes hold of Susan by the arm. Gently, but at the same time, a little forcefully.

"She wouldn't know," she insists. "Sue has had her head buried in the sand all day." She giggles. "Buried in the sand, get it?"

"I remember she was asking where her parents were," Susan volunteers.

"What was that?" Penny says. "What did you say?"

"Chloe," little Susan says, as her mother releases her arm. "Before my mom took me back to the room for my shot, she looked worried because she didn't know where you were."

"What shot?" I ask.

Claudia smiles nervously.

"My daughter has type one diabetes," she explains. "She requires two insulin shots per day."

That strikes me as a bit funny, because Susan can't weigh more than sixty pounds. But then, believe it or not, weight has nothing to do with how many injections a kid with type one diabetes might require in a single day. I'm a med school dropout, and even I know that. What's important here is that, for the first time since we discovered Chloe isn't where she's supposed to be, Penny's face loses all its color. And that, to me anyway, is worrisome.

"I told Chloe where we were going," she says, more to herself than to anyone else. "Why would she ask where we were if I already told her where we were going?"

"Listen, Pen," I interject. "Since she's not on the beach, let's go around the front of the hotel and look there."

"Maybe she went to the indoor pool?" Claudia suggests.

Some of the color returns to Penny's face.

"Of course," she says. "That's where she must be. My daughter can't live without the indoor pool."

"Thank you very much, folks," I say, as I begin making my way back up the beach toward the rear hotel doors. Double time.

CHAPTER 4

"WAIT FOR ME, Doc!" Penny calls out. "Wait up already. We need to stick together."

I stop, turn.

"Sorry, Pen," I say, exhaling. "I don't know what's gotten into me today. Panic attacks." Overwhelming stress. Fear.

"I get it," she says, breathing hard. "No need to apologize. Chloe is your daughter and you're not used to the emergencies that can go with fatherhood."

"And I thought prison was stressful."

"You ain't seen nothin' yet, Doc. Believe me. Every day a pre-teen brings you a new surprise on a silver platter. Not all of them so nice."

Approaching the hotel door, I pull it open for Penny.

"Kinda hope you're wrong about that, babe."

"Me too," she says, passing on through. "Me . . . too."

A small plastic sign that reads POOL is mounted to the wall at the opposite side of the vestibule. Below the sign is an arrow pointing in the direction of a long corridor. The vestibule houses a couple of overpriced vending machines. One selling sodas and bottled water, another selling salted snacks and candy bars. For a second or two, I imagine finding my polka-dotted daughter standing here, stuffing spare change into the slots. How disappointing to find out that she isn't.

Here's what I'm learning real fast: when you're in search of somebody, every door you pass through presents a new hope. Every corner you round offers a new opportunity. Every room you enter for the first time is a resolution. But these things also give you crushing frustration when they turn out to be dead ends. You want to think logically about where she ran off to. But it's not easy thinking logically when your adrenal glands are working overtime.

"Fingers crossed," Penny says, glancing at the sign.

"Let's just hurry," I insist, taking hold of her hand, racing her down the corridor.

We pass by a dozen or more ground-floor rooms, until we come to a glass door, which is located at the end of the corridor. The glass on the door is somewhat fogged up. I pull on the door, praying it won't be locked. But then, why would it be during a hot summer's day?

. . . Another door, another possibility . . .

The door opens. Penny and I step through.

Disappointment.

*　*　*

The pool is empty, other than a man who appears to be swimming laps. He's wearing a rubber cap on his head and swimmers' goggles over his eyes.

"This isn't funny anymore, Sidney," Penny mumbles under her breath. "Where did our little girl go?"

She's back to referring to me by my real Christian name instead of Doc. It means the anxiety is settling in. If we don't find my daughter soon, there will come confusion, and following that, anger. Then will come the outright terror if she's absolutely no-where to be found by nightfall.

. . . Stop thinking, Sid . . . Just do . . .

Chewing my bottom lip with my two front teeth. Tasting the blood.

. . . Hold it together . . .

To my right-hand side, a table stacked with white bath towels. Beyond that, a door that leads into the ladies' and men's locker rooms. Also a sauna.

I turn to Penny.

"You check the locker rooms, Pen," I say. "I'll talk to the man in the pool."

"Agreed," she says, heading for the ladies' locker room.

Stepping over to the very edge of the pool, I lower myself and take a knee. Instead of shouting, I wait the few seconds it takes for the man to take notice of my presence. He swims toward me. When he comes to the pool's edge, he stands up straight since the depth is only four feet. He removes his goggles, pushing them up onto his latex-covered brow. It's then I can see that he's at least seventy years old, but in very good shape, no doubt due to his ex-ercise regimen.

"Help you, young man?" he says, the water dripping off his nose and chin.

It's been a long time since someone referred to me as a young man. During my ten-year incarceration, I went from soft young man to hard middle-aged man. In some respects, I'm even older than that. If nothing else, prison ages a man far faster than nature intended. Constant, battlefield-like stress will do that.

"I'm looking for a little girl," I explain. "Blonde, blue eyes. About five feet two inches tall. She was wearing a yellow polka-dot bikini."

"Like the old song goes," he says.

"Exactly. Have you seen her?"

He slowly shakes his head. Squeezes both his nostrils as if to force pool water out of his ear canals.

"Been swimming pretty much all alone for almost an hour," he says. "A few people have come and gone, mostly to use the sauna or the toilets. But I haven't paid much attention."

Me, feeling a tightness in my sternum.

"You're sure about that?"

"I'm sure, young man." He looks at me for a bit, as if trying to size me up. His eyes can't help but gravitate to my tattoo. "Can I ask what this is all about?"

"It's my daughter," I say. "She seems to have gone off on her own and we're having trouble finding her."

"We, as in . . ."

"My wife and I."

Just then, the ladies' locker room door opens.

"Nothing," Penny says, dejectedly. She goes to the Men's. "I'm going in," she adds. She knocks on the wood door, opens it tentatively. "Anyone in here?"

She waits. No response. She enters.

"That her?" the old swimmer asks.

I nod.

"She looks worried," he says. "Anything I can do to help?"

"Just keep an eye out. We're staying at the hotel. If you happen to spot our daughter, let her know her parents are looking for her, and to go straight back to the room."

I stand, feel the blood rushing back into my head.

Penny comes back out of the men's room. She's shaking her head. She might not be using words, but it feels like she's screaming at me. She comes to me.

"What are we going to do, Doc?" she begs.

"Take a breath and search the hotel," I say. "Up and down."

"Maybe you should check your room before you do anything else," the old man suggests. "Maybe your daughter is back there waiting for you right now."

His suggestion, however simple, makes total sense. It also tells me we're not being smart about this search. What should we have done in the first place? As clichéd as it sounds, start at the start. Search our hotel room first and branch out from there.

"Why didn't we think of that?" I say.

"Let's go," Penny says.

We turn, start for the pool door.

"Hey!" the swimming man shouts out.

"What is it?" I say, looking over my shoulder.

"What's your name?"

"O'Keefe," I say.

I can tell I look familiar to him. Maybe he's been watching the news.

"Good luck, Mr. O'Keefe," he offers. "I've got my good eye out."

"Thanks. I appreciate it."

We pass on through the doors. We're in a race to get back to our room. Desperate for some good news. Desperate for resolution.

CHAPTER 5

WE DON'T WALK. We run the length of the bottom-level corridor. Sprint.

We cross over the vestibule with its vending machines, the entirely imagined image of Chloe standing in front of them, buying candy and soda. The image is already ingrained in my brain like a bad dream I can't shake.

"I've been looking all over for you guys?" she'd say. "Why did you leave me alone on the beach?"

. . . Get the image out of your head, Sid. Keep moving . . .

My breathing is labored, my heart pounding. When I come to the door, I pull the credit card–style opener from the little pocket sewn into the interior of my swim trunks.

"Hurry," Penny presses.

I shove the card into the locking device. There's the mechanical click of the bolt releasing, and the illumination of a little green light. Grabbing the opener, I lift it up and open the door.

Fragments of the famous song plays over and over in my brain.

"Well let me tell you 'bout the way she looked
The way she acted and the color of her hair . . .
But she's not there"

I push the door open only to find the room as empty as when we left it. Even when Penny shoves passed me and into the bathroom behind the open door, I know that Chloe isn't inside there either.

She's gone now. And that's all.

CHAPTER 6

FOR THE FIRST time, Penny breaks down, begins to cry. She sets her forehead on my shoulder, wraps her arm around my chest, pulls me in tight. I can feel her trembling. Or is it me who is trembling? She's afraid. Chloe has only been gone for an hour and she's panicked. I'm panicked.

But we have to think straight. We can't fly off the handle, jump to any conclusions that are the product of overactive imaginations. We can't allow our emotions to eat away at us.

"Listen, Pen," I say, looking into her wet eyes. "Let's look at this logically. A little more than an hour ago, we decided to come back to the room for a few minutes. We were alone for what? Ten minutes. Fifteen tops. Something must have happened to Chloe in that time. She must have walked off on her own. And if that's the case, she couldn't have gotten very far."

She wipes her eyes with the backs of her hands.

"But what if she was kidnapped, Doc? What if someone abducted her in broad daylight?"

"On a crowded private beach behind a big hotel?"

"The beach wasn't that crowded."

"Okay, but there were two responsible parents watching over her. Plus, I think their daughter would have spoken up if some big asshole picked her up and dragged her off the beach."

She sniffles, unwraps me, runs her fingers through her hair.

"You've got a point. I'm losing my shit. Nice responsible parent that I am."

"Don't be silly," I say. "I couldn't wait to give you that stupid ring, and I *really* couldn't wait to get you in the sack and you know it. This is all my fault."

"Both our faults."

"Fair enough."

"So what we need is a plan, Sid."

In my head, seeing Chloe walking around town, her earbuds in, music blaring, teenage boys eyeing her in her bikini. Maybe she's drinking a Slurpee through an orange straw, or munching on a hotdog, or a McDonald's cheeseburger. No, wait, Chloe doesn't go for cheeseburgers. She likes hamburgers. How does she do it? She buys two hamburgers, removes the burger from one of the buns and slips it onto the other patty, making it a double burger. If this were March, she'd wash it all down with a green Shamrock shake.

I might not have lived with my daughter for the past ten years, but she's sent me letters and visited. Enough so that I know her habits. As a prisoner, I found comfort in thinking about her habits. Dreaming about them. The foods she liked, the movies she went to see, the shows she watched, the music she listened to, the way she brushed her teeth—all of it was like candy to a man deprived of his child.

"Here's the deal," I say, looking at my watch. "It's ten after three. Let's throw some clothes on and walk into town. Dollars to donuts, we find our little girl chatting it up with some kids her own age at the McDonalds or the Starbucks or who knows where."

She nods.

"Okay," she says. "Deal."

But Penny is losing faith. I can see it, hear it, feel it.

We get dressed in a hurry.

Penny in a pair of Levis jeans, tank top, and gladiator sandals. Me in a pair of blue jeans, black t-shirt, and worn combat boots.

"You don't look like you're on vacation, Doc," Penny says, looking me up and down. Like my clothing is of paramount importance right now.

"When we get home, I'd better make a Target run. Buy a new wardrobe."

But to be honest, I don't give a damn about my clothes right now. Right now, I've got other things on my mind.

"You'd better get a job before you do that," Penny adds.

Her words, however truthful, are also a reminder. I'm required to check in with my parole officer today. By five o'clock. I could do it now, but I don't want to waste any more time. More importantly, I don't want to give him the impression that something is wrong. I've only been dealing with him for a short period of time, but thus far, anyway, I've found him to be perceptive. As if he were trained to recognize trouble brewing, even when simply speaking with a parolee over the phone.

I open the door and Penny goes to step back out into the corridor. But before she does, I stop her by grabbing hold of her arm.

She looks into my eyes, a bit startled.

"Hey, Pen," I say. "I love you."

She sighs, works up a sad smile.

"I love you too," she says. Pulling her arm free, she walks out into the empty corridor as if walking all alone.

CHAPTER 7

WE DO THE smart thing, or what we convince ourselves is the smart thing. Instead of walking back outside via the back door, we make our way up the stairs to the hotel lobby. Perhaps Chloe decided to chill out in front of one of the computers reserved for hotel clientele. The lobby is big and spacious. Like a wide-open log cabin with a tall cathedral ceiling. Some of the logs that create the walls still have bark on them. There's a massive stone fireplace that's two stories tall and a long reception counter located at the front end of the lobby.

The open floor contains chairs, couches, and wood coffee tables covered with magazines, newspapers, and paperbacks. The wall that looks out onto Mirror Lake is made entirely of glass; its top portion triangular to fit the cathedral ceiling. It offers a panoramic view of the entire beach and lake beyond it.

Penny and I automatically gravitate toward the glass wall and peer out onto the beach.

"You see her?" I beg.

I see Penny's reflection in the glass. See her pensive eyes, her tight anxious face. I wonder if she sees my reflection.

"I don't see her, Doc," she says. "I just don't see her."

"That bathing suit of hers would stick out," I suggest. "Yellow polka dots. They would reflect the sun."

The sun, which will be going down in a few hours. God help us.

"Do you see the Stevenses? Burt and Claudia?" Penny asks.

I look for them, in the spot they occupied all morning and much of the afternoon.

"I don't. Must be their little girl . . . what's her name, Susan? Must be she got tired or needed another shot, or both. Diabetes treatment can be tricky, I guess. I didn't really get too far into it in med school."

Something wasn't right with her, I want to add. The little girl didn't seem all there. Something in her eyes, something in her blood. But I decide to let it go, concentrate entirely on Chloe.

Turning.

"The front desk," I go on. "Maybe they've seen Chloe."

Once again, hope settles in. Dare I say it?

But the hope is staged. A ruse designed to torture us, steal greedy bites from of our souls like hungry sharks circling a bleeding fish. The man tending to the desk hasn't seen a pre-teen girl matching the description we give him. At least, not in recent hours. This is a family hotel, he adds. There's dozens of little girls running around who might match that same description.

"Is there anyone in the office in back who might have noticed her?" I beg.

He's kind enough to make the effort of actually leaving the counter to head into the back office to inquire with the staff. I can see him through the glass window that separates the office from the front desk. A woman seated at a desktop computer turns to eye Penny and me. She says something I can't possibly understand, shakes her head.

The man returns. He's short, a little overweight, with receding blond hair. Casually dressed in tan slacks and white button down. Probably of German descent like the original owners of this hotel before they sold out to a major chain.

"I'm so sorry," he says, his face masked with concern. Perhaps he feels liable for my daughter getting lost. Maybe he sees a lawsuit in the making. "Shall I contact the house detective for you?" He goes to pick up the phone, like he's deciding for me.

... *Police* ...

I'm on parole. Only a few days ago I was incarcerated in prison for first-degree murder. For the execution-style death of an entire family of Chinese immigrants. Sure, I was just the driver. But somebody had to take the rap after the two killers who accompanied me on the mission, Wemps and Singh, were killed by the Albany cops.

I'm not out of prison because of my good looks, or because the courts finally decided that I'm one hell of a good guy after all, or because of Jesus or luck. I got out because after ten years in gen pop trying to avoid rape, stabbings, beatings, sickness, and men who were being paid to silence me for good, I'd finally had enough. I called my lawyer, told him I wanted a meeting with the Albany DA. I revealed everything I knew about Rabuffo, his operation to export Chinese illegals, to sell drugs not only out of his many tailor shops, but also out of the many Chinese restaurants and food trucks he owned. He was making a fortune on crystal meth and the human trafficking slave trade.

I told them that the Chinese family who lived in that house were owned by Mickey Rabuffo, and that he ordered the hit that was carried out by Wemps and Singh. It wasn't exactly the truth, but it wasn't like my two old high school buddies were alive to refute my version of the story. It was me versus a suspected trafficker of hard drugs and human beings. Innocent human beings who just wanted a better life than the shit sandwich they were dealt back in China.

Soon enough, the FBI will have enough on Rabuffo to put him away for good. But until that time, the last thing I need is the cops breathing down my neck. All it will take is one false move or a hint of suspicion that I'm up to no good, and I'd find myself back behind bars so fast my head will perform a full *Exorcist* spin. Once that happens, there will be no chance of getting out ever again.

What it all comes down to is this: I need to find my daughter and I need to do it without the help of the police or even a rent-a-cop, like a hotel detective. If at all possible, I'm going to keep organized law enforcement out of it.

"You can put the phone down," I say.

"Excuse me?" the desk manager says.

"I said, you don't need to call in the house detective." I'm trying to put a smile on my face. Something to put him at ease. "I'm sure my daughter just went out for a walk in the village. Probably to grab a snack or meet up with friends. We're going to find her right now."

He slowly sets the phone back into its cradle.

"If you say so," he says, somewhat under his breath. "But if you need help, let me know. We're here for you. We wish to make your stay as enjoyable as possible, Mr. O'Keefe."

"Thank you," I offer.

As I back away from the desk, it hits me that he knows precisely who I am. He knows that I've just been paroled from a maximum-security prison. That the whole wide world thought of me as nothing more than a homicidal maniac. A killer with no remorse.

"What did he say?" Penny asks, as we make our way to the front, heavy wood door of the hotel.

"He wanted to call in the house detective," I say, a little under my breath.

"Maybe we should bring him in," she says. "Or is it a her?"

Me, shaking my head.

"Whatever," she goes on. "The point is that we should do everything in our power to get our daughter back, Doc. You said it yourself, we need to be smart."

Once again, I take hold of her arm. Maybe I'm a little too rough, because she makes a noise that sounds like a squeal. Her face assumes an expression of alarm. I glance over my shoulder to see the desk manager staring at me. Behind him, the woman who was working at her computer is looking at me through the back office glass window.

Suddenly I feel like I'm living inside a fishbowl. I let go of Penny.

I whisper forcefully, "I'm sorry, Pen. I didn't mean to be so rough."

She rubs the spot on her arm where I grabbed her.

"What the hell is the matter with you, Sid?"

Penny's afraid of me. I feel the shame fill my veins like a poison injection. Maybe she's been afraid of me all along. Maybe she's been trying her hardest not to be afraid. Maybe she dreaded my coming home. Maybe she didn't want me to come home at all.

I open the wood door.

"Let's just go," I insist.

She hesitates.

"Please," I beg. "Penny, please, let's just go now."

She walks out.

I follow, my convict's tail between my legs.

CHAPTER 8

WE STAND TOGETHER just outside the hotel entry, under the overhead that protects the drive-up. I'm pretty certain the desk manager can see me on CCTV, but somehow, I feel better now that his eyes aren't peeled directly on me, live and in person.

"I'm sorry for grabbing you like that, Pen," I say. "It's just that I really feel like we need to do our best on our *own* to find Chloe."

"But the house detective will be trained—"

I raise my hands and she does something that breaks my heart. She backs away. Backs away out of fear.

"Pen," I add, my throat closing in on itself, voice choking. "What are you doing?"

Her eyes fill.

"Oh my God," she says. "I'm so sorry, Doc. I didn't mean to."

She reverses course, steps into me, kisses me on the cheek.

"You're afraid of me. I don't blame you. I've become a monster. Prison can do that."

I never actually murdered anyone. But what Penny doesn't realize is that something like sixty-five percent of all paroled murderers end up killing again.

"No, I do not accept that," she affirms while anxiously twisting the metal ring on her finger. "I am most definitely *not* afraid of you. And you are not a monster. You are my husband and I love you very much."

Her words are sweet. Like a cool drink of water for a parched man who thirsts for reassurance. This is a big bad world I've reentered, and with Chloe missing, it's only getting bigger and far more volatile. Maybe the whole world is a prison. I need for Penny to know she can trust me. Otherwise, we share nothing together. We are adrift, lost in a sea of dread and suspicion.

"Where do we start looking?" she asks.

I gaze across the parking lot onto Lake Placid's quaint village and the main street that runs through it.

"Let's be smart and start at the start," I offer, not without a smile.

"You're a poet."

"Don't I know it."

Penny takes hold of my hand and together we make our way across the parking lot, like two lost souls making their way through a thick, dark wood.

CHAPTER 9

To our immediate right is the hotel bar. A glitzy affair that years ago served as the most popular biker bar in the village. I recall hanging out there not long after the 1980 Olympics when I was a young teen and you could easily buy a beer with a fake ID. Tough, leather-clad bikers would carve their names into the tables with their Bowie knives and switchblades. Loose women would pull up their t-shirts, show you their wears for a buck. It was a great place to waste away an afternoon, day drinking, playing darts and pool, and listening to ear-piercing classic rock n' roll. But now all that's been replaced with bright lights, glass, stainless steel, and colorful plastic.

"Is this even worth it?" I pose. "I don't see an eleven-year-old being welcome at an adult bar like this one."

"Let's at least ask the bartender if he's seen her," Penny suggests.

"Leave no stone unturned. I get it, Pen."

She pulls out her smartphone, pulls up a recent photo of Chloe in the gallery. I'm not able to look at the picture for very long. Maybe a few fleeting seconds. Somehow seeing Chloe standing at the bus stop in her short white dress and pink Converse sneakers, her sandy blonde hair pulled back into a tight ponytail, her Selena Gomez backpack strapped to her shoulders, her eyes full and

bright and optimistic because it's the first day of school, robs me
of my breath, fills my stomach with a pile of stones. Have I been
absent from her life for that long?

*. . . You've been absent from Chloe's life for her entire eleven years,
Sid. Stop fooling yourself into believing that the phone calls, the few
scattered letters, and the occasional visits made up for not physically
being there for her . . .*

And now she's gone.

Penny steps into the bar through the already open door. I'm
right behind her. She hasn't even said a word to the young man
tending bar before she's holding up the digital photo of Chloe for
him to view. The act catches him a little by surprise. He squints his
eyes, gazing at the cell phone–sized photo, and wipes his hands
with a white bar rag.

"Can I help you?" he inquires.

"Have you seen this girl?" Penny asks.

My eyes focus on her slim body, the way her bare knees are
knocking together, the heel on her sandal-covered foot tapping
the tiled floor like she's keeping time to some frantic tune she's
been playing over and over again in her head.

"She's our daughter," Penny goes on. "And we can't find her. Did
she happen to come by here?"

The bartender, sensing the importance of what's happening,
cocks his head over his shoulder. He's young. Maybe twenty-five,
his thick black hair combed back on his head and held in place
with gel, or what does Penny call it? Product. He gently sets the
towel back down onto the bar, and then sadly, infuriatingly, shakes
his head.

"I'm sorry," he says.

Penny peels her eyes away from him. She scans the entire
horseshoe-shaped bar. A young couple occupies two stools at the

opposite end. They're still dressed in their bathing suits, having obviously just come up from the beach to enjoy a nice quiet late afternoon cocktail.

"What about them?" Penny says.

"Miss," the bartender says, "they only just came in. Maybe it's better if you—"

"They have eyes, don't they?" Penny snaps.

She goes around the bar to the young couple.

I follow.

"Pardon me," Penny says, holding up the phone for the young woman and her partner. "I'm sorry to disturb your drink, but our daughter is lost and we were wondering if you might have happened to see her. She was on the hotel beach with us just this morning. But now she seems to have disappeared."

The more Penny talks . . . the more she attempts to explain herself, her situation . . . the more her voice rattles, her throat chokes, and her emotions take over. We're only just starting our search and she's becoming a wreck.

I take a step forward, try hard to plant a smile on my face.

The woman is attractive, with dark hair, accented with streaks of blonde. I can't tell whether the blonde is natural or the result of a dye job. Her partner is in shape, head shaved, with a tattoo on his left bicep that says Semper Fi. A Marine.

He shakes his head, presses his lips together.

"Sorry," he says, following up with a swig of his beer. "I haven't seen her."

"Neither have I," the young woman reveals. Then, reading the desperation in our faces, "Say, do you need my help with anything?"

"Just keep an eye out if you can," Penny pleads. "If you should happen to spot her, tell her this: her mother and father are desperate to find her. Tell her to go straight to the hotel lobby." She looks at me while patting her pockets. "I need a pen, Sid."

I look around. Finally, calling out to the bartender. "You got a spare pen, pal?"

He reaches into his shirt pocket, pulls out a pen, tosses it to me. I snatch it from out of the air, hand it to Penny. She takes hold of a bar napkin. She writes down her cell phone number along with the names Penny and Sidney. She hands it to the young woman.

"Like I said," Penny goes on, "just keep an eye out, if you can."

"We will," says the Marine. "You have my word."

We leave the bar feeling no better off than when we entered.

CHAPTER 10

OUTSIDE, PENNY WALKS away from the bar's open door.

She cries, "Shit! Shit!"

Several passersby can't help but crane their necks to see who's doing the shouting. A few speed up as they move on past, as if Penny is about to explode for real. A couple others stop and gawk. Two teenage boys in particular.

"Keep moving," I say to them, muscles tense, my expression hard as a rock.

"No wait," Penny says, once again pulling out her cell phone. She shows them the digital photo of Chloe. "Have you boys seen our daughter? We're looking for her."

The scruffy, t-shirted boys look into one another's eyes.

"Ummm, that's like a negative," the first one says, his voice mock surfer dude. "Sorry."

"If you see my daughter," Penny says, "let her know her mom and dad are trying to find her. Spread the word."

"We will, for sure," says the second kid.

I thank them. They run off.

Penny shoves her phone back into her bag, bends over, both hands planted on her knees. It's like somebody sucker punched her in the stomach. I place my hand on her back, run it gently up and down.

"This is all wrong, Sidney," she utters, her voice sounding hoarse and painful. "Something's not right." She's breathing heavily, in and out. "We're not going about this the right way."

She stands up tall, her face pale and tear-streaked.

"We're doing all we can," I insist. "We're looking for our daughter, Pen."

"We need the police. We can't do this ourselves. Why can't you see that, Sidney?"

Gone is the reference to my nickname, Doc. And all the affection that went with it.

Exhaling. "I'm fresh out of prison, Penny."

"Meaning what?" she begs.

"Meaning we have to be smart about this. I just spent ten years in prison for being an accomplice in the murder of an entire family. Now, I'm not out of the joint a full week and my daughter goes missing. How the hell is that going to look to the police?"

My teeth cut through the already tender flesh on my bottom lip. Just enough to cause some blood to seep into my mouth. I taste the salt, feel the pain. It's what keeps me in check. Keeps me from exploding. From doing something I'd rather not do, which, right this second, is tear this town apart, inch by inch, until I find my daughter. I need to stay in control or this mission is shot to shit before it even gets started.

Penny, still breathing hard.

"Are you okay, Pen?"

"You know the answer to that, Doc, so why bother asking it in the first place?"

Back to calling me Doc. We're making some progress here with one another. People are passing us by on the sidewalk. Husbands and wives, boyfriends and girlfriends, entire families on vacation. They're eating hotdogs or licking ice cream cones. They're carrying shopping bags and pushing baby carriages. They're laughing, playing, and not caring about anything.

"This is my fault," she says, after a bit. "I should have bought her the phone."

"I don't understand."

She sniffles, once more finger-combs her hair.

"Just before you got out," she continues, "Chloe was begging me for an iPhone. As an early birthday present." Her eyes rolling around in their sockets. "You heard her this morning."

I also remember little Susan on the beach, arguing with her parents over their refusal to buy her an iPhone, just like Chloe argued with Penny earlier.

"An iPhone seems a little extravagant for an eleven-year-old girl," I say. "I don't know a lot about it, but I think she's too young."

Penny, nodding.

"That's what I said. I told her she could have one when she got into high school and not before. It's a mini computer, which means creeps can text her, email her, Snapchat her." She looks at me with wide, wet, pleading eyes. "You see what I'm saying here, Doc? I was trying to protect her. I was raising her all alone and I was trying to do the right thing for her safety. Her survival in a messed-up crazy world." Sighing, sadly. "Now this."

I wrap my arms around her, pull her into me.

"You did your best," I say. "You are a fantastic mother. Take it from me. A man who regrets the day he was born."

"But don't you see, Doc?" she says. "If I'd gotten her the phone, all we'd have to do is call her." Shaking her head in frustration. "Just like that kid Susan said, it's a safety issue, one way or another."

Something flashes through my brain. Once more, a shred of hope injected into my veins.

"What about Chloe's iPad? Can you somehow text with her or email?"

I release her. She steps slowly back. She's thinking it over.

"Jesus," she mutters to herself. "It never dawned on me that I might be able to WhatsApp her."

"What's WhatsApp?"

"It's a kind of texting service. You can call with it, too, but you have to have internet or Wi-Fi for it to work. It's for people who don't want to pay to text or make phone calls. It's all free."

"Can you WhatsApp with your phone? The one my lawyer gave me is an old flip top. It was old ten years ago."

"Yes, I have WhatsApp on my phone."

"What have we got to lose, Pen?"

She pulls her cell back out of her bag, finger taps onto an app. I can't be sure what she's doing, her fingers are going so fast, but it looks like she's typing Chloe's name into the WhatsApp search engine.

Her eyes light up.

"Oh my God, she is on WhatsApp. I can call her."

"Do it now," I plead. "Don't wait."

She taps a button and puts the phone to her ear. Gritting her teeth, she waits and waits. Then, shaking her head.

"She's not answering," she grouses.

"At least leave her a text message," I insist. "Like I said, what have we got to lose?"

She rapid fires a text into the WhatsApp message sending portal. Hits SEND.

"What did you write, Penny?"

"I told her we're looking for her. To go to the hotel front desk immediately."

"You told her we love her, Pen?"

"You gotta ask, Doc?"

There it is again . . . the feeling of wanting to tear the town apart. Penny is staring down at the face of her phone, as if this will make Chloe text us back all the faster.

"So what do we do now?" I go on.

When my cell phone rings, my heart nearly ceases to beat.

CHAPTER 11

HEART POUNDING AGAINST sternum, I pull the phone from my jeans pocket. I don't need to see the number to know who it belongs to. Aside from my lawyer, Joel, and Penny, the only other person who has this number is my parole officer, Drew Lochte.

I gaze at the number anyway.

It's him. Drew.

The phone is ringing and I'm hesitating. I know I should be answering it. That the last thing I should be doing is letting it ring and ring. Ignoring your parole officer after you've been paroled from a maximum-security prison just days ago is not exactly the best course of action. But I'm entirely stressed out. My daughter is missing. She's my responsibility. Also, I've been issued another mandate that I've ignored. Like job hunting, for instance.

Under normal circumstances, a man newly paroled after incarceration for such a serious crime would be required to live in a government-run halfway house. I'd be allowed outside the house for working hours only. The rest of the time I'd be required to be present and accounted for inside house walls, under strict supervision. I might even be required to wear an ankle monitor.

But Joel worked out a sweet deal for me. An impossible deal.

In exchange for my testimony and for naming Rabuffo and everyone who surrounded him, I was offered a lenient parole. After all, I hadn't actually killed anyone. I was just the driver. But that didn't mean I didn't have to play by the rules. Just one screwup . . . just one seemingly unsightly situation like my missing daughter, for instance, and the State of New York could demand my immediate re-incarceration. What I mean is, what if the police suspect I had a hand in her going missing?

"Doc," Penny says, breaking me out of my spell. "Are you going to get the damned phone?"

It stops ringing.

It's answer enough.

I pocket the phone, knowing that I must call Drew back as soon as possible. Even if we don't find Chloe, I must call him back within the hour. I picture the wiry, half African American, half Caucasian man seated behind his desk in the parole offices. Maybe the top button on his button-down shirt is undone, the ball knot on his tie hanging down low. He's seated inside a cubicle that's identical to the other fifty cubicles that occupy the floor of the downtown Albany state government building. Phones ringing, fax machines spitting out paper, computer keyboards click-clacking, the perpetual monotone banter of voices all competing with one another. I see him pressing the tip of his ballpoint pen against a box on a standard black-on-white form. I see him checking the box on the phone call log. "No answer."

It's a check against me. Against my future as a free man.

Putting the phone away, I inhale a deep breath. I check my wristwatch. It's after four in the afternoon already.

"The WhatsApp text," I say. "Has Chloe responded?"

She whispers, "No." Shakes her head. "If she had her iPod on her, which she always does, she would have responded by now."

"Maybe she's in a place that doesn't have Wi-Fi," I suggest.

"Like where?"

The woods? The trunk of a car? The bottom of Mirror Lake? The bottom of Lake Placid? For Christ sakes, if only I could stop my imagination from working. From torturing me with bad daydreams.

"We're wasting time, Penny," I say after a beat. "Let's get searching."

"Promise me something first, Sidney," she says, looking into my eyes.

"What is it?"

"If we don't find Chloe here, in the downtown, we go to the hotel detective. Agreed?"

"Do I have a choice?"

"Not on your life," she says.

I watch her back as she starts walking.

* * *

We make a check on almost every clothing shop, bookstore, fly fishing outlet, food shop, bakery, coffeehouse, pizza joint, and bar on both sides of the strip. We look inside the old stone chapel that's located in the village center atop a small hill and we even poke our heads into a Chinese takeout joint. But other than the Chinese employees, it's empty.

We stop people on the sidewalk, show them Chloe's photo, ask them if they've seen our daughter. Everyone seems to react the same way. They purse their lips, scrunch their foreheads, and look away, as though ashamed of themselves for not having spotted the missing child.

By the time we've exhausted our search, it's going on six in the evening.

"It's time," Penny says, her body shaking, trembling. "You promised. Remember?"

The house detective.

"You're right," I agree. "It's time. But first, let's make one last check on the beach behind the hotel. For all we know, Chloe will be sitting there on a beach chair waiting for us to come back. Maybe she thinks we're the lost ones."

"We *are* lost," she says.

"No truer words," I say to myself. "I've been lost inside my head for ten years."

CHAPTER 12

No one occupies the beach at this hour of the evening. The lounges are still there, but they're empty. The small roped-off shallow area designated for little children is also empty, as is the little wood dock that's perched beside it. Now that the angle of the sun prevents its rays from warming the beach, the Adirondack air is cooling down. It makes me worry even more for Chloe, as though the onset of night brings not only darkness, but cold despair.

"Let's walk the beach," I say. "Just a quick inspection to see if Chloe left anything behind that might give us a clue to where she took off to."

"This is so damned silly," Penny says, acid in her tone. "We need to be involving the professionals by now. They're going to think it's strange we waited so long."

"Just look around for a minute or two, Pen."

She takes in the south end of the small, narrow beach, while I walk to the north end. I'm seeing nothing but crushed sand castles, small craters dug into the sand, discarded candy wrappers, an empty beer can, and even a pair of discarded swimming goggles. I feel like one of those amateur treasure hunters who scours the beach after hours with a metal detector in hopes of uncovering some spare change or discarded jewelry. But in this case, I'm searching for a sign of my missing daughter.

We walk and we search, but there's nothing to be seen, nothing to be discovered or uncovered.

No choice but to give in.

"It's time to call in the house detective," I whisper to myself, maybe a half second before Penny screams.

CHAPTER 13

I RUN.

Run toward the sound of the scream. Run along the water's edge to where Penny is standing, my boots kicking up the sand and clean lake surf. My jeans are soaked through by the time I come to her.

"What is it, Pen? What did you find?"

My breathing is rapid, shallow, pulse pounding in my temples.

She holds a single object in each of her hands. In her right hand, she holds a yellow polka-dotted bikini top. In her left hand, an iPod. The bikini top is soaked and covered in sand. The iPod screen has been smashed and lake water has seeped into it.

For a moment or two, the adrenaline and extra oxygen that fills my veins and arteries makes me feel like I'm levitating off the beach floor. I want to scream and rip somebody's head off, spit down his throat. But who exactly? Rabuffo? Is this his revenge? The abduction of my daughter? Does he know for sure that I exposed his entire operation to the authorities?

People talk.

Doesn't matter that I gave away everything I could under the guise of confidentiality, which, in the end, wasn't very confident since I retained my real name and my true identity—I didn't qualify for the federal witness protection program since mine were state offenses. So, like I said, people talk. Words matter. Words have consequences. Chloe's abduction could be that consequence.

Penny is swaying, her knees knocking together. I grab hold of her before she drops to the sandy ground like a sack of cold blood and bones.

"I . . . can't . . . breathe," she says.

"Listen, Pen," I insist. "Your lungs are constricting. Breathe easy. Just breathe . . ."

She's trying her hardest to listen to my instructions, but her eyes are rolling up into the back of her head and I'm almost certain she's about to pass out. I hold her all the tighter, and soon she's supporting herself on her own two feet again.

"How can this happen?" she says, her voice weak and wobbly. "Who did this, Sidney? Who took our daughter?"

I swallow something that feels and tastes like a rock.

"Let's talk to the hotel detective," I insist.

"Something we should have done a long time ago," she says.

CHAPTER 14

OUR HANDS LOCKED together, we head back into the hotel, up the single flight of stairs to the lobby. We don't approach the front desk; we throw ourselves at it.

"The hotel detective!" I holler at the portly blond desk manager I spoke with earlier. "Get him. Now!"

In my free hand, I'm holding Chloe's bathing suit top and her destroyed iPod. He glances at the items, swallows something, and breathes in deeply.

"Can we please keep our voices down?" he asks, with an anxious grin on his face while pulling his belt up over his soft underbelly. "Other hotel customers occupy the lobby."

My veins are on fire. I feel my biceps squeezing through the tight skin that covers them. I hand Chloe's things to Penny, clench my fingers and hands into rock-hard fists. I'm tasting the salty blood now that I've bitten through the flesh on my lip.

My right hand is raised and reaching across the counter even before the act can register with my brain. I grab hold of his shirt, pull him into me. The entire hotel lobby seems to go mannequin still, while I pull his face into mine.

"My daughter is gone," I whisper, forcefully. "I don't give a flying fuck about your damned clientele. Got it?"

"Sidney," Penny says, voice steady and serious. "Let the man go."

Suddenly, like waking up from a bad dream, I realize what it is I'm doing. An electric shock wave courses through my nervous system, and I release him.

"I'm sorry," I say. "It's the stress. My wife and I, we're very worried."

The blonde woman from the office in back emerges from out of the open office door. She steps up to the desk.

"The hotel detective is on her way," she explains. "Please wait here, Mr. O'Keefe."

"Her," I say, like a question.

"Is there a problem?" the manager poses.

How am I going to respond? That I just spent the last ten years surrounded by human-growth-hormone and steroid-injected male New York State corrections officers?

I feel my insides going south fast. My head is spinning. I'm biting down on my lip again. I glance at Penny. Her worried eyes are locked on mine. I must be a sore sight to behold.

It's then my bowels turn to water.

*　*　*

The public men's room is located on the opposite side of the lobby, off the long corridor that also accesses the second-floor rooms. I head inside, find that it's empty, and lock the door behind me. Pushing open the stall, I drop my jeans, and get rid of whatever poison has infected me. My brow is covered in sweat and my gut feels like somebody kicked it with a steel-toed jackboot.

When I'm done, I get dressed, then stand before the bathroom mirror and wash my hands in steaming hot water. Turning the hot water off, I turn on the cold water. I cup my hands together, fill them, splash the water on my face. Again and again. Gazing into the mirror, I watch the water bead and drip off the skin. My face is tight and stressed, the five o'clock shadow having evolved into a salt and pepper scruff.

The equally salt and pepper hair on my head is closely cropped. So close, it looks like I cut it myself with scissors. There's a pinky finger–sized scar on my scalp, above my right eye. It's where some-body broke a plastic food tray over my head back when I was em-ployed in the prison kitchen. I nearly drowned him in a fifty-gallon vat of yellow potato salad. I spent three months in the hole for that one. Didn't matter that it wasn't my fault. What mattered is that I threw the last punch, so to speak. The COs never see the first punch. That would be too fair.

I close my eyes, breathe deeply.

"Get it together, Sid," I say aloud. "You don't get it together, you're going back. You go back with Rabuffo knowing you testi-fied against him, you're a dead man. Christ, you just might be a dead man now. You know Rabuffo's style at this point in the game. Let the father live just long enough to see his family die. Could be Rabuffo is starting with Chloe, then Penny will be next. He'll do it to make you suffer, to tear your heart and soul apart. Finally, he'll finish with you. But it won't be quick. He'll make it hurt. He'll have one of his Chinese bosses perform Lingchi on you. Cut bits and pieces off of you, until you'll resemble one hundred ninety pounds of raw meat. Until your heart finally has had enough and it ceases to beat."

One more splash of water to the face.

I turn off the faucet. Standing straight and stiff, I pull a fist full of paper towels from the wall-mounted dispenser, dry my face. Tossing them into the receptacle, I can't help but steal one more glance in the mirror. They're standing behind me. All four of them. The Chen family. The Chinese father and mother, and their two kids. One a boy, the other a little girl, not much younger than Chloe. They're staring at me in the mirror, not saying anything. They're alive but their heads and faces are bleeding.

There's a hole in the father's forehead. So wide you can see the whiteness of his brains. His wife's left eye has been shot through. The entirety of the little boy's cranial cap is blown away, while the little girl's left lower jaw is shredded from an exit wound. Yet somehow, they are able to stand there, eyeing me, like they want something from me.

I'm not sure how much time has passed since I first saw them standing there, but my head feels like it's spinning out of control. Until the father opens his mouth, whispers one word.

"Revenge."

I close my eyes, whisper, "Go away. Go the hell away. I never touched you. I told them not to kill you. Wemps and Singh, I told them, damn it."

The loud knocking startles me.

A fist pounding on the wood door. I open my eyes and dread the reflection I'm going to see in the mirror. But the Chinese family is gone. Of course, they were never there in the first place. I dreamt them up.

. . . Get it the hell together, Sid . . . Stop living inside your head . . .

"Sid, are you okay?" Penny inquires through the door. "What's taking so long?"

"Sorry," I say, reaching out to unlock the dead bolt. Then, opening the door, looking into her face. "I felt sick. I'm okay now."

I step out into the corridor.

"You look pale," she says.

"It's okay. There's no time to worry about a stomachache."

"The detective is here. She's in the lobby, waiting."

I start walking.

"Sid," Penny says, stopping me.

I turn and eye her.

"It's getting dark, Sid," she goes on. "It's getting dark and our daughter is out there somewhere."

. . . Rabuffo . . .

"We're gonna find her, Pen. If it's the last thing we do on God's earth, we're gonna find her. Tonight."

Turning, I head back into the lobby, my eyes searching for the hotel detective.

CHAPTER 15

SHE'S TALL AND slim with straight dark hair parted over her right eye. She's got a leather bag slung over her shoulder and she's wearing a tan, lightweight business suit, her skirt cut just above the knees, her matching jacket covering a tight white button down. She's wearing black pumps for footwear, which makes her even taller. She recognizes me before I realize who she is. When she holds out her hand, I catch a glimpse of the firearm that's holstered on her waist.

"I'm Giselle," she says, taking my hand in hers, gripping it tightly, with confidence. "Giselle Fontaine. I understand we've got ourselves a situation."

She releases my hand, offers Penny a nod.

"This is my wife, Penny," I say.

Giselle shakes her hand. Then, "Why don't we head to your room, folks. We can talk in private there and I can get a look at the place."

Without waiting for an answer, the detective turns and heads into the stairwell that leads back downstairs to the ground floor rooms.

Pulling out my keycard, I open the door for her, half expecting to see Chloe sitting on the bed, watching television. But I've already given up hope on her just suddenly showing up like that.

Still, my heart jumps up into my mouth when I open the door. I'm almost tempted to utter the name, Chloe. But the room is dark and silent and all too dead.

Here's what I do.

I flip on the light switch, which engages every ceiling and wall-mounted lamp in the room. Together the three of us head into the room, which contains two beds, three suitcases, numerous electronics chargers plugged into the outlets, plus a cooler filled with beer and cold soft drinks.

Immediately I'm attracted to the cooler. I pull out a cold bottle of Dos Equis.

Penny gives me a look. So does Detective Giselle.

"I'm sorry," I say. "I know this isn't the time, but after a day like today, I really need one."

Giselle grins, holds up her hands.

"Hey, don't mind me. I'd have probably downed a fifth of vodka by now if any of my rug rats had gone missing. Knock yourself out." She reaches into her pocket, pulls out a notepad. "Now I'm going to ask you some vital questions about your daughter, then I want to get a sort of timeline idea of what occurred."

Penny holds out the bathing suit top and the iPad like she's presenting evidence to a court of law.

"Our daughter's gone," Penny interjects, acid-like. "That's all we know."

"I understand that," Giselle says, locking eyes on the items in Penny's hands. "But the more information I have, the more I can help."

I pop open the beer, steal a deep drink.

"We found that stuff on the beach in back of the hotel, just minutes ago," I offer.

Giselle takes the stuff in hand, stares at it for a long beat.

"Your daughter's?"

Penny nods.

Giselle's eyes go wide. It's a while before she blinks. That's when she stuffs the items into her bag.

"It's state's evidence now," she explains. "I'll make sure the police get it tonight, as in immediately."

"Show her the picture of Chloe on your phone, Pen," I add.

Penny pulls out her smartphone, presents it to the hotel detective who stares down at it.

"Very fine-looking young lady," she says while eyeing Chloe's face as though committing it to memory. Then, reaching into her jacket pocket and coming back out with a business card, "Here's my cell number. Please forward the picture to me so I can send it on to the hotel staff. While we're talking, the staff will be making a sweep of every room, space, crawl space, nook and cranny in the facility. No area will go unsearched. Do we have an understanding?"

Penny and I both nod. Somehow hearing that the detective is being proactive fills me with the dreaded H word again. Hope.

She hands Penny the card.

. . . Hope is but a dream . . .

Giselle makes specific inquiries about Chloe. Her age, height, weight, school, hobbies, social media site subscriptions including her WhatsApp account, you name it. She writes the pertinent stuff down. Then she asks to see my daughter's things.

"You mind if I go through her suitcase, Mr. and Mrs. O'Keefe?"

"Why?" Penny begs. "Even I don't do that. It's a privacy thing."

"You should," Giselle says. "Kids your daughter's age can sometimes get involved with people and things they shouldn't. Kids Chloe's age are dying."

"Are you saying my daughter is doing drugs?" Penny says. "She's only eleven."

"Oh gee, I'm not saying that at all," Giselle offers. "But what if there's a receipt for a train ticket, or heck, even a plane ticket? What if there's a note from a girlfriend or boyfriend that indicates she had every intention of running away? What if she's not doing drugs, but has a secret boyfriend who is? You gotta think about all the possibilities."

I drink some more beer, wipe my mouth with the back of my hand. I might have been incarcerated for a long time, but I'm very much aware that the death rate among teens and pre-teens has increased by almost thirty-five percent during those ten years. Oxy, fentanyl-laced heroin . . . it's killing kids Chloe's age, and their parents are blind to their addiction. They're not recognizing the signs. The death stare, the weight loss, the insomnia, the mood swings.

"Let her check, Pen," I say. "The detective is right."

"We'll look together," Giselle says. Then, her eyes shifting to me, "Oh, and one more thing, folks. If we don't come up with anything in our search through the hotel, it is my duty as hotel detective to call in the police. That iPod and bathing top in my bag is reason enough to call them in right this second. But because of your special, let's call them circumstances, Mr. O'Keefe, perhaps it's better that you and your wife pay a personal visit to the police chief himself. His name is Joe Walton."

"What special circumstances?" I ask, already anticipating the answer before she annunciates it.

"Now, darn it all, Mr. O'Keefe, I know who you are, and what you were accused of doing all those years ago. I know that you are newly paroled and I'm happy for you and Mrs. O'Keefe. You seem like fine people to me and my heart aches for you. But procedure is procedure, and I'm going to tell you right now that you both should have come to me sooner with this. I can only assume you did not want to rock the legal applecart, so to speak. The last thing you need right now is a hotel full of cops. Am I right?"

My heart sinks from my mouth to somewhere around my feet. When I look at Penny, I'm not sure if what I see is disappointment in her face or just plain disgust. I want to say something in my defense. But I don't. What the hell am I going to do? Explain to her that I exposed a mob boss and now he might be enacting his revenge on me?

"But let's not dwell on the past," Giselle suggests. "Let's see that suitcase and go from there. And listen to me, closely. I can assure you that between me, the hotel staff, and the village police department, we will do everything in our power to find your daughter. Understood?"

A teardrop falls down Penny's cheek.

She stands, pulls Chloe's pink overhead compartment-sized case from off the floor, drops it onto the bed.

"Go for it," she says.

It takes all of two minutes to rummage through the clothes and underclothes. But in the end, we find nothing to indicate our daughter has run away with a girl, boy, or the circus. Nothing to indicate she's into drugs, hard, soft, or prescription based. While the women were going through the case, I could hear someone from the hotel knocking on each door of the floor in their search for Chloe. Naturally, they skipped our room.

"Listen here folks, let me check in with some of the staff." Giselle pulls the radio from her belt, calls on a man named Frank, asks him if the crew has uncovered Chloe yet.

After a beat or two, a tinny voice responds.

"Negative on that, G."

"Percentage of task completion there, Frank?"

"Closing in on one hundred percent, G. Wish I had better news."

The dreaded H word.

. . . *Hope. Hope is but a dream* . . .

Go to hell.

Detective Giselle Fontaine purses her lips, pulls out her cell phone from the interior pocket on her jacket.

She says, "Before I call Chief Walton to get going on a possible Amber Alert and to file a missing person's report, can I ask you one last question?"

My mouth goes dry at the mere mention of an Amber Alert. I nod since I don't have enough saliva in my mouth to form a word.

"Was Chloe angry at you for anything? Was she maybe upset over a boyfriend? Girlfriend? Anything like that?"

Penny shakes her head. "No. Nothing was wrong. She's just a normal eleven-year-old kid, playing in the beach sand and poof, she's gone."

"But then, she's not a normal eleven-year-old kid," Giselle interjects.

"What are you implying?" Penny asks.

"What I'm implying is that she's the child of a man who went to prison for a violent action."

My stomach goes tight because the detective is spot on and she knows it, as much as it hurts to hear it.

"She wasn't upset about your husband coming home?" Giselle presses. "It can be a traumatic thing for a child to never know what it's like to live with her father, and suddenly he's home."

"In other words," I add, "is Chloe afraid of me? You insinuating I might have had something to do with her disappearance?"

My blood is getting hot and Penny is aware of it.

"Calm down, Doc," she cautiously says.

Giselle looks into my eyes. "Well, gee, that's not what I'm getting at, Mr. O'Keefe."

"Funny," I say, "because that's the way I feel."

"And, Mrs. O'Keefe," Giselle goes on, "were you seeing anyone romantically before Mr. O'Keefe came back home? Someone your daughter liked and had gotten used to? Someone whom you cut ties with in order to welcome Mr. O'Keefe back with, ummm, open arms?"

Penny's face goes stone still. Like Giselle didn't just ask her a rapid-fire series of personal questions. More like she stomped on her feet.

"I assure you, Detective," Penny utters, "nothing of the sort has occurred."

Penny looks at me like she's asking me if I believe her. What choice do I have but to believe her?

Giselle nods, then proceeds to speed-dial a number on her cell phone. But instead of completing the call inside the room, she takes the phone with her outside into the corridor. Curiously, that's when my own phone starts to ring.

"You have to get that," Penny insists. "If it's your parole officer, you can't just blow him off."

Biting my bottom lip, trying not to break the thin vermillion skin any more than I already have.

"No choice," I say, stating the obvious.

Flipping the phone open, I press the little green SEND button and place it to my ear.

"This is Sidney O'Keefe," I say.

CHAPTER 16

"WHERE YOU BEEN, Sid?" Drew Lochte says from down inside his Albany office. "Been searching high and low for you."

I picture the forty-something man seated at his cubicle desk, black loafer-covered feet resting up on the desktop, tie hanging low, sleeves rolled up. It's late in the day before the weekend starts and I'm one of the last, if not *the* last call he's going to make. If I didn't answer, there's a good chance he would have no other option but to pay a personal visit to our North Albany apartment first thing Monday morning. Or hell, Saturday morning. Perhaps he's planning on doing that anyway.

"Sorry, Drew," I say, my eyes on Penny, trying my best to keep my voice free of alarm. "I took a ride with the family up north. We were out of cell phone range for a while."

I picture Lochte drumming on the desktop with a Bic pen. I picture him not believing a word I say. I've done some checking up on the parole officer, and I believe he is a straight-up guy. Not a bully, like so many power-hungry parole officers can be. But I also know Drew Lochte is trained to be skeptical at best, to see entirely through the bullshit at worst.

"Sidney," Drew says, "did you forget that if you leave the city, you're to notify me first?"

Penny staring back at me like, *Get rid of him already.*

"My apologies, Drew," I say. "I haven't been close to them in a while. Penny suggested a quick trip and I thought it would be fun. We weren't exactly thinking about the rules."

"So where are you exactly?"

"Lake Placid."

"Lake Placid," Drew repeats, like he's having an *ah-ha* moment. "Nice this time of year. And how's the job hunting going? Speaking of rules, you'll recall the rules of your parole as stipulated in the over-the-fucking-top ridiculously lenient deal your lawyer struck with the district attorney. You are to gain employment as soon as humanly possible or at the very least provide me with a list of potential employers you are actively seeking out, or else risk a serious violation of said rules." He pauses for effect. "So where's my list, Sid man? It's been almost a week. I should have a list with a dozen employer titles on it, plus the corresponding days and times of your interviews. I don't care if you get a job washing dishes at Jack's Diner on Central Avenue. I just want to see that you're trying." He exhales. "Guy with your build and solid guns, you should be able to get a job as a forklift."

Me, trying to swallow. Saliva glands shutting down.

"I promise, Drew, I'll have something for you next week. Just cut me a little slack. My family hasn't seen me in forever. I need to spend a little time with them, alone. Away from the city. It's important to them. Important to me."

Another pause. Longer this time. More weighted.

"I get it," Drew says, after a while, his voice more sullen, less insistent. Then, after a beat, "How's your daughter doing? How's she taking to your being home? No trouble?"

An electric jolt to my heart. Jesus, is he playing with me? Is my parole officer messing with my head? Does he know something about Chloe's disappearance and playing dumb?

My eyes, still locked on Penny's. I'm not sure that I've blinked the entire time I've been on the phone with him.

"She's . . . fine," I lie.

Another pause that's as painful as it is long and drawn out. A slight commotion on his end of the connection, like he's removed his feet from the desk, and sat up straight.

"Listen, Sid," he says, his voice low, as if he's talking to me with his hand cupped over the mouthpiece. "You realize it's my job to give you a hard time, right?"

"I guess so," I say. "I've never been paroled before. But then again, I've never been accused and convicted of murder before either."

"I know you didn't kill that family. That you were just the driver, that you were trying to pay your debt off to a man who would cut your neck from ear to ear and think nothing of it. Or, it's what I want to believe anyway. But the rules are the rules, and I need this job and I'll lose it if I don't do it to the best of my ability."

"I understand."

"That's why I have to insist that you be truthful with me. No lies, no deceptions and we'll get along just fine, capice?"

"Capice, Drew."

"Think of me as your new dad. The kind of dad you can come to about anything. I won't yell at you and I won't smack you up-side the head. I'll simply listen to what you have to say and then take the best course of action. Sound fair, Sid man? Or what do they call you? Doc?"

"Sure," I say. "Sure thing. And yes, you can call me Doc. It's probably as close as I'll ever get to being a real doctor."

"Now here's the prescription I'm gonna write up for you, Doc," Lochte goes on. "I want you to enjoy a nice few days with your family. Get readjusted. Spoil them a little. I know you don't have a whole lot of money, or maybe you buried a stash before you went away. Whatever . . . Spoil them with hugs, kisses, and love if you've got nothing else. All I ask is that you check in with me as soon as you get back. Then we can get back on the job hunt." He snickers. "Hey, you gotta put food on the table now, am I right? You're the man of the house again, Sidney. Be proud. You made it out of the joint. You made it back to something that most cons would give up their left nut for. Hell, both nuts."

"Thanks, Drew," I say. "Goodbye."

"Hasta la vista, Doc Sidney," he says. "I'm out."

He hangs up.

For the first time in what seems forever, I breathe.

CHAPTER 17

PENNY AND I head back out into the corridor. Giselle is standing there, her cell phone in her hand.

"Chief Walton is expecting you." Shifting her gaze from me to Penny and back again. "I would go with you, but I need to stay here and continue to monitor the situation."

"What about Chloe's things?" Penny inquires. "The things we found on the beach."

"I've already sent them on to the police station," Giselle informs. "No worries there."

It sounds absurd when she says, *No worries.*

"Remember, folks," the detective goes on, "just because your daughter hasn't shown up yet doesn't mean she won't. Which is why I need to stay put. I need to keep on top of my people."

"Where do we go?" I ask.

"The Lake Placid village precinct is only a five-minute walk from here. Go left outside the main doors of the hotel. Head south on Main Street until you come to the Olympic Training facility. The police building will be on your left. You can't miss it."

Both Penny and I politely thank Giselle. As we begin making our way down the carpeted corridor, she calls out for us. We stop, turn.

"You really should eat something," she suggests. "I'm guessing you haven't eaten a thing all darn day. You need your strength."

Penny takes a step toward Giselle.

She says, "Right now my daughter is out there somewhere with nothing to eat. Food is the last thing on my mind."

We turn back around, begin our journey to the police.

*   *   *

Just like Giselle promised, the walk to the police station takes only five minutes. The two-story brick building dates back maybe to the Second World War. Several police cruisers are parked out front. Not sedans, but more rugged 4X4 SUVs painted black and white, and adorned with a decal of a triangular mountain with a snow-flake in its center. Lake Placid is a downhill skier's paradise, after all. The precinct's front doors are made of glass and wood, and as soon as we enter through them into the vestibule, we're greeted by a guard sergeant who mans a counter to our left-hand side.

"Help you?" the older, heavyset man inquires.

"We're here to see Chief Walton," I announce.

"He's expecting us," Penny interjects.

Instead of using his intercom, the sergeant pushes his chair out, and stands. There's a pair of bifocal reading glasses hanging off his neck by a leather lanyard. They sway and slap against his barrel chest when he crosses over the precinct floor and into an interior office located all the way in back.

For a long beat, Penny and I stand stone still by the front counter while the scattering of uniformed officers who occupy the room type away on their old desktop computers, or chat away on the phone. When the beefy guard sergeant comes back out of the rear office, he issues us a wave.

"The chief will see you now," he says.

As instructed, we make our way to the back of the precinct.

For the chief of police, the office is small and cramped. But that's more the result of the overall diminutive size of the police headquarters than it is the status of the individual who occupies it. To our right as we walk in is a bulletin board with mug shots tacked to it. Below the mug shots are photos of missing persons. Little kids mostly. Little girls and boys with sad, milk carton faces. I can't help myself. I picture Chloe's face pinned to the board. Just the thought of it makes me at once livid, but at the same time, sad and rock-bottom low.

. . . Turn the damned imagination off, Doc . . . Do it now or you won't make it through the night . . .

To the left is an old leather couch that looks like it dates back to the 1932 Lake Placid Olympics. Mounted to the wall directly above it is a flat-screened television, which is presently turned off. A wood desk takes up the majority of the office. Seated behind it is a fifty-something man who's clean shaven but balding. Judging by the way he's seated in the old swivel chair, he's maybe five ten or eleven and carrying more than his share of beer weight. What's left of his reddish hair is sporting some gray at the temples. Big blue eyes, an average nose streaked with a few broken blood vessels, and a rather pronounced chin complete the face. If I were made to describe his head at gunpoint, I'd say it looks like a big block of granite.

He stands for a moment, introducing himself simply as Joe Walton, with his right hand outstretched in the direction of the couch. Penny sits, but I choose to remain standing.

"Please take a load off," he says, while sitting himself back down. He pulls a pair of reading glasses from out of a plastic case that's stored in his chest pocket, slips them on. Staring down at an open manila folder, he adds, "Sidney and Penny O'Keefe. Your daughter is Chloe, I'm told. Eleven years old. Student. Good kid. Never been in trouble. Been missing now for, how many hours?"

"Over six," I inform.

He nods, runs his fingers across his nose like it itches.

"Missing Persons reports usually go out after twenty-four hours, but in the case of a minor we've already issued an Amber Alert. As soon as House Detective Fontaine forwarded Chloe's photo and vitals, it went out across the wires and the internet. Even the electronic signs along Interstate 87 are helping spread the word. The system has worked more than once for us, Mr. and Mrs. O'Keefe."

"Let's hope it works again," Penny says, her hands pressed together in her lap, like she's praying.

He says, "I'm not going to bother you for Chloe's vitals since Giselle already sent those over, too, along with the things you discovered on the beach. But I would like to get some more information from you both before I instruct my people to head out on patrol."

"We understand," I say, glancing at Penny.

Walton clears his throat, nods as if answering a question he's silently posed to himself.

He says, "Has your daughter been acting strange as of late?"

Once more, Penny and I glance into one another's eyes. She clears the bullfrog from her throat.

"It's like I told Detective Giselle," she says, her voice sounding like a defeated whisper. "Chloe is a good kid. A normal kid. A happy kid." Then, throwing her hands up in the air, "Jesus, why aren't you out there trying to find her?"

Walton holds up both his hands, palms out.

"I understand your frustration, Mrs. O'Keefe, I really do. When I was a boy, my little brother, Timmy, went missing for three days.

Turned out he was living up in the hayloft of the neighbor's barn. He ran away because my mother bought me a pair of sneakers and got him nothing. Converse high top Chuck Taylors, if I recall. Black. She couldn't afford to buy us both a pair at the same time, and while his were still in pretty good shape, mine were held together with duct tape. So you see, Mrs. O'Keefe, kids, as normal as they seem, will sometimes do the damndest things. Especially when puberty is starting to hit. And I imagine that, at eleven years of age, your daughter is riding on the dramatic precipice of young adulthood."

Penny nods.

"Yes," she says, somewhat shyly. "In some ways, she's there already."

"So perhaps I should rephrase my question," Walton goes on. "Has there occurred anything in Chloe's life that's given her cause for being upset? Any dramatic changes, moves, or shifts? Anything that would cause her to, say, run away, just like my little brother, Timmy?"

This time, Penny and I do not communicate through eye contact. This time, I simply keep my mouth shut and allow her to do the talking.

"Yes," Penny says. "My husband is back after being gone for a very long time."

Walton forms a grin. He sits back in his swivel chair, as if he's happy with the way he's beginning to pry the truth out of us.

"And where were you, Mr. O'Keefe?"

For a change I'm not biting on my bottom lip. I'm nibbling on it. I'm also feeling the burn start at my toes, run all the way up the backs of my legs, up my spine into my head.

"You know exactly where I've been, Chief Walton," I say. "Prison."

The grin becomes a big smile.

"I just wanted to hear it from you," he says.

For a weighted minute, the room turns as still and cold as a morgue. But then Walton breaks the ice by leaning up in his squeaky swivel chair. "Who was the last to see Chloe before she disappeared . . . let me see, here . . . on the beach behind the Golden Arrow Hotel?"

"A man and a woman by the name of Stevens," Penny offers. "Claudia and Burt. Chloe was playing in the sand with their little girl. A girl about her own age."

"A stranger?"

"Yes," Penny goes on. "Chloe is very friendly like that."

"Sounds like you have done a stellar job of raising her under very difficult and stressful circumstances, Mrs. O'Keefe," Walton offers with a wink of his eye. His irony does not go unnoticed.

He writes something down, then looks directly at me.

"Question," he says. "Why were the Stevenses the last people to see Chloe before she went missing?"

The room falls quiet for a moment because he's just asked the one *Gotcha* question I've been hoping to avoid.

"Of course, we had our eye on her, too," I say, feeling the blood fill my face along with the lie.

"Oh, Sidney," Penny interrupts with a shake of her head. "Let's just tell him the truth, for God's sakes."

Chief Walton gazes at Penny, then at me.

"Which truth?" he asks.

Me, exhaling. "Penny and I had taken a moment to be alone. In the hotel room. It was the first time in years. Ten years."

Holding up his hands again.

"Okay, okay," he says, once again sitting back in the swivel chair. "I get it. You left your daughter alone on the beach with some strangers so you could get some action."

"It wasn't *exactly* like that," Penny protests. "Chloe is very mature, and our room is located on the bottom floor, beach level. We were literally just a few feet away. Sidney had a small, very personal gift he wanted to share with me while we had a brief spare moment alone."

She doesn't show him the metal ring, but she does twist it on her finger, self-consciously.

"But you *weren't* watching her," he clarifies. "Technically speaking. I'm just trying to paint a clear picture inside my head here."

"No," I confirm. "We *weren't* watching her. We were together in that room, with the curtains closed. That answer your question . . . *Chief?*"

"Take it easy, Mr. O'Keefe," Walton says after a long beat. "No need to get all worked up over nothing. Best to keep that temper in check, wouldn't you agree?"

. . . *worked up over nothing* . . .

He slowly, dramatically, sits back and then up again, the swivel chair sounding like it's about to collapse under his weight. His eyes on the desk, he shuffles through Chloe's file, taking a second or two to study her photo. He picks up the pen, taps out a few beats on the metal desktop, then quite abruptly, stands.

"Mrs. O'Keefe," he says, both his thumbs jammed into his black leather utility belt. "Would you mind stepping outside for just a moment? I'd like to have a word with your husband, alone."

He follows up with a polite smile. But other than politeness, there's nothing in the smile that conveys friendliness or happiness. Penny rises, nods, and heads for the door, but not without brushing the fingertips on her right hand against my left hand. The touch sends a kind of electric wave up and down my spine.

"I'll be right outside, Doc," she whispers.

The door opens and closes hard, the loud violent noise startling me like a gunshot to the heart.

CHAPTER 18

WALTON STARES AT me for a while. It's not like he's eyeing me so much as MRI'ing me with his special eyes. Trying to see inside me, see what it is I'm hiding.

"What's this all about?" I say, not hiding my anger. "Or is this just another stall tactic to keep you from looking for my daughter?"

"Love the attitude, O'Keefe," he says, gritting his teeth. "But I'm gonna lay it on the line now that your wife is out of the room. I know exactly who you are, what you're all about, and what you did to that Chinese family back in '07."

"I didn't do anything to that Chinese family."

He rolls his eyes around in their sockets, sticks out his already pronounced chin.

"You pick the devil you sleep with, O'Keefe," he says. "If I had a dime for every asshole I put away who says, *Gee, I didn't do it*, or *I swear, I'm really not a bad guy*, I wouldn't be working this shitty job chasing out-of-town drunk drivers every weekend. I don't really give a crap who killed them or why. What I do give a crap about is a little girl who's apparently gone missing in my village while her parents were busy fucking their brains out inside their hotel room, and it don't sit right with me."

He goes quiet for another beat, but his words are somehow still bouncing off the walls like ricocheting bullets.

"So what are you getting at, Chief?"

"I've made a few calls, your parole officer being one of them . . . what's his name." He shuffles through the paperwork again.

"Lochte," I say. "Drew . . . Lochte."

"Yeah, Lochte. That's it. We discussed your parole and why you were able to get such a sweet deal on the outside." Smiling again. "Yeah, that's right, I know about the pricks who came after you in the joint. I also know how you managed to put them down, Sidney *Van Dam*. You got the bleeding-heart tattoo on your bicep. Whad' you do, tell your old lady it was a heart to remember her by?" He snorts. "You're a badass motherfucker, O'Keefe. A killer. You should be proud of yourself. Men, women, and children fear you."

"But not you, Chief."

He grins. "Now we're making some real progress."

Heart beating, pulsing, pounding. I'm swallowing something hard and bitter, my mouth entirely dry, my teeth digging at my bottom lip. Severe agitation, clinically speaking. Severe restlessness, aggravation, anxiety. I'm absolutely seething, and Walton knows it because Walton is going out of his way to provoke me. Non-clinically speaking, he's pulling every one of my triggers.

I inhale a breath, release it slowly.

I say, "Wow, guess you've done your homework after all, Chief."

"Yah, I have. 'Cause that's what I do." Picking up the file and releasing it so that it drops back down on the desk. Then, "Here's what I'm guessing about you, O'Keefe. As lucky as you've been at keeping your own neck from being cut wide open, you knew that your luck was about to run out. That Rabuffo was gonna get to you sooner or later, just to make sure you kept your mouth shut for all eternity plus one hundred years. To make sure you suddenly don't start mouthing off about his not so legal business affairs." He smiles. "How's that TV jingle go? You seen it yet since you been out?"

"Rabuffo's Custom Clothiers . . ." I half sing, half mumble.

"That's it, O'Keefe," he says. "You can carry a tune. That damn jingle runs every five minutes on TV and radio, I swear. I sing it in my goddamn sleep."

"Daylight's wasting, Chief."

"Okay, so Rabuffo knows that eventually your dick is gonna get itchy and you're gonna one day wake up and it's gonna be Popeye time. You're gonna look in the mirror and scream, *Enough is enough, and enough is too much!* So what do you do?—"

"—I make contact with my lawyer, tell him to tell the DA I'm ready to talk. It's Rabuffo's worst nightmare."

"I love it when somebody like yourself is on the same page with me," he says. "Makes this shit so much easier."

"Glad I can help."

"So you went to Albany, got down on your knees, sucked the DA off, swallowed his load, and now you're free and the FBI is building up its case against that rich-as-Jesus trafficking asshole." Tapping his temple with his index finger. "He knows you spilled everything, and in my mind at least, he's not happy about it so now he's going after you in a different way. He wants to make you suffer. He wants to torture you. So what's he do? He follows you up here, or one of his goons follows you up here anyway, and they snatch your daughter off the beach while you're getting your rocks off. Sound like a logical possibility to you?"

My eyes lock onto his. They're so focused I can make out the jagged lightning strike–like broken blood vessels that mar his whites. My guess is that Walton likes his beer and whiskey chasers so much, he's a shorthair away from a stroke, or at the very least, minor myocardial infarction. If his tired eyes don't give him away, then his wheat belly and friendly demeanor do.

"You listen to me, Chief," I say, my voice low, but somehow screaming. "Penny doesn't know shit about Rabuffo. All she knows is I worked for him as a driver that night in 2007, and because of it, I did time. I'd very much appreciate it if that's the way it stayed."

He crosses arms over barrel chest.

"So she really doesn't know, does she?" he says. "She doesn't know the extent of it. How the hell does she think you went from incarcerated for pretty much life to suddenly scot-free with the snap of a finger? She doesn't know the things you know about Mickey. Some of his deepest, darkest secrets."

"Like what?"

"I can bet Rabuffo has quite the stash stored away in a vault somewhere. Maybe even a vault kept deep down inside the basement of his house. You two were as close as a father and son, I'm told. Might be reasonable to suspect you know more than you're letting on about when it comes to accessing that little fortune."

In my head, seeing myself side by side Rabuffo, riding an elevator down into the subterranean depths beneath his mansion, where the true Rabuffo operation was run. How is it the chief of an upstate mountain backwater is privy to all this?

"Mickey Rabuffo," he goes on. "Must be he let you in on lots of secrets. How he operated his various smuggling ops, his Chinese restaurants, the tailor shops, who he trusted, who he didn't. Maybe even, where he kept his money." He laughs. "Because he damn sure didn't keep it all in the KeyBank down the road. I imagine he saved you from a whole lot of hurt from those card shark assholes you owed. Maybe . . . just maybe . . . Mickey Rabuffo saved your life when it needed saving the most."

*   *   *

I see myself walking the grounds behind Mickey's house in North Albany. We're surrounded by woods. There's an Olympic-sized swimming pool that's a girl magnet. A few of them are lounging around it, their tops off. Beautiful girls with long blonde, red, and brunette hair. They tease one another, drink champagne with one another, snort lines off one another's flat bellies, kiss one another's Botox-injected lips. The house beyond the pool is a large white Colonial. There's a separate wing for the maids, butlers, and cooks. Rabuffo is living in a decadent Caligula-like world long since passed and he's loving it.

He's wearing a white robe over long red swimming trunks. He's got these big sunglasses on that look like something Elvis would have worn back in the mid-seventies. Hanging off his neck is a thick gold chain. He's smoking a big cigar delivered from Cuba via his own plane, which also made a pit stop in Mexico City. No doubt the plane contained a good-sized shipment of El Chapo love powder. He sets his hand on my shoulder, gives it a pinch. Something a loving father might do to his young adult son.

"Sidney," he says, "I like you. I like paying for you. I like helping you. You know why?"

"Why's that, Mick?" I say, staying close to him, answering only when spoken to.

"Because you're smart. You're not like the other morons who work for me. That fucking Wemps and Singh. Meatheads. They are loyal, I will admit. But you. You've got class. You're educated. You have manors. You're confident, even after that bullshit your ex-wife pulled on you. You don't even like carrying a gun."

"Why would I need a gun, Mick?"

He stops, laughs, pulls the cigar from his mouth.

"Now that's funny," he says. *"You, the young man who could have been a surgeon or a heart doctor or the guy who cured cancer, if only you'd stayed in med school. But then that horrible bitch came into your life and robbed you blind. But now you're going to have a new life. I'm going to take you into my confidence, Sidney. In exchange for your loyalty, I'm going to let you work off your debt, and in the process, I'll make you rich beyond your wildest dreams. I'm going to make you one of my own, like my very own son."*

*   *   *

My thoughts, drifting back to the here and now.

"She knows," I say.

"Who knows what, O'Keefe? You're talking in riddles."

"Penny," I say. "That I leveraged my inside information on Rabuffo in order to negotiate parole. And a very sweet parole deal at that."

"Didn't you just tell me she thinks you were the driver and that's all?"

"Let me be clear," I say. "She hasn't exactly come out and said she knows what I did in order to get paroled. But trust me, she knows. I feel it in my gut that she knows. How could she not know, Chief?"

"And she knows Mr. Custom Clothier-slash-Chinese restaurant mogul is about to face FBI arrest any minute? Thanks to you."

"She knows I was working for him at the time of my arrest, but I always kept my true connection to him a secret—to protect her. To protect my baby." Shaking my head. "Christ, I only started in with him because I needed the money. I was a bag man. Nothing dangerous. Then, I guess, one thing led to another. Like you said, I slept with the devil and got burned."

"It's quite possible that it led directly to your missing daughter, Sidney." He allows his arms to fall by his sides, purses his lips, glances up at the acoustical ceiling. "Unless, of course, something else happened to your daughter."

"What kind of something else?"

"You were a violent man in prison," he says, a little under his breath, his eyes now back on me. "Some men have difficulty adjusting when they get out. Little things annoy them. Like a little girl, for instance. Kids tend to agitate some people, get under their skin."

The fury once more mainlined into my veins.

"What are you accusing me of, Chief?"

He grins, bearing those chewing-tobacco-stained teeth.

"Nothing much," he says with a wink. "Just theorizing is all."

"My daughter loves me," I say, my voice raised a decibel or two. "We had a loving relationship when I was away. We have one now."

Inhaling, biting down on my lip.

He holds up his hands. "Hey, take it easy, Doctor Sid. I'm just talking out loud is all. We're all friends here. We both want the same thing. We wanna see Chloe returned to the arms of her adoring family."

I say, "So since we both want the same thing, what's the plan, Chief? Are we going to find Chloe? Or do you wanna keep talking?"

"I'll do everything in my power to see that she's found. I'm in touch with Canadian authorities up north and the APD down south in Albany and everywhere in between. If she's out there, we'll find her, Doctor Sid."

Turning, I go for the door.

"Oh, and Sid?" Walton calls out.

About-facing. "What is it?"

"Watch your back. Rabuffo probably has one of his goons Scotch-taped to your ass. Probably has since the moment you walked out of prison a free man."

"Thanks for caring. I feel better now."

"And one more thing."

"You've still got my undivided attention."

"On the subject of how you handled yourself in the joint. You've become one formidable dude. Like I said, a badass motherfucker. Do not take the law into your own hands. You might live through it, but it will most definitely get your little girl killed." He pokes his temple with an extended index finger. "Be a smarty. Go back to the hotel, eat something, get some rest. Keep your cell phone by your side. Anything comes up, we'll call you right away. And check in with Lochte tomorrow. He'll want to hear from you."

"Duly noted, Chief," I say.

Opening the door, I step out into the corridor, fingers crossed.

CHAPTER 19

PENNY IS ANXIOUSLY waiting for me. She's got her phone in hand. She's staring at the screen, wide-eyed.

"What's wrong now, Pen?" I ask.

"It's the Amber Alert, Sid. I'm looking at it. Can't keep my eyes off of it. There's our daughter's picture, plain as day. Her grade school picture. It doesn't seem real, Sid. It's like I have to convince myself that it's Chloe."

She shows me the photo. It's my little baby's smiling face. Above the face are the words, "Amber Alert. Americans Missing: Broadcast Emergency Response." I'm looking at the face and feeling the pain of her separation from us. It's like a knife is stabbing me in the gut again and again and again. Only I never bleed out. The wound automatically cauterizes and heals. The torture never ends. It's just like being caught up in a nightmare, but your brain refuses to wake up. Just looking at Penny's pale, withdrawn face, I can tell it's the same for her, too.

The pain will only go away when we get Chloe back.

If we get Chloe back.

* * *

We exit the police station like we've just walked out of a wake. We begin our slow walk along the Main Street sidewalk back to our hotel. It's the walk of the doomed. Not long ago, we were panicked, our bodies running at high speed on adrenaline. But now, it's as if concrete has been poured into our veins. The concrete is hardening, making every single step a labored effort.

"My God, Sid," Penny utters through her tears. "What the hell are we going to do? Chloe's out there somewhere. She's out there, and she's alone, and hungry. Do you think she misses us?"

I've been missing my daughter for ten years. It was the price I paid for keeping my mouth shut inside prison. Truth is, I never feared for my own life, so much as I feared for the lives of my family. I knew that if I were to blow the whistle on Rabuffo once and for all, it would put them at risk. In the end, when I did finally talk, it had to occur only under conditions of the utmost security. It's what the DA and the FBI had to agree to, or I would have chosen to remain in prison for the rest of my life if need be.

But it's all backfired.

Just five days reunited with my wife and daughter and I'm convinced the bastard has struck back. He's abducted my daughter, and now it feels like there's not a goddamned thing I can do about it.

I know Rabuffo. I know the men who work for him. Human life is cheap to them. The value of human life is measured only in how much money it can earn them. When that life suddenly stops being profitable, it is cut off, sometimes in the most brutal and violent of manners.

I look up at the clear night sky. Up this high in the Adirondack Mountain country, the sky is so clean and clear it's like you can reach out and touch the stars. A billion stars.

"Star light, star bright," I whisper to myself, wiping a tear from my eye. "First star I see tonight. Please watch over my little girl. Let her live so that I might see her again."

CHAPTER 20

WE'RE PASSING BY a coffee shop when I feel it.

Someone following us.

No, I don't have eyes in the back of my head. But what I have developed over the past ten years of incarceration is a sensitive built-in-bad-guy detector. It's as simple as this: when in the penitentiary, you don't watch your back, you're a dead man. You don't join Jesus; you join the devil. The devil is by far the more feared.

We move on, slowly. Agonizingly slow. On our right, a takeout pizza place. The smell is drawing me in, yet I can't fathom eating anything knowing my little girl might be going hungry tonight. But like Detective Giselle said, it's important that Penny and I maintain our strength. No, that's not right. It's *imperative* that we maintain our strength. Not for us, but for Chloe.

I take hold of Penny's hand, stop her.

"Whaddya say, Pen. Maybe we should grab a couple of slices, take them back to the room, sit by the phone."

"How can you think of food at a time like this?"

It's the question I anticipated most.

"Strength," I say. "We're going to need it. You know that. It's not like I'm asking you to head out for a five-course celebratory meal. I'd hoped we would be doing that as a family tonight, but it will have to wait until we get Chloe back, safe and sound. And we *will* get her back."

"What about your stomach?"

"It's better now." It's not entirely the truth. But I'm thinking of our endurance, our ability not to collapse under the strain, the pressure.

"Okay, okay." She nods. "But we make sure to get a big slice for Chloe. I mean, what if she comes back soon? She'll be hungry."

For the first time in what feels like forever, I feel myself smiling.

"Of course," I say. "We should get her two big slices, a large Coke, and a chocolate chip cookie."

Letting go of my hand, she heads into the pizza place. I follow, one eye on her, and the other on the man who's following us.

The bagged box of pizza slices in hand, we continue along Main Street toward the hotel. I manage to walk a half step behind Penny. I don't want her to notice the way I'm looking over my shoulder, just enough to increase my periphery. Whenever possible I use the glass storefronts as mirrors to see what they might be reflecting. In every case it's the same man.

He's a slim white guy, maybe five feet nine. My height, in other words. He's wearing a thin black leather coat over a black t-shirt. There's writing on the t-shirt in big white block letters. I'm pretty sure it says CBGB, which I recognize as the name of a long defunct punk rock nightclub in New York City. He's wearing black jeans and a pair of black combat boots. If he's trying to look like a thug, he's doing a really good job of it.

So here's the twenty-thousand-dollar question: Do I confront him now while we're walking back to our hotel? Do I risk the mistake of confronting an innocent guy who just happens to be walking the same path we are along Main Street? Do I threaten a man who's merely minding his own business? Or do I play it cool? Not confuse my built-in-bad-guy detector for paranoia?

I think the answer is obvious.

Keep your good eye on him while you let the police do their job. God willing, in just a few short hours or maybe even minutes, Chloe will be located and this hell will already be a memory. A bad dream best forgotten.

*   *   *

We enter back into the hotel through the lobby. The same desk manager is standing behind the counter. He looks up at me as I walk through the door.

"Good evening, Mr. O'Keefe," he says. "Any luck finding your daughter?"

It's a hard thing to admit, but I half expected him to burst out with a smile as soon as we came through the door. I hoped against hope that he might tell us Chloe showed up at the desk and she is now in the room waiting for us. If Penny expected the same thing, she's not saying anything about it.

"We're still looking," I reveal.

"The police are on it," Penny adds, both her hands gripping the pizza. "They've issued an Amber Alert."

"I'm aware of it," the man says. "The night manager comes on soon. I'll make sure he is fully abreast of the situation."

"Thank you," I say. Then, "Is Detective Fontaine still around?"

"She's gone home for the night. But if there's a problem, or you feel the need to speak with her, just contact the front desk, and we will contact her on your behalf."

I should have asked her for a card when I had the chance. My brain is not working right. Human nature tells us that under times of extreme duress, our minds overwork themselves. We tend to overthink situations, imagine the worst. But at the same time, the brain's overworking process can cause temporary memory loss. It can also cause a breakdown in lucid thinking.

"Thank you," I utter, not sure if I mean it.

Penny goes to the staircase that leads down to the ground level. She silently descends the stairs, not like she's making her way back to our room. But more like she's entering back into the lowest depths of Dante's Inferno.

CHAPTER 21

THIS ISN'T A happy, fun hotel room on the lake.

This room is lifeless and empty. It's cold for the summertime and it reminds me of the first time I visited a morgue as a young med student and examined my first corpse. The dull pain that suddenly emerged inside my gut. The feeling of finality when gazing at the lifeless flesh and bones. Like a famous writer once said, the dead look really dead when they're dead.

If only I could stop thinking for a while.

Chloe's suitcase is still laid out on the bed, wide open, her clothing strewn about from House Detective Giselle's search. Setting the pizza onto the desktop, Penny immediately goes to the case. She begins folding Chloe's clothing, piece by piece, repacking it, nicely and neatly.

"If I told Chloe once, I told her a thousand times," she says, her voice taking on a strange inflection, like she's not herself, but another woman entirely, "don't throw your clothes all over the place. Keep them nice and organized in your suitcase. That way you don't lose anything. You don't leave anything behind."

She's folding feverishly now, packing them almost violently.

"That girl will be the death of me, I swear," she barks, her words verging on shouts. "Maybe it's time I took the iPod away. That will get her to listen to me."

I go to her, take hold of her hands. I remove the article of Chloe's clothing that she's holding, gently set it into the case.

"Penny," I say, "listen to yourself."

Her face scrunches up like a woman who's been stabbed in the back with a surgical scalpel. The pain is that bad, that severe. I pull her into me, her face pressed against my chest. But she battles me. The pain has become like a demon and it's showing itself. She makes tight fists, pounds them against my chest.

"It's you, Sidney!" she screams. "You did this! Everything was all right until you came back. Why did you have to come back in our lives?"

A trap door opening underneath me. I'm falling into a lake of fire and remorse.

"Penny, please," I say, feeling my heart break. "You don't know what you're saying. You're upset is all."

She punches me in the chest, tries to claw my face. No choice but to hold her back, so tightly I fear I might break her arms.

"I'm not upset, I'm enraged. You did this. Do you hear me? You . . . did . . . this. You *made* our daughter disappear. You did something in prison. You talked to the police and the district attorney about Rabuffo. You told them everything they wanted to know. You did the one thing that would place us in danger. That's why you got out when you should be doing life for murdering that family. Don't tell me I don't know what you did to get out. You told them everything you know. And because you told them everything, somebody is having his revenge. Before this is over, we're all going to be dead."

"Penny, you're hysterical."

"Fuck you, Sidney. Fuck you for what you've done to us."

"Penny, stop it. Stop it now."

"I'll never stop. I won't stop until you're gone again. Until you're dead."

My heart is splitting in two, but I'm also feeling the anger build up inside me, like steam heat rising up out of a boiler. That's when the bad dream suddenly gets a whole hell of a lot worse. I'm about to do the one thing I should never consider doing. But I do it anyway. I raise my hand, slap Penny across the face.

The hotel room becomes a still life.

Penny is silenced. She stares up at me with wide, unblinking eyes, the mark on her face where I've hit her, red and painful looking. Slowly, she brings the tips of her fingers to her face, touches the tender place on her cheek. She sits herself down on the edge of the bed.

"You're right, Doc," she says, her voice reduced to a hoarse whisper. "I'm hysterical."

Someone occupying the adjoining room knocks on the wall, tells us to "Keep it down." Instinct takes over. I go to the wall, pound my own fist against it, shout, "Go to hell!"

Maybe it's the sight and sound of me yelling at a blank wall, but when I turn back around, Penny is slowly working up a smile.

"Now that's what I call *hysterical*," she says.

I stare down at my own fist. One of my knuckles is bleeding. But I don't care. I welcome the pain. Welcome the distraction. My face . . . I can feel the anger radiating from it in the form of heat and bursting blood corpuscles. I go back to Penny, sit down beside her.

"I've never raised a hand against a woman in my life," I say.

"We're *losing* it," she says, exhaling. "It's only been eight or nine hours, and we're losing our minds."

"Can you blame us, Penny?"

"No," she mumbles, "I cannot blame us. I cannot blame us one bit."

I set my hand gently on her thigh, lean into her, kiss her on her red cheek. She slips off the bed, reaches into her bag, pulls out her cell phone. Looks at the screen.

"Nothing," she says.

I pull out my phone, flip it open.

"Same. But then, I'm not sure Chloe even has the number."

She goes to the table, sets the cell phone down onto the desk, then opens the pizza box.

"Are you hungry?" she says. "Can you eat something?"

"Sure," I say. But it's a lie. A lie meant to passively aggressively demand that Penny eat. But she's too smart. She sees right through it.

Taking a slice from the box, she bites into it, places it back down. She goes to hand me a slice. As I'm reaching out for it, I hear something coming from outside the sliding glass doors. It's a voice. It sounds like a little girl calling out for her mommy.

CHAPTER 22

PENNY DROPS THE pizza box onto the desktop. She goes to the sliding glass doors. I practically leap over the bed, plant myself directly beside her. I pull the curtains open just enough to see out into the dark.

"Too much artificial light in here, Pen," I say. "I can't see anything outside."

Penny goes to the opposite side of the room to the wall-mounted universal light switch, kills the overheads. Now I can see out onto the beach. It's dark and empty, but the lights from the buildings on the opposite side of Mirror Lake create two silhouettes. The first is a tall person. I can't tell if it's a man or a woman. The second figure is far shorter.

"Is that her?" Penny cries, having returned to the glass doors. "Is that our Chloe?"

She grips the door opener with both hands. But I reach out with my left hand, press it against the aluminum doorframe.

"Wait," I insist. "Something's not right."

It's my built-in-bad-guy detector speaking to me again. Telling me not to blindly jump even when sufficiently provoked.

"Listen, Pen," I say, heart pumping a paradiddle against my sternum, "if that's Chloe, why isn't she running toward us? Why isn't she banging on the door, begging us to let her in? Why would she be standing there on the empty beach next to someone else? An adult? I know it sounds crazy, but it feels like a trap."

I can hear Penny breathing hard. She so badly wants Chloe back, it's like she's lost all reason. All ability to see behind her wish. Desperation is consuming her. The same holds true for me. But I learned over the years not to take the bait. At least, not at first. You need to swim around it, nibble it, test it, before committing to that one, final decisive bite. The one that hooks you, reels you in for good.

"Stand back," I tell her.

It takes her a moment, but eventually she lets go of the door, takes a small step back. I put my hand on the closer and slowly pull the door open. Just enough for me to step outside into the dark of the cool Adirondack night.

My eyes focus on the two silhouettes. One big, one little.

They're not moving. They're not speaking. It's like they're not alive, but instead, cardboard cutouts of live human beings.

"Chloe," I call out. "Is that you, sweetheart?"

"Daddy?" says the voice of the little girl.

. . . Oh, sweet Jesus, it's her . . .

"I'm coming, baby!" I shout. "Don't you move!"

Instinct kicks in once more. I take a step forward, then attempt to break out into a sprint. But I'm on the ground before the abrupt collision to the head registers with my brain.

CHAPTER 23

BLACKOUT.

Maybe for a full minute. Maybe for only a second or two. Head trauma can be a tricky thing. Even a minor bump in the right place can cause unconsciousness for a short or long period of time. But as I'm regaining consciousness, I make out the blurry movement of someone pulling the little girl ... *my* little girl ... back across the beach and into the darkness, until they disappear.

I see something else too. The image of a man. He's dressed all in black.

He blends in with the night.

I reach for him, try to grab his ankle. But he backsteps at just the right moment. I don't possess the strength to try again.

"Who ... are ... you?" I ask, the words peeling themselves from the back of my throat like dead skin. "Where ... is ... Chloe?"

"You'll be hearing from us," he says.

He runs off.

The sliding glass door opens. Penny shrieks and comes to me. She drops to her knees, takes my head in her hands.

"Sidney, my God," she exhales. "What have they done to you?"

"Chloe," I say, my head ringing like a bell. "That had to be Chloe."

I lift myself up onto my knees. The dizziness still swimming around my brain, I nonetheless manage to stand up straight.

"Stay here," I say.

"Where are you going?" she begs.

"I'm going after the son of a bitch who took our daughter."

CHAPTER 24

THE MAN IN black can't be that far ahead of me.

He ran off in a northerly direction.

Head fills with a thousand screaming voices, veins on fire, blood boiling, searing. The rage consumes me. I make chase to the sound of Penny screaming at me. Screaming *for* me. This is not me being smart. This is not even me losing my cool. It is me acting on raw emotion. It is acting on the survival instinct I learned inside prison. It is something you cannot understand, nor comprehend. That is, unless you've spent any time inside a maximum-security prison yourself, and done so as a perpetually hunted man. You don't become the victim of another attacker. You face the attacker head-on. You attack the attacker. You use your brain, but you also use brute force. It is survival of the fittest in its purest form. Prison Darwinism.

Penny screams. "Stop! Wait! Sidney, we need to call the police!"

But I can't help myself, can't ignore the anger. It's the instinct of an animal. A rabid animal. It's all consuming. I don't feel myself moving, don't feel myself breathing. It's as though I am dreaming this moment rather than living it for real. It's all about finding this man who cold cocked me over the head. Finding out what he knows about Chloe, where they're keeping her. Finding out the identity of the bastards who stole her.

I come to the edge of the beach and the hotel property. A storm fence lines the perimeter of the property. Nowhere to go other than to the right and into the lake, or go left in the direction of Main Street.

That's when I spot him.

The same man who followed us back from the police station. He's climbing the storm fence, trying to make his way to the safety of the other side. I run to him, thrust myself at him like a line-backer trying to make an impossible tackle. I grab hold of his legs, yank him down from the fence.

Throwing him onto his back, I jam my knees into his shoulder joints, cock my right arm back, land three swift back-to-back tight-fisted punches to the face. His bottom lip pops like a water balloon filled with blood. His nose snaps. His left eye swells up like a plum. When you're trained to heal someone, it's easy to damage them. You know precisely where it hurts, precisely where the most damage and the most bleeding will occur while expending the least amount of effort.

I see his left hand reaching. He comes out with a snub-nosed revolver. I slap it away, wrap my right hand around his throat.

"Where's my daughter?"

"Go to hell, killer." He spits blood in my face.

I punch him again. A short, sharp, powerful jab. Then, pulling his right hand up, I grab hold of the index finger.

"Who sent you?"

"Fuck . . . you . . . killer."

I pull the finger sideways, as far as nature will allow the proximal phalanx and the middle phalanxes to go without dislocating. I feel the flexor digitorum profundus tendon pop at the center knuckle, just a split second before the bone snaps like a dry twig. At the same time, I cover his mouth with my free hand while he screams into it.

"Where are you hiding my daughter, you ugly bastard?"

Lifting my hand off his mouth.

"Go ahead," he spits. "Kill me, killer. That's what you do. You sick, violent killer. Go ahead. You succeed at that, you'll never see Chloe again. You understand me? You kill me, you call the cops, you so much as breathe in the direction of the hotel house detective, your little teeny-weeny polka-dot bikini-wearing daughter will die a slow, agonizing death."

Raising up my fist, I'm about to plow it into his face again. But his face already looks like raw hamburger. If facial symmetry is an important component to one's perception of physical beauty, this guy is truly screwed for a while. His procerus, or what you and I recognize as a nose, is definitely leaning left, and I might have broken his left orbital plate. Not to mention his lips, which resemble rare sausage with punctured casings. And that finger on his hand will require surgery to repair. Perhaps several pins. I guess I've made my point.

"What the hell do you want?" I ask, swallowing a lump of concrete.

"You'll find out when we're ready, killer. And not before." There's pain in his voice. Fear. But he's not backing down. He's a professional. I know the type.

I slide off of him. Stand.

"You tell Rabuffo I had no choice."

"Maybe you can tell him that yourself." He stands, awkwardly. "Or maybe this ain't about Rabuffo at all, killer."

He turns, begins limping toward the parking lot and Main Street.

"Why'd you do it?" I shout. "Why'd you come to me?"

He turns. "So that I could deliver a message. An untraceable message. Cell phones aren't safe."

"And what message is that?"

"It goes something like this: If you want to see your daughter alive again, you will do as we say."

"And the little girl? That was Chloe? *My* Chloe?"

He wipes the blood from his nostrils and lips with the back of his one good hand.

"What the hell do you think, Inmate number 03C2258, Sidney O'Keefe?"

Turning, he runs off, taking his damaged face and hand with him, but mistakenly leaving his gun behind.

CHAPTER 25

GRABBING HOLD OF the snub-nose revolver, I stuff it into the back of my pant waist, conceal it by pulling my t-shirt over it. Then I jog back to the hotel room, before someone does the lawfully right thing and calls the police. It's entirely possible they already have.

Maybe, in terms of being a free man, I am already a short-timer.

Sliding open the door, I step inside, shut the door behind me, lock it, pull the curtain closed. Penny is so visibly upset, she's trembling.

"What the hell was that?!" she barks.

I hold up my hands, like I'm telling her to get ahold of herself.

. . . *Do not touch her again, Sid. Do not lay a hand on her . . . Get your emotions in order . . . Rein your instincts in . . . Prison Darwinism no longer applies on the outside . . .*

"Chloe," I say. "She's alive, and from what I can tell, unharmed."

For the first time since this ordeal began down on the beach, real optimism paints her tired face.

"My God," she says. "That *was* her . . . Down on the beach, I mean."

I nod. "Yes, I think so . . . Oh Christ, I *know* so."

"Then what's going on?" she pushes. "Who was that man?"

The face of Rabuffo fills my head. Him taking me into his confidence all those years ago. Him taking me down into the protected basement operation below his house. Showing me the safe or bank vault, where he kept millions of dollars in unmarked currency, gold, and silver coins. He would make me a soldier in his army.

The top soldier.

He would even share the combination to the vault with me. Our relationship was one of mutual trust, but not admiration. I had acquired a gambling debt to an organization that would cost me my life if I didn't pay it all off. Rabuffo stepped in, paid it off on my behalf. Which meant he owned me, like a slave and his master. But in that ownership sprung a kind of love, too.

The love for a son he never had.

But then Wemps and Singh killed that family. They were shot dead by the cops in the aftermath. I was arrested and bore the brunt for the quadruple homicide. Didn't matter that Rabuffo loved me like a son. What mattered was that I kept my mouth shut while doing my time on the inside. But how long can a man—a human being—physically and mentally hold out? With that in mind, he tried his best to silence me for good.

The father killing the son. A tragic story as old as the Bible itself.

A loud knock on the door.

"Mr. O'Keefe?" the voice on the other side of the door barks. "Hotel security. Please open up."

More knocking. Pounding.

I go to the door, open it. I see a middle-aged man in a gray uniform. He's heavyset and packing a gun on his utility belt.

"Guests are reporting a disturbance coming from this room, and outside the room. I'm going to have to ask you to keep it down or else vacate the premises. Is that understood?"

I nod, like an inmate swallowing a verbal scolding from a corrections officer.

His brown eyes zoom in on my hand. The bleeding knuckles. I quickly hide the hand behind my back.

"'Night," I say.

"'Night," he says, with a smirk. "Make it a calm one, please."

I close the door, lock it, apply the dead bolt, locking us inside our cell of a room. Then, turning to my wife.

"Listen, Pen," I say. "Sit down."

"Why?"

"It's time I came clean about something."

"Clean about what, Sid?"

"The whole story behind why I was paroled from prison."

CHAPTER 26

IT TAKES ALL of twenty minutes, but when I'm done, Penny knows everything about my relationship with Rabuffo. The details. Some of them retreads, but some of them brand new to her ears. About my first wife emptying our bank accounts before she took off. About the gambling debts I entered into with some pretty bad dudes who ran an operation that competed directly with Mickey's. About my crawling to Rabuffo to bail me out, and in the process, save my pathetic life. About his hiring me in exchange for paying them off. About his taking me under his wing, treating me like the son he never had. About the truth behind my final job with him, and how my old high school buddies-turned-Rabuffo-employees, Wemps and Singh, killed that Chinese family. How they were shot dead by the cops when they tried to make a run for it. How I took the blame for it all, and how Rabuffo wanted to hush me while I was doing my never-ending time. About my loyalty, until that loyalty wasn't enough. How Rabuffo wanted me dead, to guarantee my silence. About how I never stopped worrying that, one day, he would go after her and Chloe. About how I finally had no choice but to plead my case to the DA, knowing that one day my survival skills would fail me, and Rabuffo would succeed in having me assassinated. Once that happened, he would surely come after my family. Or maybe he would come after them first, just to torture me. I wouldn't be around to protect them when the killers finally came for them. It would be the worst torture any one man could ever bear.

"So now I'm here to protect you," I confess, "and all I've managed to do is get Chloe abducted." Me, shaking my head. "I'm completely useless, Pen. You're right, this is all my fault."

She places her hand on my thigh.

"I was wrong, Doc. This isn't your fault. You were only trying to shield us from danger. I see that now. I also see why you withheld the whole truth about Rabuffo for so long. I'd always assumed you were just one of his drivers. One of his bag men. But, you're right. If I knew too much, it would make me a liability. Make Chloe a liability."

"That was my thinking, my reasoning. I would stop at nothing to see you safe."

She goes to her suitcase, which is set out on the stand by the door. She digs through it, comes back out with a small bottle filled with medication.

"What's that, Pen?"

"Valium," she says, straight faced. "Would you like one or two to calm you down?"

I think about the possibility of being up all night. How even a few hours of sleep will be crucial if we're going to maintain some sort of sanity and strength through this thing. But I also know that swallowing a sedative like Valium, especially after suffering a blow to the head, will take away my edge, inhibit my natural ability to maintain optimum neuronal function. In other words, it could very well dull my built-in-bad-guy detector, dull my survival instinct.

"I'm good," I say, in the end.

She opens the cap, pops a couple into the palm of her hand, downs them with a glass of tap water from the sink in the bathroom.

She comes to me then.

For moment, we stand stone stiff, just facing each other. It's almost like we're looking into one another's eyes for the first time. After a long couple of beats, our bodies come together. We hold one another tightly. We drop slowly onto the bed, on our sides, never letting go. This isn't only about stress and distress, it's about love and needing one another like never before. We're holding onto each other so tightly, it's not like we want to press our bodies together. It's as if we wish to become one person. Our tears are streaming down are faces. The tears are combining. I taste the tears on my lips and tongue.

Soon, I feel a steady breathing coming from Penny. When I angle my head so that I'm able to get a look at her face, I can tell she is sleeping. Exhaustion and Valium overtake her, and I am so damned happy about it. No mother should have to go through the torture she has endured all day long. But will her dreams be sweet? The answer to that one is plain enough.

The room is quiet.

The lights are still on, but I don't dare let go of Penny to get up and turn them off. Instead, I close my own eyes, try my hardest to clear my throbbing head. To fall asleep, if only for a few minutes.

*   *   *

I see them standing inside the room then at the end of the bed. The Chinese father and mother. Together, they flank both their children. They're covered in blood, each of them with a different version of the same execution-style head wound.

The little girl takes a step forward, holds out her hands, like she wants me to grab hold of them. But I can't. I'm paralyzed on my back.

"Why did you do this to us?" she asks.

I want to tell her that I didn't do it. That I was just driving the car. That Wemps and Singh killed them. That I had nothing to do with it. The frustration builds up inside me and I'm trying to scream at her. Scream the truth. But all I can do is lie there and watch them bleed out . . .

*   *   *

A loud bang.

A fist against the front door.

I sit up fast, eyes wide open, my spine a heavy-duty spring. Another knock. Louder this time.

"Mr. O'Keefe, you up?"

I shake my head, try to shake the cobwebs from it. I know the voice.

"Mr. O'Keefe, it's Giselle . . . Hotel Detective Giselle Fontaine."

Penny is startled awake. She slowly sits up.

"What's . . . going . . . on?" Her voice is sleepy, groggy. "Is it Chloe?"

"It's Detective Giselle," I answer.

Glancing at my watch. Five in the morning. Holy Christ, we've been asleep for hours. Is it possible grief and excessive anxiety can have that effect on the human body? My med studies would have suggested otherwise. But then I've never had a child kidnapped before by a band of human traffickers. This is all new to me. Or maybe I'm suffering from the effects of a concussion. Or hell, I learned to sleep in prison with one eye open, the other shut.

"Hang on," I shout, slipping out of the bed.

I'm still fully clothed. I immediately go the door, open it.

Giselle is standing there, her big blue eyes intently looking into my own.

"Tell me you've found Chloe."

"Not exactly, Mr. O'Keefe. But may I come in?"

"Of course." I step out of the way. "Penny is still in bed. By some miracle we actually slept."

"Gosh, that's a blessing to be sure," she says.

She's showered. Her long hair is still damp and her blue suit is professionally pressed.

"Do you mind?" she says, picking up the remote off the desk, turning on the television.

"What's going on?" I beg through a haze of sleep and confusion.

"This is going on," she says. The TV is already tuned in to the local 24-hour news station. "It's time for the headline rundown, so pay attention."

I glance at Penny out the corner of my eye. Her eyelids are at half-mast. Somehow, during the night, she must have snuck under the blankets, and now she's holding them up to her chin.

A commercial for a local Lake Placid boat manufacturer is just finishing up. Then the news comes back on, a female news anchor presiding.

"Back to our top story," the young African American anchor announces. "A local man was assaulted last night and badly beaten just outside a popular Lake Placid–area hotel. Tom Bertram, 53, of Boat Landing Road, has testified that he was taking a walk along a moonlit Mirror Lake on the beach located behind the Golden Arrow Hotel, when he was suddenly attacked by a man he identifies as recently paroled convicted murderer Sidney O'Keefe."

My insides drop. It feels like my organs are spilling out of my body.

"What the hell is she saying?" Penny asks. "*You* were attacked by *him*."

"Hang on," Giselle insists.

The news report shifts from the anchor to video tape that must have been shot only minutes after our physical confrontation on the north side of the hotel. That is, judging by the fresh blood pouring out of his lower lip and nostrils.

"You see this?" Bertram says, pointing at his own face with a finger that's been stabilized with a stainless-steel splint, and bandaged with gauze and surgical tape. "This is what happens when you let animals out of prison before they're supposed to get out of prison. Innocent people like me get attacked. I was just minding my own business when that monster came up on me from behind, tackled me, started beating me." He starts to tear up, really pouring it on. "I appeal to you, the police of this village. Find Sidney O'Keefe before he skips town and does the same horrible thing to someone else."

"This isn't happening," I whisper, more to myself than anyone else occupying the room.

"There's more," Giselle says.

The video ends and the broadcast switches back to the real-time anchor.

"Sources tell Channel 9 that Thomas Bertram was able to identify O'Keefe from the very recent news reports of his surprising parole from Green Haven Maximum Security Penitentiary, which occurred this past Monday." A mug shot of my face appears on the screen over the anchor's right shoulder. "Back in September of 2007, O'Keefe was arrested and convicted as a coconspirator in the murder of four Chinese undocumented immigrants. He was paroled suddenly, after serving ten years of a twenty-five to life sentence. His defense lawyer, Joel Harwood, was unavailable for comment. In other news . . ."

Giselle, lowers the volume.

"So now what?" I ask.

"Customers staying in the hotel reported a violent scuffle last night on the north side of the hotel." The house detective glances at the wall. "The people staying in that room reported you fighting. That you punched the wall, Mr. O'Keefe. That you hit Mrs. O'Keefe."

Penny slides out of bed. Like me, she is still fully clothed.

"You listen to me, Giselle," she says, her tone now defiant and angry. "I saw what happened. Chloe was out there last night, on the beach. Somebody was holding onto her. A big man. When my husband went outside to check on the situation, he was attacked by a second man. The injured man on the television."

"And you didn't call me?" Giselle says, shaking her head. "You didn't call Walton?"

"He clobbered me on the head." Me feeling the lump left behind by his .38 caliber revolver. "I was knocked unconscious for a few seconds. But I chased the bastard, and when I caught up to him, I demanded answers. He told me if we involved the cops, Chloe would die. My daughter would fucking die. He wouldn't give me any answers. He wouldn't give me anything but threats. So naturally—"

I hold up my dominant hand. The knuckles are scabbed.

"—Naturally you beat the living snot out of him," Giselle answers in my stead. Then, exhaling, "But here's the darned thing. The police are going to want to pick you up. Walton is going to arrest you. And you know what that means."

"You can't do that!" Penny barks. "You can't take my husband away from me when our daughter is still missing. When we have bad men out there threatening us. Threatening to kill Chloe."

"Listen," I say. "I know who has my daughter, and I can prove it."

Giselle looks at me, like she's not sure whether to believe me or not. She shifts her gaze to Penny.

"Is this true?" she says.

"We need to tell her," Penny says.

"Tell me what?" Giselle says.

"About the man who used to own me," I say. Then, my eyes suddenly attracted to the television. "That man," I say, pointing at the flat screen. "That son of a bitch."

CHAPTER 27

HE'S BEING LED out of his North Albany mansion by a crew of men and women wearing navy blue FBI windbreakers. An unmarked cruiser is parked at the top of the drive, the doors open. The FBI agents shove the big, white-haired Rabuffo into the back seat, slam the door closed. The car then zooms off, no doubt on its way to the downtown FBI headquarters.

The volume on the television is turned way down. But on the screen, the name Paul "Mickey" Rabuffo appears. Below it, "Arrested for racketeering, human and illicit drug trafficking along with multiple counts of murder."

Penny takes a step toward the television.

"Jesus, that's him," she says. "Rabuffo is finally going to prison."

"Thus, our missing Chloe," I say. "And thus, that son of a bitch Bertram who tried to knock me cold."

Giselle shakes her head.

"So, if I were to put two and two together, I'm guessing you took the rap for this fella a long time ago and it cost you a lengthy prison stay. But he tried to quiet you, for like forever, and eventually you got tired of looking over your shoulder. So you organized a come-to-Jesus with the Albany DA."

"In so many words, that's the story," I confirm.

She scrunches her brow.

"Cheese Louise," she says. "Usually all I do around here is look for missing wallets. But this is some serious crap. Even I know Rabuffo's clothing shops are just a front. Same goes with his Chinese eateries, one of which is now located on Main Street in the heart of the village. He is not a man to dick around with." Then, catching herself, "Oops, sorry about my French, Mrs. O'Keefe."

"Don't worry about it," Penny says. "We've been cursing our fucking brains out since yesterday early afternoon."

My phone rings, startling me so badly, I nearly hit the ceiling. I go to the bedside, retrieve the phone, flip it open.

"Shit," I say. "My parole officer calling on a Saturday."

"At this point," Giselle says, "maybe it's best to speak with your lawyer first."

Now coming from outside the building, the faint but indiscernible sound of cop cruisers. I flip the phone closed, pull it from its charger, stuff it into my pocket.

"Oh no," Penny says. "It's got to be Walton."

"And I can bet he's got the entire village police department with him."

I pull the curtain open on the sliding glass doors. Instinct once more kicks in. The will to survive. To fend off the attackers. I glance at Penny, then at Giselle. I see Chloe's silhouette on the beach near the water. I can give myself up to the police, risk being locked up for what I did to Bertram. Or, I could take another route. Perhaps not the smartest route in the world, but the only route available.

I pull out the pistol from my jeans.

"Where the hell did you get that?!" Giselle snaps. "You've got to hand that over right now."

"I can't," I say, the words barely making it out of my mouth. "This is something I have to do. For Chloe."

I look out back. The beach is empty this early in the morning, with the sun's rays only now peeking out over the mountaintops to the east. No police occupy the immediate vicinity, as far as I can see. But that doesn't mean they're not there.

"Penny," I say. "Grab your phone from off the charger. Pack a couple of water bottles and some of that pizza into your daypack."

"Why?" she asks, her voice verging on weeping. "What are you talking about, Sid?"

"If the police pick me up, they'll toss me back in prison. That's not going to happen." I retract the revolver's cylinder, check the six-shot load, then slap it back home. "Don't you see what's happening here? I'm being set up."

"By who?" Penny begs. "Rabuffo is already arrested."

"He's got a restaurant up here. It means his people are here. We actually looked inside the place when we were scouring the village for Chloe. They've infiltrated paradise like cockroaches. This is revenge, pure and simple. They put me back in the joint, they'll kill Chloe and then they'll kill you. It's all a part of their plan to torture me. They'll make sure I live to see my family die."

"Mr. O'Keefe," Giselle says, pulling back her jacket to reveal her sidearm, "I must ask you to stand down. Think about what you're doing."

The police cruiser sirens are louder now. Closer. A Lake Placid cop SUV pulls up outside the back door. Then, coming from outside the room's front door, a sound of jackboots slapping against the corridor floor. I hear car doors opening, weapons being locked and loaded. The entire room goes silent and still, as if my execution is imminent.

Like I said, I have a distinct choice here.

I can either surrender the gun to Giselle, and surrender myself to the Lake Placid Village PD, which means a sure one-way trip back to prison. Or I can take the one shot I have left to get my daughter back safe and sound. In the end, it'll mean I either die trying, or at the very least, go back to prison anyway. But at least she'll be safe and back in the arms of her mother.

. . . .So what's it going to be, Sid? Door number one or door number two?

Two always was my lucky number.

Giselle isn't expecting it when I wrap my left arm around her waist, press the barrel of the .38 against her temple.

"Penny," I say, "grab her gun."

My wife has become a mannequin.

"Penny," I shout, "grab the detective's gun! Now!"

She breaks herself out of her spell, comes toward us, reaches into Giselle's jacket, steals her gun. It's a 9mm Sig Sauer short-barreled semi-automatic. Nice piece for a hotel detective. An expensive piece.

"Thank you very much, Pen," I say. "Now, take a look outside the curtain and tell me what you see."

"You really know what you're doing?" Giselle whispers, her tone hard as nails and just as sharp. "You're gonna fry like bacon when the village finest finally nail you, fella."

"Please, Detective Fontaine, I'm well aware of just how wrong this is. But what would you do if it was your daughter? I just want to get my Chloe back. Somebody took her right off this beach, and then that somebody actually had the nerve to show their face, or faces, after they did it. It tells me they aren't all that afraid of the law enforcement around here. And that includes you, Detective."

I can feel her trembling in my arm. My guess is nobody has ever pointed a gun at her before. Not in this vacation utopia.

"So what's your plan, Mr. O'Keefe?" Giselle asks.

"I'll let you know as soon as Penny gives me the lowdown."

I focus on my wife, who is looking out onto the back of the hotel through a narrow slit between the curtains.

"I see two police SUVs," she says, "and four policemen wearing their uniforms. One of them is Chief Walton. All of them are holding guns, Sidney."

"Okay," I say. "Here's what we're going to do. Penny, grab the stuff."

She goes back to the bed, grabs the daypack.

"Now," I go on, "Giselle, you're going to be a good kid and walk with me to the sliding glass doors."

"What's this train wreck all about, Mr. O'Keefe?" she presses, while I push her toward the doors. "Did *you* do something to your daughter? Did you get mad at her? Did she do something bad by mistake like step on your big toe? Something that threw you into a rage? Are we going to find her remains somewhere on the hotel premises? Are they going to dredge her body out of the lake?"

The once nice and helpful hotel detective has now turned into someone I do not recognize. But then I guess the same can be said of me. I'm the one holding the gun on her. Maybe she's suspected me all along of doing something horrible to my daughter. By the looks of it, the entire town suspects me of kidnapping and killing my own little girl.

"Just please shut up," I say, burying the barrel into her skull. So hard, I can hear her wince.

"Now, Penny," I go on. "On the count of three, I want you to open the curtains and the door, you understand?"

She's wide-eyed, her eyes incapable of blinking. It's the stress, the absolute situational shock. She's not saying a word, but I know what she's thinking. *This is crazy. This could land us in prison for a long time. But our daughter is out there, abducted, and the police aren't looking for her. They're looking for my husband . . . We have to do what's right for Chloe, no matter what . . .*

"I understand," she says. "But, Sidney, I am so, so scared."

"Just do what I say and we'll be fine, Pen."

I shift my hold on Giselle so that I grab hold of her left arm, pull it behind her back, pushing upwards on it, applying severe pressure to the rotator cuff. It's exactly the kind of move the COs would pull on us when things got rowdy. Once more she winces, and once more, she's powerless to do anything about it.

"Ready, Penny? On three . . . One, two . . ."

When I get to three, she swings back the curtain, allowing the bright morning sunlight to fill the room and allowing our eyes to take in the cops pointing their weapons at us. Acting in one single, fluid motion, she grips the opener with both hands, yanks the door open.

"Stand down, O'Keefe!" Chief Joe Walton shouts.

Yanking on Giselle's arm, I whisper for her to step outside. She does it.

"You stand down, Walton!" I shout. "You never had any intention of looking for my daughter. You set your sights on me, and that's as far as it went."

Standing maybe a dozen feet away, I make out the elderly man who was swimming laps in the indoor pool. He's staring me down with wide eyes and an ashen face. I also spot the young couple we spoke to in the bar yesterday. The couple who offered their help. The young blonde woman and the Marine with Semper Fi tattooed to his bicep.

"That's them," the young woman says. "He was drunk as a skunk, and they were upsetting the whole bar. Accusing us of taking their daughter."

"You're full of shit!" Penny shouts. "We did no such thing. And my husband wasn't drunk."

"Shoot him!" Giselle spits. "Shoot the darn bastard, Joe, while you have the chance."

Walton's gun is raised, the bead planted on my head.

"You do that, Chief," I say, "and Giselle's brains are blown all over the beach." But I can only hope that Walton doesn't call my bluff because I'd rather run than shoot Giselle.

"What do you want, O'Keefe?" the chief begs.

"My wife and I just want to walk out of here unmolested. You got that, Chief?"

Walton doesn't respond. The other cops keep their weapons trained on us. But I can also see that they're looking to one another for guidance. They've never encountered a hostage situation before. I get the sense that this is all new to them. Never mind pre-med or my med school classes in human nature and bio chem. It was prison life that taught me how to sniff out another man's fear. And right now, I'm smelling a whole bunch of it. It's not a fight or flight situation for these cops since choosing flight would mean the loss of their jobs or, worse, humiliation. But I can see the whites in their wide, unblinking eyes and the Adam's apples bobbing up and down in their necks, like turkeys about to face the hatchet. Their faces bear a pale pallor.

"I'm gonna tell you one more time, O'Keefe," Walton states. "Stand down. Or we will fire on you."

"No, you won't," I say, working up a smile.

Pulling the pistol away from Giselle's head, I pull the trigger, fire a shot over Walton's head. Across the bow, as it were.

The police hit the dirt.

One cop screams, "Don't kill me!"

"This is gonna hurt me more than you, Giselle," I whisper into her ear. "But I'm not leaving Lake Placid without my little girl."

That's when I pistol-whip her upside the skull, behind the temple so as not to cause her any concussive damage. She automatically drops to her knees, distracting the police.

"Penny!" I shout. "Run!"

CHAPTER 28

WE SPRINT AROUND the hotel, to the parking lot. There's a gathering of cops positioned around the front door. But the village PD have obviously concentrated their efforts on the back of the building where our hotel room is located and where we had easy access to the exterior.

"We need a car," I say, gazing at all the vehicles parked in the lot. "We can't just hop a bus."

We'd taken the bus up north from Albany. The car Penny and I had before I went to prison was sold off a long time ago.

"We don't have keys," Penny stresses. "How the hell we gonna steal a car, Sidney?"

"I learned a thing or two in prison, Pen. Plus, I have the fingers of a surgeon. Problem is, I need to find an older model to work with."

We still haven't been spotted by the cops positioned in the near distance. But that doesn't mean we're not being spotted on the hotel's exterior mounted CCTV cameras in real time. Then, Penny raises her arm, points.

"What about that one there, Doc?"

I turn, spot the vehicle that's caught her attention. It's an old Jeep. A CJ Wrangler, probably dating back to the early eighties.

There's no top on it, hard or soft, and no doors. It means we don't have to worry about door locks.

"Good eyes, Pen. Now let's just hope it's got enough gas."

We go to the Jeep, which is parked in between a Mercedes sedan and a brand-new Ford F-150 pickup truck.

"Hop in," I say. "We're gonna make this quick."

Reaching under the steering column, I feel for the spaghetti of wires with the index fingers and thumbs on both my hands. I pull them out, exposing them. There's a series of four wires, but it's the wires that bookend all the others that have my full attention. A red wire and a blue wire connected to the starter. What I need to do, in theory at least, is tap their ends together, and that should create the spark needed to fire up the engine. Problem is, I need something metal to create the proper bridge between the wire ends.

Turning to my wife. "Pen, you got a safety pin or anything like that?"

She reaches into her bag, rummages around, comes back out with a paperclip.

"How about this?"

"Perfect."

I bend the paperclip so that one end is touching the blue wire, the other hovering over the red. I'm just about to touch the red wire when I hear the shouts.

"That's him!" comes the voice of a man. "That's O'Keefe there!"

I shift my focus on the gathering of cops at the hotel entrance. Standing in the middle of them is the desk manager. He's pointing at me.

"There's the murdering son of a bitch!" he shouts once more.

The cops turn towards us, draw their weapons, enter into a sprint. Pressing both feet against the rubber floor mat to ground myself against electrocution, I touch the paperclip to the red wire. Sparks shoot out, but the Jeep starts up with a hearty roar.

Left foot on the clutch, the right on the gas, I grind the gear into reverse, pull out of the parking space. Hitting the brakes, I throw the shift into first, and burn rubber. The cops go down onto their knees, combat position, the black barrels on their service weapons staring us in the face.

Reaching out, I grab hold of Penny's shirt, pull her down into my lap. I lower my head as the pop, pop, pop of discharged weapons fill the air and the bullets whiz past my head like hornets.

"Why are they trying to kill us?!" Penny screams. "They're supposed to be on our side."

"Don't talk!" I shout, as I speed the length of the parking lot, knowing the only thing standing before the Jeep and the open road is four Lake Placid police officers.

"I'm not going to stop!" I scream, throwing the shift from second to third, the big V6 engine roaring.

I'm convinced I'm about to run all four officers down when, at the very last second, they leap out of the way. Peering into the rearview, I see them take aim once more, fire their weapons at will. More bullets whiz past, one of them bursting through the windshield, making a nickel-sized hole, from which several cracks emerge.

Heading out onto Main Street, I hook a left, and gun the engine past Olympic Center on our right and the Village Police Station on my left. From there I turn onto the road that will take us south and into the Adirondack mountain range.

State Highway 73.

The highway through the forest.

"You can get up," I say to Penny, pulling on her shirt.

She rises, slowly, cautiously, as if the police are right on our tail. Something that will happen sooner than later. That is, if I can't find a suitable place for us to hide while we try and make sense of this whole thing.

"Where are we going?" Penny asks as we pass by the old, massive Olympic ski jumps and head into the thickly forested region.

But I don't answer right away. I haven't eaten anything of substance in almost twenty-four hours. But that doesn't prevent the nausea from overwhelming me. I pull off the side of the road, jump out, bend over, vomit a stomach full of clear, burning bile.

"Doc, what's the matter?" Penny pleads. "We have to keep going."

It takes a long few seconds, but eventually, the nausea abates, and I make my way back to the Jeep, slip behind the wheel.

"We've just fled from the police," I say, still somewhat dizzy and sick. "I assaulted Giselle when I slapped her with the gun. This . . . this situation we're in . . . it's getting worse by the minute." Wiping my mouth with the back of my hand. "The decisions I'm making. I'm worried they're all wrong."

"We're doing it for Chloe," Penny says.

"That's what I keep telling myself. And it's the truth. But listen, Pen, if we don't find her, and the police catch up to us, I'm done, finished. I'll never see the light of day again."

"We won't let that happen."

"You say that. I say that. Maybe even God says that. But the smart thing to do would be to work with the cops, not fight them, run from them."

"Then why are we running, Doc?"

"Because I don't trust them. I don't trust Walton as far as I can throw him."

In my head I'm thinking about the lecture he gave me inside his office after he insisted Penny step outside. Him telling me about Rabuffo, about his vault, then accusing me of hurting my own daughter.

"Then we're doing the right thing," Penny goes on.

I attempt to work up a smile.

"God willing," I say.

I pull back out onto the road.

"Where exactly are we heading?" Penny asks after a few beats, the cool sweet-smelling breeze blowing against our faces, my stomach calming down.

"We're going to head down into Keene Valley and the Mount Marcy range. There's a lot of abandoned cabins in that area. We get lucky, we'll find a secluded spot that will take the police forever to find."

"Then what?" Penny asks.

I shrug my shoulders, feel the cool wind against my face.

"I'm not sure," I say. "I've never been a fugitive before."

"What's that mean, Doc?"

"It means there's people out there who want to kill us. And if we die, Chloe dies. So we need to hide."

But I pray the forest is big enough to hide us from the law. But not so big that we can't find Chloe before the sun sets a second time.

CHAPTER 29

THE FARTHER WE drive into the mountainous Adirondack wilderness, the more alone we seem to be. But I know the sensation of isolation is nothing more than an illusion. A dream. When I spot the police SUV coming up on me fast, the dream is completely shattered. With flashers flashing and sirens blaring, the far speedier black and white vehicle pulls up on my tail. So close I can make out the smooth-shaven face of the uniformed cop who's doing the driving. I can also make out the round face of Chief Joe Walton riding in the passenger seat.

One eye on the road, the other on the rearview, I see him pull the mic from the dash, bring it to his face.

"Sidney O'Keefe," he barks out the SUV rooftop-mounted loudspeakers. "We demand that you stop your vehicle. Get out. Hands raised high above your head."

I punch the gas, try and pry more speed out of the Jeep. I set my hand back on Penny's shoulder.

"Be prepared to lower your head!" I shout, the wind buffeting our faces in the open-topped Jeep. "They start shooting again, they just might hit something this time. They're that close."

"Sidney O'Keefe!" Walton says, his voice loud and tinny. "This is your last warning. Stop your vehicle or we will fire on you!"

Up ahead, a trail marker for one of the many high peaks that can be accessed on both sides of the narrow, winding road. The idea hits me like a lightning strike.

"Penny," I say, "grab hold of the roll bar. Don't let go until I tell you. You got it?"

Slowly, she raises up her right hand, grabs hold of the roll bar. With her left hand, she reaches out, grabs the horizontal bar mounted to the dashboard directly above the glove box.

"What are you going to do?" she asks.

"I'm going to get us out of this."

Tapping the breaks, I make it look like I'm obeying Walton's commands. I even raise up my left hand as if to indicate a kind of surrender. As we come upon the trail marker, I continue to slow the vehicle as the cruiser behind me also slows while keeping close on my tail. So close, we're nearly trading paint.

"Hang on tight!" I yell.

The green sign is nearly upon us on the right-hand side.

"Here we go!"

I turn the wheel sharply to the right, the back end of the Jeep fishtailing, the tires spinning on the pavement as I give it the gas, but catching and propelling us onto the trail. Behind us, the cop piloting the SUV slams on the brakes, sending the vehicle sliding off into the ditch on the opposite side of the road.

I throw the Jeep into the 4-wheel drive by pulling back on the floor-mounted transfer case stick shift. The Jeep bounces and bucks along the uneven, mostly vertical trail, but manages to negotiate the terrain like a mountain goat in full gallop.

In the rearview I see the passenger-side door on the SUV open and Walton emerge from it, his service weapon in hand. He aims the piece in our direction, but we're already too far gone, the trees and brush shielding us.

I take on elevation until the mountain becomes too steep and slick even for the Jeep. With the LPPD having a very good idea of our present location, I maneuver the four-wheel drive vehicle along the base of the mountain until I find a logging road. I used to hike the Adirondack peaks back when I was kid. I know for a fact that logging roads snake their way through the entire Adirondack forest and most of them lead deep into the wilderness. We drive the road for maybe ten minutes until we come to a fork. That's when I stop.

"Well, Pen," I say. "Right or left?"

"How does the old poem go?" she says, both of her white-knuckled hands still gripping the dashboard bar. "The road less traveled?"

"And that will make all the difference," I say, picturing the old, scraggy-faced photo of Robert Frost that hung above the blackboard in my high school English class. "The one on the right definitely looks less traveled."

Pushing the gear shift back into first, I hook a right onto the road less traveled, hoping that it not only makes all the difference, but that it's also a road that accesses shelter.

The gas gauge reads half full, which in my mind is more optimistic than considering it's also half empty. It's good to maintain a positive attitude in these situations. I'm not one for the new wellness fad or alternative medicines, but it's been proven that a positive attitude can most definitely not only reduce significant stress, it can actually heal wounds.

Despite the optimism, the midday sun is quickly becoming obscured by thick rain clouds. Thick gray and black clouds, the rumbles from which are noticeable even above the roar of the engine.

"We'd better find something soon, Pen," I point out, "or we're in for a soaking."

But what I'm not telling her is that hypothermia can kick in even in the summer and in relatively high temperatures. Once the skin and flesh get rain-soaked, the body temperature can take a nosedive. Which means we need a roof over our heads quick. A cabin, shed, lean-to, or at the very least an awning of some sort.

Anything.

A lightning strike off in the near distance. Wait for the thunder. When it comes, it's loud and forceful, the noise bouncing off the mountain range like a pinball in a pinball machine. The first rain-drops follow. I see Penny wipe one of them from her cheek like she's wiping away a tear. Suddenly the dread of knowing that Chloe is being held against her will fills my veins again like a poison, and the serenity of the forest becomes a kind of living hell.

"Look," Penny speaks up suddenly. "There, on the right."

"What is it?" I say. "What are you seeing?"

"I think it's a cabin. Use your special eyes, Doc."

I tap the brakes, focus my eyes on the linear spaces between the trees. She's right. There's a wood shack or cabin set inside a clearing beyond a thick stand of old pine trees. I pull around the pines and the structure reveals itself. A single-story cabin made of logs with an old tin roof. Behind it is a sort of open-walled shelter for wood and tools. Its plywood overhang is large enough that I can pull up under it, sheltering us from the rain.

Downshifting, I pull onto an overgrown two-track that serves as a driveway, and come to a stop under the shelter. Another lightning strike illuminates the sky, and a few seconds pass before the thunder pounds the region like live artillery shells. Penny hops out, her pack tossed over her shoulder, the gun she took from Detective Giselle stored in her pants waist. Her eyes are peeled on the cabin, the front door to which is shuttered with a piece of old gray plywood.

"Looks abandoned to me, Doc."

"More than likely it's a deer hunting cabin," I point out. "Which means it's pretty much unoccupied most of the year except for the fall."

"You sure about that?"

"No," I say, cocking my head over my shoulder. "But it feels good to say it."

The rain starts to pick up. Another lightning strike. Closer this time. The thunder that follows rattles our bones. My bones, anyway.

"We need to get inside, Doc," Penny insists.

I slide out of the Jeep.

"Shall we add breaking and entering to today's list of high crimes and misdemeanors, Pen?"

"Do we have a choice, Doc?" she says.

CHAPTER 30

THE SKY GROWS darker, more ominous, the fine hairs on the back of my neck rising up from the static electricity in the air. The rain is growing harder, verging on coming down in sheets. In the back of the Jeep, I find a tire iron. I grab hold of it, bring it with me to the front door, shove one end of the tool into the narrow space between the door and the screwed-on plywood.

Gripping the bar with both my hands, I plant my booted foot against the exterior wall. Inhaling a breath, I yank on the bar. Turns out the plywood is rotted. It comes away from the log wall so easily I almost fall onto my backside. Pulling the entire board off the doorframe and tossing it to the side, I try the doorknob. It turns. I push on the door. It opens.

"No wonder the owner boarded the place up," I observe. "No working locks." Then, stepping inside, "Stay close behind and leave the door open, in case we gotta make a quick exit."

Setting the tire iron against the interior wall, I pull out the gun and slowly step into the open room. To my right is a log wall with a set of wood-framed bunk beds pushed up against it. A gun rack is mounted to the wall beside the beds. A pump-action shotgun is stored on the rack, along with a .30-30 lever-action rifle. Something John Wayne would have carried in one of his old Westerns.

Whoever owns the place isn't all that concerned about the safety of his firearms.

To my left is a big stone fireplace. Thick spider webs shroud the black cast iron hearth, telling me it hasn't been used in months or maybe years. I step farther into the room located on the opposite side. But then, the word room is too generous. More like a galley kitchen, attached to a small bathroom that also contains a stand-up shower.

Stepping into the kitchen, I wipe away the spider webs that hang from the ceiling.

"Hope you're not afraid of spiders, Pen."

"You know I am. If there's a broom, I can get rid of them while you make a fire, Daniel Boone."

I nod, begin making my way back across the front room to the open door.

"You know what I think?" I say, closing the door on the rain and the storm. "I think this place is abandoned. I can bet whoever lived here either couldn't take care of it anymore, or maybe died. Places like this are scattered all over the Adirondacks. With no surviving relatives, the places are soon forgotten and simply rot back into the earth like your average corpse."

Penny comes back out of the kitchen with a broom. Already she's swiping at the spider webs.

"There's a pile of dry wood by the hearth," she says. "Now all we need is a bottle of wine."

"And our daughter," I add.

Luck hasn't entirely abandoned us. Good luck, that is. Because the chimney is clear. The dry wood catches quickly and burns hot and bright from the unobstructed draw. All too often you hear about critters getting stuck in fireplace chimneys that are underutilized, but not this one.

With the burning wood going snap, crackle, pop inside the fireplace, I pull out my cell phone, flip the top. No calls, but I know that sooner than later, my parole officer is going to call me and tell me I'm a wanted man. Or perhaps at this point, he's not even bothering to call me.

Penny pulls up two wood stools. One for mama bear and one for papa. We both take a load off.

"Okay," I say. "Who gets the first call? Parole or the lawyer?"

"Toss-up," she says. "That is, if we even have service out here."

"Never thought of that. What about you?"

She's holding her phone in her hand.

"Two bars," she says. "You wanna use mine?"

"Let's see how I do with mine. I have the numbers on speed dial. You don't think I've actually memorized them, do you?"

I decide to contact Joel first. He's my legal counsel, after all. Could be he doesn't want me to contact Drew Lochte at New York State Parole in the first place. Thumbing the speed dial for my lawyer, I press the phone to my ear and wait.

Electronic rings fill my ear. The rings are clouded by pulses of static coming from the bursts of lightning striking all around us. The ringing stops as someone picks up.

"Mr. Harwood's office," comes the faint voice of Joel's secretary. "How can I help you?"

My heart rate begins to climb. I know the wrath I'm about to face down, even over the phone. To a man like Joel, the abduction of my daughter by a man like Rabuffo is secondary to the fact that I have taken the law into my own hands. Gone vigilante. Or perhaps secondary is not the right word. Perhaps it's more accurate to say that he will consider the move stupid and reckless. But what he can never know is the desperation that fills my veins. Mine and Penny's. And desperate times call for desperate measures, it's true. I simply can't risk being locked up by the police or anyone else.

I tell the secretary my name, then I ask for Joel. She nervously tells me to wait one second. I picture the blue-suited Joel seated behind his big mahogany desk in his glass-walled office on the top floor of a downtown Albany tower. He'll have a glass candy bowl filled with Good & Plenty within reach, and not one computer monitor, but two, one of them dedicated to real-time stock market quotes. He'll be relaxed, leaning back in his leather swivel chair. But when he hears my voice, he'll instruct his secretary to hold all calls. He'll straighten up, and concentrate entirely on me and my situation.

He picks up the phone.

"Jesus Christ, Sidney," he snipes, in the place of a hello. "Where the hell are you?"

I must admit, I'm taken aback. It's almost like Joel is somehow able to punch me in the gut from a distance of two hundred miles. Under normal circumstances, his demeanor is even keel, even tempered, and by the book. Even when parole negotiations got heated with the DA, Joel always maintained total professionalism. The sudden change in tone tells me he's worried. Maybe more than worried. Maybe in fear of what could happen to him and his practice, his having been such a strong advocate for my release.

"They took my daughter, Joel," I say. "They took my daughter, and I'm going to get her back."

"The police will get her back, Sidney," he asserts. "You must trust the system. You must go back. You must turn yourself in. Do you understand me? Do it now."

"Joel," I say. "Rabuffo's people revealed themselves. Last night. Someone was holding my daughter outside our hotel room. They let her speak to me. When I took the bait, I stepped outside and one of his goons knocked me over the head with a pistol. I was knocked out for a few seconds, but when I got up, I chased him.

When I got to him, I beat him. I couldn't help myself, Joel. I completely lost it. You would, too, if you were in my shoes. I just want my daughter back."

He pauses for a beat or two. Long enough for me to make out his breathing.

He says, "Why would they bait you like that, Sidney? Why not just send over a note, an email, or a text, listing their specific demands? Why do something so risky like that?"

"You tell me," I say, my eyes looking into the hot fire, but seeing the silhouette of my daughter as she stood on the beach beside the big unidentified man. "If you ask me, it was to taunt me. To torture me. To let me know they have power over me."

"You notice anything missing from your pockets? Your wallet maybe? Maybe they baited you so that they could search you. Find something you keep on your person at all times."

I pat my back pocket. My wallet is present and accounted for.

"What could they be looking for, Joel?"

He pauses once more. Then, "You and Rabuffo were pretty damned close. Like a proud dad and his only boy. That's the way you've always described it to me."

In my head, standing side by side Rabuffo in the basement of his house. A basement that was like a fortress located within a fortress, with its own alarm system, CCTV system, emergency lockdown system, enough firearms . . . long and short gun . . . to wage a small war. And of course, the vault where he stashed his cash and booty. Everything from diamonds to gold coins. Enough to purchase a small country in West Africa.

"So what's your theory, Joel?" I go on. "Where's this going?"

"Well now that the big boss has had his legs cut out from under him by the FBI, could be his lieutenants want their fair share of the Rabuffo fortune. Maybe the only way they can get at it is through you. You ever think of that, Sidney?"

I'm standing, even before I feel myself making the conscious decision to stand.

"Why, Joel?"

"Because, like I've already said, you and the big boss were pretty cozy before you got sent away."

"I owed him."

"And he, in turn, employed you. Reciprocity at its purest. Until . . . well, you know what happened."

"Yah," I say, "I was there."

In my head, the flashes of gunfire lighting up the windows of the bungalow the Chinese family lived in. Four gunshots in total.

"So let me get this straight," I go on. "This isn't about revenge for exposing Rabuffo. Instead, this is about something his people want from me."

"Maybe a little of both," he says, exhaling so deeply even I can feel it. "None of this matters, Sid. What matters is that you turn yourself in to me, and then we can let the police do their job, get Chloe back safe and sound."

"So far all they've been concentrating on is me, and *not* my daughter."

"That's because you're giving them reason to concentrate on you. Sources said you grabbed hold of Penny inside the hotel lobby. That when you approached a Marine and his girlfriend in the bar, you were drunk and belligerent. There's reports of you fighting and getting violent inside your hotel room. Then that goon . . . what's his name, Bertram . . . showing up at the police station and on the local news, his face destroyed, his finger nearly yanked off. I won't even bring up what you did this morning, for God's sakes, taking that hotel detective hostage and assaulting her. You're not even supposed to be in Lake Placid. By law you're supposed to remain in Albany where you're to be looking for a job and reporting in to your parole officer."

"I needed to spend quality time with my family. It's been a while, you know? It was Penny's idea, and to be honest, I jumped at the chance."

"Yeah, well, how's that quality time going for you, Sid? You've broken enough laws to put you back in the pen for four back-to-back life sentences."

"Do I have to answer that?"

"No, but you do have to answer to parole and the Lake Placid Village law enforcement authorities. And after all the work we did to get you free, I can bet it's all for nothing. They're going to want to incarcerate you again, Sidney, and this time it will be for good. So why not turn yourself in to me now, and at least plead your case to the courts? You're under obvious duress because of the abduction of your daughter, and you acted out of emotion. Any red-blooded man and father would do the same thing. That will be our defense."

I find myself looking at Penny. Rather than concentrate on me, and my conversation with Joel, she seems fixated by her smartphone. Something she's watching on the little digital screen.

The thoughts race through my head. Maybe Joel is right. Maybe Penny and I should get back in the Jeep, head back to town, turn ourselves in, leave the rescue of Chloe up to the cops. Maybe that's the only way out of this mess. The only way I can guarantee that I will not be transported back to prison.

"What about contacting Lochte?" I pose.

"I'm already on it," Joel says. "He's of the opinion that you need to turn yourself in right now. Like me, he understands your state of mind. But the goddamned law is the law, Sidney. You can't make it all up to suit your own purposes. Only God can do that."

Me, nodding. Penny turns to me, her eyes wide open, her face withdrawn and pale. Filled with a sudden burst of stress. She stands.

"Get off the phone, Sid." Her words are forced, emphatic.

I look into her eyes, whisper, "What? Why?"

"Get off the phone . . . Get off the damned phone!"

"Sidney," Joel says. "You there?"

"Ahhh yeah, Joel . . ."

"Sidney, what's happening?"

Penny, stepping toward me, her face practically in my face. She grabs the phone out of my hand, thumbs the END CALL button.

"Why did you do that, Penny? That's Joel. The one man we have on our side."

She hands me back the phone.

"You're not . . . *We're* not turning ourselves in," she states.

"Joel said it's the best move. I believe him."

"It's too late for that," she says, holding the screen on her smartphone up to my face.

"It's never too late," I say.

"You're now wanted for murder, Sid," she cries. "Two . . . fucking . . . counts. The murders of our daughter, Chloe, and Giselle."

CHAPTER 31

THE WOOD FLOOR beneath my feet goes soft. Like I'm no longer standing on something solid, but instead, sinking into quicksand. This nightmare is only getting worse. The burning wood pops. It startles me, like a gunshot I didn't expect.

Penny presses PLAY on the video that's now appearing on her smartphone screen. I see a field reporter standing outside the Lake Placid Village Police Station where Chief Joe Walton is holding a press conference in the rain.

"We are saddened by the events of this morning," he says into the multiple microphones attached to the wood podium before him, the rain pelting the visor on his police lid. "Namely the presumed loss of a little girl, Chloe O'Keefe, eleven years old, the child who'd been reported abducted by her parents yesterday afternoon, and the loss of one of the village's most prominent citizens and a former decorated member of this police force, forty-five-year-old Giselle Fontaine. While Fontaine was found dead in her bathtub only a few hours after her harrowing abduction ordeal with the accused, we have not yet uncovered the body of Chloe. Although based on the physical and circumstantial evidence at hand, we are suspecting and expecting the worst."

The press lobs questions at the cop, but he holds up his meaty hands as if to say, *Not now*.

"The photos we're about to show you are disturbing," he warns. "You should all be cautioned." He turns, nods to one of his uniformed policemen who pulls out a big white poster board that serves as a backdrop for six full color eight-by-ten-inch glossy photos.

"Can you all make these out?" Walton asks.

The cameraman working the presser for the news channel broadcast on the digital smartphone zooms in on the first photo. It shows a woman who is most definitely Detective Giselle Fontaine, her face bruised and battered, her mouth gaping open, along with her blue eyes. There's something wrapped around her throat. It's a pair of yellow polka-dot bikini bottoms. The bottoms are bloodstained, if not blood-soaked.

"Oh God," I mumble to myself. "What the hell has happened to our little girl?"

Penny's eyes are rolling back in their sockets. She begins to fall. She's overwhelmed, physically, emotionally. Her heart is palpitating. She's going into shock. I grab onto her.

"Penny," I say. "Breathe, honey, please breathe."

Each photograph is broadcast over the news channel, one by one. All a different version of the same thing. Giselle dead, her face and neck horribly black and blued. Her neck choked by Chloe's bathing suit.

The chief moves in closer to the microphones.

"Currently, our number one suspect in the double homicide is a fifty-year-old male and the father of the suspected deceased, Chloe O'Keefe, namely Sidney O'Keefe. Released from a downstate maximum-security penitentiary only last week for which he had been doing a twenty-five-to-life sentence in the murder of four undocumented Chinese aliens back in 2007, O'Keefe is proof that some natural born killers should never be paroled. And I can't stress the word *never* enough.

"As I've already indicated this morning, O'Keefe and his wife took Fontaine hostage, holding her with her own gun, which they took off her person. They then fled the police who'd arrived on the scene to investigate the beating of one Tom Bertram, who identified O'Keefe as his attacker late last night. While the O'Keefes fled to the woods located in and around Keene Valley, it appears they doubled back to exact their revenge on Fontaine as she was heading home. At this point, we can't be certain when O'Keefe assaulted his daughter, but said assault was likely deadly, and the primary reason behind his false story of her having been abducted right off the beach on Mirror Lake.

"As of this moment, both local and state police have joined in the hunt for O'Keefe who, at present, is at large with his wife, Penny. Penny, it should be noted, is considered coconspirator in the double homicide. Like her husband, she should also be considered armed and dangerous. If anyone within the vicinity of Lake Placid and/or the Keene Valley should accidentally come across the two perpetrators, we urge you not to engage in any open contact with them, but to instead immediately dial 911 and contact local police authorities."

Chief Walton walks away from the mic to the shotgunned questions lobbed by the many reporters present. That's when the video ends.

*   *   *

"What the hell just happened?" I say, my voice barely exiting my dry mouth.

"They killed her. They killed them both. And they're blaming us, Sid."

"But that's impossible. The only pictures they showed were of Giselle, and even then, we can't be sure she's dead."

"What are you saying?"

It hits me with all the intensity of the electrical storm still waging outside the log walls of this long-abandoned cabin. Setting the smartphone onto the stool, I grab hold of Penny's shoulders.

"Don't you see what's happening here, Penny? We're being set up. We're being made to look like murderers. Or, at the very least, I'm being set up."

"But why, Sidney? Why go to the lengths they are going to? I mean, it's the police for God's sakes. I thought you said it was Rabuffo who wanted his revenge. But we're running from the very people who should be helping us. Helping our daughter."

I think about my phone call with Joel. About the reason they baited me with Chloe outside the hotel room last night. About them needing something from me in order to get at what they want.

"Because they want something," I say.

"What exactly can they want that bad, Doc?"

Realization . . . It's like a bright white light that suddenly turns on over my head. Joel wasn't lying when he said Rabuffo's lieutenants are going after their fair share of his fortune.

"They want Rabuffo's cash, Pen. And they think I alone hold the key to it."

"So you think it's possible our daughter is alive?"

I nod.

"I do," I say. "They want us to think she's dead so that we'll come out into the open. It's their leverage. But we're not going to take the bait. We're going to stick it out right here until we can figure out a way to get back to town, find out who knows where they're keeping Chloe, and then we're going to get her back. Only then will we turn ourselves into the police."

"With Joel's help."

"With Joel's help," I agree.

CHAPTER 32

I TOSS TWO more logs on the fire. It sparks while the dry logs take to the flame like tissue paper.

"So what do we do now, Sid?" Penny begs, her hands trembling. "I'm going crazy here. I feel like my skin is peeling off my body. I need to see Chloe. I need to know she's alive."

"They got us up against a wall, Pen. Like I just said, they believe my only choice . . . *our* only choice . . . is to give ourselves up."

"Are we going to do that?" Penny begs. "Give ourselves up, I mean?"

"Here's what's going to happen, Pen. Whoever is doing this to us . . . whoever is masterminding it . . . is going to make contact with us. They're going to try and make a deal. Our freedom in exchange for something else."

"What about Chloe?"

"That's the thing," I add. "We don't negotiate for anything less than Chloe's release."

"In exchange for what, Doc?"

"Who's the common denominator in all of this?" I pose. "What's the reason the DA let me out of prison in the first place?"

She thinks about it for a moment. But she doesn't have to think long.

"Rabuffo," she says.

"Rabuffo has a treasure trove hidden away, Pen. My guess is that our enemies believe I not only know precisely where to find it, but that I know the combination to the vault itself."

She looks at me for a moment. Rather, not at me, but into me.

"Well, Sidney," she says, "do you?"

I hear it then.

Something coming from outside other than the weather. The sound of rotors chopping through the air. I go to the front door, open it, poke my head out. Just enough to get a look without being spotted. But then, they can see the smoke. If it's a police chopper, they can pick up the heat signal from the fire on their infrared equipment. They can pick up our voices with basic over-the-counter sound equipment you can purchase at the local Radio Shack. They know we're in here regardless of my exposed face.

We're sitting ducks.

"What is it, Doc?" Penny asks. "Is it the police?"

"A helicopter," I say. "They're on to us, Pen. They know where we're hiding out."

I head out into a rain that's eased up now that the bulk of the storm has passed. The black-and-white Lake Placid police chopper makes a low-flying pass, like they're buzzing the place. I do the only thing I can do. I raise up my right hand, hold my middle index finger high.

Back inside the cabin, I stare down Penny.

Choices.

Surrender to the police. Head outside with our hands held high. Or stand our ground.

Penny's eyes locked on mine.

"We're screwed, Sidney," she says, her voice trembling, big tears falling. "We've got nowhere to go. We have to give up."

My chest tight, mouth dry, temples pounding. Instinct kicks in. The survival instinct. It overrides all reason. But it's not just my survival that's at stake here. Nor Penny's. It's Chloe's. Nothing matters more than Chloe's life. I'll do whatever I have to do to make sure these bastards do not harm a single hair on her head.

I go to the gun rack at the opposite side of the room. I pull down the shotgun, examine it. It's not in bad shape. It could use some oil, but otherwise in working order. Pulling down the .30-30, I can see it, too, is in working order.

The chopper buzzes overhead as it makes another pass. It sounds like it's about to crash through the roof.

"We've got to do something, Doc," Penny insists. "Do it now."

"Like go outside and hold our hands over our head?" I respond. "Surrender? Only to lose our daughter forever?"

"They'll have no choice but to return her to us."

"You don't know what we're dealing with here, Pen," I say. "It's Rabuffo. Doesn't matter if he's in FBI custody. He has people who will not only make sure Chloe dies, but that she suffers in the process."

She begins to cry again.

"Oh, sweet Jesus," she weeps. "This isn't happening. This is all a bad dream."

"I need bullets," I say more to myself than to Penny. "I can do without the oil, but bullets would be nice. And shells for the shotgun."

Setting the .30-30 back on the rack, I once more grab the shotgun, slide back the action, open the bolt. Like I said, decent shape. Racking the gun, I head into the kitchen, examine the shelves mounted to the wall between the counter and the bathroom. Three boxes of Remington 12-guage shotgun shells. Another three boxes of Remington .30-30 cartridges. I grab hold of all six boxes, carry them into the main room and to the gun rack. Loading the .30-30, I listen to the chopper make another pass, and I see Penny once more staring at her phone.

She wipes her tears and locks her gaze on mine.

"It's a text message," she explains.

"Caller ID?"

"Unidentified caller, Doc."

"Read it to me," I say, cocking the now loaded .30-30, then starting on feeding shells to the shotgun.

"'I can make all this go away,'" she recites.

"That's it? That's all it says?"

"'I can make this go away,'" she repeats.

"What about the phone number? Is there an area code? Is it 518?" 518 being the local area code for this part of northern New York State. A code that also includes the capital city of Albany where our apartment is located.

"It's an eight-eight-eight number," Penny adds.

"Okay, Pen, that means whoever's doing this is thorough and not prone to mistakes. It also means they somehow know your number."

"What do I text in return?"

"Tell them we want our daughter back. Then we go our separate ways."

She doesn't hesitate to thumb the message into the phone.

The chopper buzzes the camp again.

So close, the thundering noise of the chopper causes Penny to shrug, as if the machine were about to take the roof off and our heads along with it.

"That's enough of that," I grouse.

Switching up the shotgun for the .30-30, I head outside onto the overgrown front lawn. I catch sight of the chopper, a Huey, about to make another pass. Shouldering the rifle, I plant a bead on its nose. As the chopper begins its dive, I wait patiently, holding my breath until it's almost directly over the tin roof. That's when I release some of the air in my lungs and fire as rapidly as possible.

I'm certain I've connected with the chopper's windshield, because I can see the chips of safety glass fly off it. The chopper exposes its belly, rapidly taking on elevation as a defensive maneuver. I fire again, this time aiming for the engine. When I see black smoke emerge from the back of the chopper exhaust, I know I've struck home.

The chopper circles over the wilderness like a wounded bird of prey. But its motor can't be that badly damaged since it's now coming back toward me. Something's different this time. The closer it comes, the easier it is to see that its side door has been opened. There's a man leaning out of it. He's dressed in black tactical gear including a helmet and dark goggles. He's also holding an automatic rifle. The automatic rifle is armed with a grenade launcher.

I take aim with my .30-30 at the exact moment I make out the flash of the grenade launcher.

"Holy Christ!" I bark as I launch myself onto the cabin two-track.

The grenade detonates maybe ten feet away from me, the concussion rattling my teeth and bones, exploded soil and grass raining down upon me. Shaking the dizziness from my head, I do my best to bound back up, and return the fire as the chopper once again zooms away from me.

But I'm so unsteady and shaken up, all I'm hitting is air.

The chopper flies another circular pattern.

It's coming back. Its trajectory is lower this time. Like whoever is doing the shooting is trying to improve his aim. It hits me then that he might be going for the cabin. Maybe he'll try to hit it with a grenade, hope for a fire, burn us out into the open for good. It's exactly how I'd do it.

"Penny," I whisper to myself. "She's inside the cabin."

I go for the front door, throw it open. My wife is nowhere to be seen.

"Penny!" I shout. "Penny, where are you!?"

"Here," she responds.

I gaze in the direction of the voice. That's when I spot her hiding under the bunk beds.

"Jesus, spiders are everywhere under here!" she barks.

I go to her, bend at the knees, take hold of her hand.

"We've got to move, baby. We've got to get the hell out."

Yanking her out from under the bunk beds, I pull her up onto her feet, and drag her to the front door, a half second before the grenade connects with the back of the cabin.

CHAPTER 33

THE BLAST PROPELS us out the open front door, onto the front lawn, flat onto our chests. For a brief second, the wind is knocked out of me. I search for Penny. She's only a few feet away from me, on my left-hand side. She's moving around, so at least I know she's alive.

My head is ringing, the ground beneath me spinning. I'm waking up from a vivid dream that's made me temporarily paralyzed. It takes all my strength to peel myself up off the ground. But when I manage to get back up on my feet, I spot the chopper making one more go-around. As it's coming back at us, I shoulder the .30-30 and open up on her with all the ammo I have left, the rounds connecting with the Huey's front end.

Flames shoot out of the exhaust, but it doesn't seem to affect the chopper's ability to fly. Just a few seconds later, it disappears beyond the tree line.

The police know our precise location. That is, if the chopper belongs to the police in the first place. Maybe it belongs to Rabuffo, or both.

What this means is, Penny and I have no choice but to get the hell out of here. Go deeper into the woods, or maybe get out of the woods altogether and head to another town or city. Someplace we can lie low, figure out a way to rescue our daughter, then expose the men and women who are setting me up as a murderer. It's exactly how I put it to Penny as the quiet of the deep woods once more replaces the mechanical blade slapping, whop-whop-whop noise from the helicopter.

"Listen and listen clearly, Sidney," she says. "I will not leave this place until we have our Chloe back. Do you understand me?"

She's right. There's no point in even considering heading to another town when it only makes sense that whoever abducted Chloe is keeping her nearby.

"Okay," I say. "Let's grab the bags, go deeper into the forest. If we're lucky we'll come upon another safe house."

We head back into the cabin. The damage from the grenade is not as extensive as I first thought. It's taken out a good portion of the kitchen, but not much else. Even the fire is still burning steadily in the stone fireplace. It's like we merely stepped outside for a nice brisk, post-thunderstorm afternoon walk in the fresh country air.

"Check your phone again, Pen," I say, heading to the bunk beds. "I'll grab the stuff."

"There's no messages," she says.

"How do you know? You haven't even looked at your phone."

I pick up the daypack, strap it over my shoulder. Then I go to the gun rack, grab hold of the shotgun and an extra box of shells. I'm about to put the shells in the daypack when I feel the solid slam against the back of my head. My brain matter bounces against the interior of my skull, and the cabin turns into a deep, dark black hole.

CHAPTER 34

DARKNESS SURROUNDS ME.

I'm falling through it. So fast I can't take a breath. There seems to be no end to the falling, until suddenly I find myself walking a beautiful property. A heavenly property. The grass is freshly mowed, the trees in full bloom. The birds are singing in the trees and the cicadas are strumming. It's a beautiful early summer day with a slight breeze blowing through the leaves. I hear giggling coming from some girls hanging around a swimming pool. Beyond the swimming pool is a house that's bigger than the high school I attended.

A man approaches me. He's tall, with thick white hair, and he carries a soft underbelly. He's wearing a silk robe over pressed trousers and black Gucci loafers, no socks.

"I want to show you something, son," Mickey Rabuffo says. "Something wonderful . . ."

We're down inside the depths of the mansion. It's like a bunker, with bright overhead lighting that illuminates the long corridor. There are rooms on both sides. Rooms filled with weapons, another with drug product ready to be shipped. One major portion of the underground facility is used as a lab to cook methamphetamine. And yet another cell-like area houses illegal Chinese who are presently on the market. Finally, there's a vault that houses the bulk of

Rabuffo's fortune. A fortune accessible only by retinal scan and a keypad access code.

"Place your left eye up to the scanner," Rabuffo insists.

I do as he says.

An electric sensor scans my eye for a few long beats, until the mechanical noise of a heavy vault door being unlocked fills the basement depths.

"This is how much I trust you, Sidney," Rabuffo says . . .

*   *   *

But then Rabuffo is gone. The long corridor becomes dark and cold. I feel the cold seep through my bones, as if my blood were no longer warm. I see someone standing at the end of the long corridor. At first, it's just a silhouette, but then the closer I come to her, I know that it's a girl.

It's Chloe.

"Daddy," she says. "Please save me."

Rabuffo appears once more. He grabs hold of her hair with his fist, throws her to the floor. She screams . . .

*   *   *

When I come to, I'm blinded.

That's because someone has laid me out on my belly, my face stuffed in a pillow. My wrists are tied or duct taped behind my back, along with my ankles. My head hurts. Hurts bad enough so that it's possible I'm hemorrhaging. It's as if the blood that soaks my brain wants to pop out of my skull. But then, if I were hemorrhaging, I'd already be dead or stroking out.

Still, I manage to slowly turn my head, just enough so that I can see out the corner of my eye. It's then I realize I'm laid out on the bottom bunk of the rickety bunk beds inside the cabin. My vision is blurry, my hearing not to be trusted, but I can make out at least three people positioned around the fire. One of them is Penny. She's not standing, but seated on one of the wood stools. She's looking up at a man. The man is in uniform. A cop's uniform.

It's Walton.

The person standing beside Walton is a woman.

The woman should not be here. As in—she should presently be occupying a cold storage drawer down inside the Warren County morgue. It's Detective Giselle Fontaine. She doesn't look strangled to me. My eyesight might be cloudy at present or, hell, I might even be dreaming. But I'm not dreaming and sure as shit if she isn't standing inside this cabin, warming herself by the fire like she just happened to walk in while out for a nature hike. It's most definitely her. I can also see that she has reappropriated her pistol, since it's currently back in her hip holster.

It's not a good sign for things to come.

I try to move on this mattress of rusted and broken springs, but I can't.

I'm hogtied. For all they know, I'm still out cold, still sleeping it off. So here's the dilemma: I don't see my daughter anywhere, which tells me she is still being held against her will in some as of yet unidentified location.

Here's the other dilemma: I'm having a tough time trying to decide whether or not my lovely bride is currently also being held against her will, or if she's . . . how shall I put this? . . . on the side of the enemy.

Here's what I'm going to do: I'm going to lie here as still as possible. I'm going to suffer through my blistering headache, and I'm going to listen to what they are saying. Then I'm going to make a determination as to my next move based upon the evidence gathered. Which, at this point, appears to be decidedly fucked up.

*   *   *

"It wasn't supposed to go down like this, Penny," Walton gripes, the frustration oozing from his pores. He's sucking hard on a cigarette, his round face red from the blood vessels that worm their way inside his skin. "You should have had the access code by now. We should have Rabuffo's stash. All of it. That's what you promised when we agreed to enter into this shit storm. We wait any longer, the feds are gonna take it, if they haven't already." He's stomping his foot. "Christ, Penny, didn't you get the text? I can make all this go away. Just deliver the access codes like you promised. Like we planned. You're playing both sides of the street here."

"The darned feds haven't taken over yet, Chief," Giselle interjects. "That crap they showed on the television news this morning with the FBI busting Rabuffo was total federal bureau propaganda. Theatrics and politics. Rabuffo is still the property of the Albany cops while they process him. But I'll bet dollars to Dunkin Donuts, that situation ends this afternoon."

"Which means what?" Penny says bitterly from down on her stool.

"It means that by the dinner hour tonight," Giselle goes on, "you're going to see a whole bunch of men and women dressed in cheap suits and windbreakers bearing the letters FBI crossing the yellow APD Do-Not-Enter crime scene ribbon, while they tear the Rabuffo estate apart."

Walton tosses the cigarette into the fire, turns his attention to Giselle.

He says, "She was supposed to have worked the damn code out of that muscle-head numb nuts by yesterday afternoon. It wasn't supposed to go this far. Shit, he shot back at our chopper. You don't fucking shoot back at a police helo. Goes against the god-damned rules."

Penny stands. "They shot at him first. They blew up the kitchen, for Christ sakes. Jesus, Walton, he's my husband and he's been through hell and back. Isn't it enough that you're using my daughter?"

"No," Walton sneers, "it's not enough. How's that grab ya? She's perfectly fine. She's got the run of my trailer, all the video games she wants to play, all the pizza she can eat."

"You give her back to me, you son of a bitch," Penny snaps. "You probably have her locked up in a cage, you creep. You creep son of a bitch."

Walton takes a step toward my wife, his right hand raised like he's going to slap her.

"Darn it, Chief!" Giselle scorns, "That's enough."

Walton lowers his hand, stares back into the fire.

"We need the codes from your husband, Penny," Giselle goes on, her demeanor softer, less demanding. "And we sort of need them now. Before it's too late."

"Too late," Penny grouses. "That why you tried to blow us to smithereens with that helicopter?"

Giselle turns to Walton, sneers at him.

"That police helicopter is the Chief's overly zealous and testosterone-charged support staff nearly messing everything up for us. Isn't that right, Chief?"

"They were only doing their job," he says. "Or what they think of as their job. They could have been killed when our killer shot back at them. That would be on him. Not me."

. . . He's got to be joking . . .

Giselle refocuses on my wife.

"There's simply too darned much at stake at this point, Penny," she says. "You see, we're not career criminals here. We're nice, peaceful, country people. But when offered a fortune that can only come your way once in a lifetime, you make amends, and you postpone your morals for a while. How did Mr. Shakespeare put it? 'Taketh now or lose it forever more.'"

"What if he doesn't know any codes?" Penny sneers. "He's been knocked out twice in twenty-four hours. What if he's lost his memory? Or what the hell, maybe Rabuffo changed them after Sid was put in prison."

"Oh, Sid knows them," Walton jumps in. "I know for a fact Mr. Muscle Head killer knows them. And he's not braindead yet. And as for Rabuffo changing the codes, we thought that over already. We're banking on the very distinct possibility he didn't change them, because why bother if Sid's going away for a hundred years or more."

"Okay, so on the off chance Rabuffo didn't change them once Sid was released from prison," Penny goes on, "how can you be so sure my husband still knows the codes?"

"Because I know a man who knows the real deal. A man who used to be as close to your killer husband as a blood brother." Walton looks at his wristwatch. "And that man should be here any minute to extract the codes to Rabuffo's vault once and for all. Someone who lives and thrives on dirty work."

* * *

Maybe a minute later, I make out the sound of a four-by-four vehicle or truck pulling up outside the cabin. I can hear a commotion as not one, but several people exit the vehicle.

"Keep your disgusting hands off me," comes a voice I immediately recognize, even if it's a voice I have not heard in many, many years. "You're not the boss of me, you weirdos."

"We're just doing our jobs," says another voice. A man's voice. Also, a familiar voice.

"Leave him alone, Burt," a woman speaks. "We were told to drive him all the way out here, and that's as far as it goes."

"Don't back-talk me, Claudia," Burt says. "I know what I'm doing. And I'm not exactly in the best of moods now that I lost my iPhone on the beach."

"You should know better than to leave it sitting out on the beach chair, dummy."

"Don't you call me 'dummy.'"

The two people who watched over my daughter on the beach before she was taken away enter into the cabin. Burt and Claudia Stevens. I gaze upon them with my eyes half closed. She's just as smiley as she was yesterday morning in her yellow summer-weight sundress, and he's just as portly in his Bermuda shorts, yellow knee-high socks, and pink Izod polo shirt.

They have someone with them. The man they were supposedly transporting to this off-the-grid location. I recognize him as someone, like Detective Giselle, who should be six feet under by now. Or someone I assumed was buried a long, long time ago.

He is Singh. And Singh lives.

CHAPTER 35

My heart is pounding. My headache is long gone. It's replaced, instead, with fury. Or maybe I'm just dreaming all this up. I'm yanking on the duct tape cuffs. There's a couple of bed springs that have snapped in half over the years and pierced the old, rotted mattress material. I'm fiercely rubbing the tape against them. I don't know if I'm doing any good, but it's worth the shot.

I've known Singh almost my entire life, only now, I feel like I am looking at him for the first time. He's not the muscular, dark-haired macho athlete I knew in high school. Instead, his left hand is missing, no doubt where the bullets from the APD severed it as he and Wemps were making their escape from the bungalow that housed the Chinese family they slaughtered in cold blood. A pinkish-purple hypertrophic scar runs diagonally across his face, crossing over his lips like an earthquake fault, and his left eye is presumably missing, since there's a black pirate patch covering it. As for the dark hair, it's long gone, replaced by a scarred, egg head scalp.

He turns to me. I'm quick to shut my eyes all the way, feign sleep.

"There he is," Singh says. "Jeeze, I haven't laid eyes, or eye . . . get it? . . . on my old buddy in over a decade. In fact, he probably thinks I'm dead. Last I saw him, a whole lot of bullets were plugging me with a whole lot of daylight. I actually died on the operating table. But that's when good ole' Mr. Rabuffo stepped in, paid off whoever had to be paid off to pronounce me dead, and then shipped me off to his private hospital down in the basement of his mansion."

Singh's got motor mouth, like he sniffed up a half dozen bumps of high-grade cocaine on the way out here. Or maybe he's been sampling Rabuffo's crystal meth now that the crime kingpin is no longer around to watch the store.

"That's some story, Mr. Singh," Giselle says. "So why is it you don't know the codes to access the Rabuffo vault like your old friend Sidney does?"

I slowly open my eyes again, enough so I can make out the expression on Singh's messed-up face. It's not all that easy to tell, what with that purple scar planted in the middle of it, but if I had to guess, I would interpret the look as one of scorn.

"That's because I wasn't Rabuffo's favorite. I didn't have the education like the *almost* doc here did. I didn't have the boyish good looks, the nice laugh, the all-around good-guy-caught-up-in-gambling-circumstances-beyond-his-control, like our passed-out boy Sidney did. I didn't look good in one of his Rabuffo's Custom Clothier's one-thousand-dollar suits." He shrugs his still beefy shoulders. "Hell, I don't know, maybe Rabuffo was queer for him."

Walton approaches Singh.

"Well, here's what you're going to do, Singh," he says. "You're gonna extract all the information we need from O'Keefe. More precisely, the code to that fancy safe he's got stored inside the basement of his big-ass mansion. And then we're all gonna take a ride and go get it."

"And my husband?" Penny says. "What happens to Sidney when this is finished?"

Walton turns to her, laughs.

"That's really rich, Penny," he snipes. "You had a chance to do things your way and we've got nothing to show for it. Now, all of a sudden you have feelings for the hubby? You kidding me? Wasn't this your idea in the first place?" He holds up both his hands like he's issuing a time-out. "Oh wait, excuse me. Allow me to correct myself. This wasn't your idea. It was your boyfriend's idea. Your boyfriend's plan."

Penny's face drains while my blood begins to boil, and my heart breaks.

"Leave Joel out of this, Walton," she says bitterly. "You hear me? He has his reputation to think about."

Okay, stop the world, I wanna blow it up. Or maybe I should find a way to blow myself up. How could I have not seen through the forest of lies and deceit before now? How could I not have realized something was entirely wrong the moment Penny had no problem leaving our eleven-year-old daughter alone on the beach? Maybe I hadn't had sex with a woman in ten years, but that didn't mean I had to do it right then and there. We might have waited another day, until we got home.

But Penny made it seem all right. She made it seem like Chloe was mature beyond her years. That she knew better than to stray. And besides, she was playing so nicely with the child of the sweet couple who were also hanging out on the beach. What harm could there be in sneaking away for a few minutes?

Wait, hold the phone, Sid . . .

What's the use in blaming Penny for the abduction? For this plot to snatch Rabuffo's fortune, if such a maneuver is even possible? The more correct and honorable thing to do is to blame yourself for being so naïve. So stupid. So selfish. Did you really have to give her that stupid ring while all alone in the hotel room? You should have stayed on the beach, your eyes glued to your daughter, where they belonged.

Singh approaches me.

He's reaching into his pocket with his one existing hand, comes back out with a black leather glove. I know what he's capable of doing with that one hand protected inside a leather glove. The destruction or, should I say, the facial reconstruction. There's forty-three muscles in the human face, all of which are manipulated by the facial nerve, or what's clinically known as the seventh cranial nerve. It's the fat nerve that protrudes from the cerebral cortex and that splits into five more nerves, the exact names of which I actually forget at the moment considering two major head traumas within twenty-four hours. But I'm guessing each and every one of those five nerves are about to get a workout.

He brings the end of the glove to his mouth, clamps onto it with his teeth, then shoves his meaty hand inside. If I'm dreaming, this is the part where I'm supposed to wake up.

I open both eyes, roll onto my side, my wrists still sawing away at the sharp springs.

"Well, look who's awake?" Singh says, smiling. "Hey, were you spying on us, old friend? Man, oh man, killer, do we have some history together or what?"

I'm pulling like a son of a bitch on the tape that binds me. My ankles are still sealed together, but there's suddenly some wiggle room in the wrists.

Singh bends down so that he avoids hitting his head against the wood bunk bed frame above me. He reaches out with his rubber-gloved hand, grabs hold of my t-shirt collar, yanks me toward him. That's when I feel a snap in my wrists. I've managed to split apart the duct tape. But that doesn't mean I want him to know that. In my prone position, with my ankles still bound together, I have no way of defending myself. That is, without getting myself killed in the process.

For now, I hold my wrists together behind me, while he pulls me forward. Cocking his head over his shoulder, he shouts, "Get me one of them stools!"

"Why?" Penny asks nervously. "What exactly do you plan on doing with it?"

"Just bring it here, bitch."

"Do what he says," Walton insists.

When Penny hesitates, Walton pulls his service weapon, aims it at my wife's face, thumbs back the hammer to show her he means business.

"Jeepers, Penny, just do it, will ya," Giselle adds. "What the hell did you think you were getting into when you agreed to this mission? A nice little picnic by the lake? I'm assuming Joel didn't fill you in on all the details. But that's neither here nor there. So either play right, or suffer the same darned consequences your husband is about to endure."

"What consequences?" Penny begs.

"Just give me that damned stool already," Singh orders. "And you'll find out."

For the first time since I've come to, I open my trap.

"Penny," I say, "don't listen to them. They're just going to kill you in the end anyway."

Singh's face goes wide-eyed. He cocks back his thick arm, belts me in the mouth.

"Owe, jeeze, Singh," I snap. "And to think I used to beat you up when we were freshmen."

"Revenge is a bitch, ain't it, killer? That's for taking my hand off."

"Hell you talking about?" I say, my head spinning, brain ringing. "I was just the driver that night."

"You leave him alone, Singh!" Penny barks. She comes rushing across the floor, raises her hand, strikes Singh. He turns fast, smacks her across the face. It's all I can do to remain lying on my side. Maybe Penny deserves to be hit for what she's done to our daughter. For her betrayal of our little family. But that's not for Singh to decide.

My head is fucking pounding.

"Penny," I say, "just do as they say, please. You don't have to worry. Walton and Giselle aren't about to kill anyone. They'll never take that risk. Take it from me. Do you know what violent cons do to police who end up in prison? It's not pretty, believe me."

Walton smiles, his teeth gray, his fat face filling with blood and oxygen. He takes a step forward, that service weapon still gripped in his shooting hand.

"That what you think, O'Keefe?" he says. "You think I don't have the stomach for taking a life in order to get what I want?" He releases a belly laugh. "Only reason you aren't dead yet is because we need information from you. But tell you what, you wanna see what I'm capable of when properly motivated?"

He turns toward the Stevenses, both of whom have been standing in the corner of the cabin between the fireplace and the front door, quiet as church mice. My guess is they expected to receive a substantial payment with the delivery of Singh and then it would be back to the beach. It's the only reason they would wait around since they don't seem the type to have been in on this plan from the get-go.

Walton takes a few steps toward the couple, his pistol aimed for Burt Stevens' face. Point-blank.

"Easy with that thing, Chief," Burt says, his Adam's apple bouncing around inside his fat neck. "You'll kill somebody if you're not careful."

"Exactly," Walton says.

When he pulls the trigger, the entire cabin lights up in a white flash while the back of Burt's head spatters against the log wall. The chubby man drops on the spot like a sack of blood and old bones. His wife's face has received the brunt of the blood spray, her perfect hair now highlighted with bits of bone and brain matter. Her eyes are wide and wet, her lips trembling.

She lunges herself at Walton, who casually steps out of the way. She smacks the opposite wall so hard, she drops onto her backside, her yellow dress hiked up onto her belly, exposing pink underpants. She screams, jumps back up onto her feet, runs left, runs right, and then finally sprints for the open cabin door.

Singh is laughing so hard at the show, he's bent over in pain.

Penny is screaming, crying.

Giselle is shaking her head in disgust, while Walton issues a kind of satisfied smile. Like all's well with his world. He gives her a short head start before heading out the door in pursuit. If I lift my head up enough, I can see out the open front door, see her trying to make it across the overgrown lawn to the logging road. But then I hear the crack, crack, crack of the semi-automatic, and she does a full face-plant in the mud.

Seconds later, Walton enters back into the cabin. He thumbs the magazine release on his gun, drops the partially empty mag into the palm of his free hand. Storing the mag in one of the narrow pockets on his utility belt, he pulls a full magazine from the belt, slaps that into the pistol grip, then pulls back on the slide.

He's once more locked and loaded, and most definitely headed for a death sentence inside some maximum-security joint. At the very least, the son of a bitch will never step foot in heaven.

"So where were we?" Singh inquires, turning back to me. "Sorry about the rude interruption, killer. But you gotta admit, it was pretty funny. You see the look on that lady's face when she kissed that wall? Too freakin' funny." Reaching down, he grabs hold of my collar again, pulls me out of the bunk. "Where's the god-damned stool?!" he shouts. "I've got work to do."

Penny brings him the stool, this time without an argument. Sets it down only a foot or two from the bunk bed. I'm doing my best not to let on that my wrists are freed. In the meantime, I catch a quick peek at the wall-mounted gun rack. While the .30-30 is leaning against the wall on the opposite side of the room, the loaded shotgun is still stored on the rack. I don't know if anybody has noticed the shotgun, or if anybody cares. All they know is they are in charge. They are in control.

My hands and ankles are bound together. Supposed to be any-way. What difference would it make if there were one hundred shotguns lying around? Once I hand over the information Singh is about to torture out of me, I'm as good as dead. Penny and Chloe, too, if my instincts serve me right.

Singh presses his hand on my shoulder, pushes me down onto the stool.

"There," he says, "that comfy, killer? Oops, sorry, I know you hate it when I call you that."

"Feels good, Singh," I say. Then, working up a smile, "But before we get started, answer me a quick question. If you're still alive, who's inside your coffin?"

"Hey, good question. None of these idiots thought to ask me that. You always were the smart one, killer, errrr, I mean, Sidney. Wemps was the dumb one. The coke head. I was always the jock. But you, you were the smart one. We always knew you'd go places." He makes a fist, rubs it against the scarred stump of a wrist that used to support his left hand. "'Course, everything kind of got fucked up along the way, now didn't it?"

"Hey, man," I say, "if it's one thing you can count on, it's a good life turning to shit."

"Amen, brother," Singh says. Then, "God, we been friends for how long, bro?"

"Forty years maybe, give or take."

He cocks back his good arm.

"Then you know this ain't nothing personal. It's all business."

"You can bet your good eye on it, Singh."

Penny quickly turns her head. Walton takes on the evil sneer once more, like he's really going to enjoy this show. Giselle crosses her arms over her chest, checks the time on her wristwatch like she's late for a church meeting.

"Can we just pretty please get this moving already?" the house detective adds. "We've got two dead bodies to deal with, and for the love of Pete, I can't imagine we're not on somebody's radar by now."

"Good point," Singh says. "The radar that belongs to the good police. If there are any of those left in Lake Placid."

This is the part where you might expect me to take my chances, go for the shotgun in the corner. But I do that now, Singh will be on me like flies on an open wound. I need to play a little rope-a-dope, wear him out a little.

Here's the thing: he's only got one hand left. If memory serves me well, he took at least two bullets to the lungs on that fateful night all those years ago. He's lost lung tissue. A lot of the tissue that remains has got to be scarred and useless, not unlike someone who suffers from idiopathic pulmonary fibrosis. Basically, what I'm saying is, no way oxygen is moving through Singh's tiny air sacks as freely as they might, say, on a man with a healthy pair of lungs. A nonsmoker preferably. It won't take very long for him to get winded. I just have to hold out for a little while, pray those five facial nerves don't give me so much pain I start spouting out the combination to Rabuffo's vault. Only then, when Singh is too winded to punch, will I make my move.

I survived ten years inside a maximum-security penitentiary. I've been beat up before. Take it from me, you only feel the first dozen or so fists. After that, the nerves tend to go numb. At least, that's what I'm hoping for.

"Ready, killer?" Singh poses.

"Can't wait," I say.

The glove-covered fist flies.

CHAPTER 36

HE SUCKS IN a semi-lungful of oxygen, then goes to town striking me maybe half a dozen times over the course of thirty seconds.

I'm not gonna lie.

My face is turning into miles of chewed-up roadbed. Feels like it anyway, thanks to those now throbbing five nerves. Both lips are bleeding. My two front teeth feel loose. My nose isn't broken . . . *yet*. But blood is dripping from the nostrils. My left eye is nearly swollen shut, and if he does damage to the right eye, I'm as good as screwed. The chances of rescuing my daughter anytime soon will be almost nonexistent if I can't see what the hell I'm doing.

"You know what we want?" Walton says. "Just a sequence of numbers, O'Keefe. You give us the code, you go home. We'll even release Chloe."

. . . *You'll also need my eye scan, you dope. But then, thank God he's not aware of it, or he'd pluck my eye out of its socket . . .*

Penny turns quick.

"I get my money, you son of a bitch," she cries out. "After everything I've been through. After everything you've done to me and my family, I get my money. Joel gets his money also."

"You'll get nothing unless I approve it," Walton speaks. "And just remember this, dead women don't need money."

Good. They're arguing. Exactly what I want. Dissension among the ranks. It was bound to happen sooner than later. Something else I predicted is happening too. Singh is noticeably winded. Tired. Spent. His air sacks sucking wind like miniature balloons about to burst. He'd never reveal his condition to Walton, because he'd become worthless in the crooked cop's eyes. My guess is Walton keeps him around to do the dirty work.

I shake my head. The blood sprays off of me like a beat-up boxer up against the ropes.

"What's the matter, Singh?" I say, my voice slurred by the swelled lips and the combination of blood and saliva pouring out of them. "You're not the epitome of athletic perfection anymore, are you? You're all worn out. Just look at you. You look like a cyborg run out of gas." I laugh just to add spice to my insult. "Go home, get some rest. Let somebody else do the man's work."

His pale, sweat-coated face goes stiff, his good eye rolling around in its socket. He's overexerting himself. Happens all the time to basketball players, and especially football players during hot summer afternoon double sessions. Even healthy high school kids have been known to drop dead on the field due to overexertion.

"You shut the hell up, killer," he says, inhaling and exhaling heavy breaths. "You always were a spoiled prick, always getting your way. I could have been like a son to Rabuffo. But after Wemps and I went out of our way to introduce you to him, you worked your charm, and as usual, got your little bratty way."

"Shut up, Singh," Walton says. "Just do the job you're hired on for. Keep your high school bullshit to yourself. Get the bastard to talk."

"You really think I know the code, Walton?" I spit. "Is that what Penny told you? Is that what all this is riding on? This house of cards? That I know the code to Rabuffo's personal safe or, what are you calling it? The vault? He's probably changed it by now."

"He knows it," Penny interjects, while running both her hands through her thick hair. Something she does when she's truly nervous. "He told me he knows the code. He . . . told . . . me. He also told me Rabuffo would never change it because he doesn't know how to change it. He needs to bring technicians in to do that stuff, and Rabuffo hates exposing his underground lair to outsiders. And now he's in jail, so what the hell chance is there of the code being changed at this point?" Then, her wet eyes gazing directly at me, "Please just tell them the code, Sidney, and we can get Chloe back and go home."

I laugh.

"Now that's funny," I say. "Especially considering I admitted the true depth of my connection to Rabuffo only yesterday. Sounds like somebody *else* promised you I knew the codes. Who would that be, Pen? Joel Harwood, my lawyer? My friend on the outside? No wonder he negotiated my release so easily."

"Leave him out of this," Penny says. "He took care of me and Chloe when you were gone."

"Now that makes me feel a whole lot better."

"You two stop your bickering," Walton orders. "It's like watching *One Life to Live*. You live through this thing, I'll personally pay for a marriage counselor." Then, pointing at Singh, "Get moving, you one-armed, one-eyed pile of shit. Giselle is right. Pretty soon we're gonna have hell raining down on us if we don't get this thing moving. I wanna be in Albany by early evening and have that vault emptied by nightfall."

"If the FBI aren't already emptying it now," Giselle points out, along with a profound sigh.

Behind my back, I'm slowly separating my wrists. All I need is a few more moments and I can make my move.

Singh cocks back his arm, punches me again. But here's the thing. This time I lower my head, chin against sternum. As his punch is being delivered, he unexpectedly nails the crown of my forehead, the absolute hardest part of the skull. Many a professional boxer has ended their career with a connection to that part of a hard head. It's an absolute wrist breaker.

I see the pain streak across Singh's already screwed-up face like an electric current as he retracts his fist.

"Come on, Singh, you pussy. Let's see what you got?" Me, egging him on.

His wrist is in so much pain, he can't even talk. Cocking back his arm, he issues a straight jab, followed by a right hook—the only hook he's capable of considering the circumstances. But he's so slow, I easily catch both of them with my forehead.

This time he lets loose with a cry and a whimper while rubbing his injured wrist with his stump. It's a pathetic scene. Tears are pouring out of his eye, and his one good hand . . . his one *existing* hand . . . is now swelled like a black balloon.

That's when I separate my wrists entirely.

"Singh, you asshole!" Walton shouts. "Why aren't you doing your job? Get to work."

"My wrist's busted up," Singh cries, shoving the swelled hand in between his thighs. "It's all fucked up."

"Jesus H," Walton grouses, holstering his sidearm. "Now I've seen everything. A torturer who ends up torturing himself. You know what? Screw this. We'll find another way to get the code. I say we just kill O'Keefe and be done with it."

"No!" Penny screams.

Walton stomps his way across the floor, shaking his arms out, his hands going in and out of fist position, bobbing up and down on the balls of his feet like he's about to enter into a boxing ring. My face might be bleeding, the vision in my one eye now nonexistent, but I'm somehow able to lock eyes on Penny. She's crying, her face filled with remorse for what she's done to me. To Chloe. Or maybe that's just wishful thinking on my part.

"I . . . love . . . you," I whisper. No matter what she's done, it's still the truth.

She doesn't say anything in return. Instead, she just nods.

That's when I jump up off the wood stool, throw myself at the gun rack, pull down the shotgun. Singh's teary eyes go wide, his mouth agape. I plant the bead on him.

"Oh shit," he mumbles.

I press the trigger. The blast nails him square in the chest, sends him flat onto his back.

Walton goes for his sidearm. I pump a second shell into the chamber, catch him in my sights. Fire. The blast takes a chunk of his shoulder along with a sizeable portion of flesh on his fat neck. But it doesn't stop him from drawing his semi-automatic, aiming it at me.

Pump another round into the chamber, the spent shell ejecting. Fire again, nail him in the beer gut.

Bastard is still alive. Still kicking.

He presses the trigger, sends two rounds up into the roof before the laws of nature take over and his body collapses to the wood floor.

Then comes Giselle, her semi-automatic already aimed for me, dead on. I'm too slow shifting the barrel in her direction. She presses the trigger. But nothing happens. The mechanical click of hammer meeting metal fills the cabin.

She presses the trigger again. Just another empty click.

Heart thumping against sternum, I pump one more live shell into the chamber, while the spent shell flies out, bouncing on the wood floor.

"Darn it all!" she cries. "Darn, fuck, fuck, darn! It's jammed!" Then, sensing the shotgun aimed directly at her, she works up a nervous smile. A pretty smile. "You wouldn't shoot a woman, would you, Mr. O'Keefe? I mean, you were supposed to be a doctor, right? Isn't there like a Hippocratic Oath? Like you're supposed to keep me alive at all costs. No matter what. Isn't that right . . . Doc?"

The lips that form her nervous smile are trembling.

"Don't call me Doc," I say.

I press the trigger.

*   *   *

Okay, I'm going to come clean here.

I most definitely pressed the shotgun trigger. I most definitely blew something away. But it wasn't House Detective Giselle Fontaine. I raised the barrel up just high enough that I blew a hole in the ceiling, sharp splinters of dry wood and bits of old, green moss-covered asphalt shingles raining down upon her head.

She's so shocked by the shotgun explosion that her face turns pale, and her knees buckle. Even Penny's jaw drops, her eyes wide and dazed. Stunned.

The eyes say, "How could my husband shoot a woman in cold blood? Even if she did try and shoot him first?"

I guess that would have made me a monster in my lover's eyes, even if I wouldn't mind turning the shotgun on her either. But then, as much as I trained myself for survival inside concrete and razor wire prison walls—as much as I had to deal with violence or, what was worse, the promise of violence on a constant, twenty-four-seven basis—I still could never get myself to kill a woman. Especially a woman who is unarmed. Or, in this case, a gun that's pin is malfunctioning counts as unarmed.

Instead, here's what I do: I once more point the shotgun barrel at the detective's pretty, but still pale face. I tell her to drop the gun, in as calm and collected a voice I can muster. As if I were asking her to open her mouth and say, "Ahhh."

I then tell her to leave.

Her knees are still trembling. She's wearing a skirt and high-heel shoes.

She shakes her head.

"What do you mean *leave*?" she says, taking on a smirk. "Jeepers, I can't just walk out of here dressed like this. I don't . . . I've *never* gone much for hiking . . . I've never been a woods walker. How about I take Burt's truck or Walton's SUV?"

I pump the shotgun, the expended shell exiting the chamber, doing a couple of midair spins before dropping to the floor.

"Giselle," I say, "you've got a choice. The next time I pull the trigger, you can die. Or you can take your chances and *walk* back to Lake Placid, like Little Red Riding Hood." My eyes back on Penny. "How's the song go again, Pen?"

She looks like she's about to cry again. And she is.

"Over the river and through the woods to grandmother's house we go . . ." Her voice is trembling while the tears drop down her cheeks. "But that's not Little Red Riding hood, now that I think of it. It's a Christmas song, I think."

"I stand corrected." My eyes back on Giselle. "So, what's it going to be, Detective? A nice hike through the Adirondack Mountains or an early grave?"

It somehow pleases me to use this "early grave" bit. Like I'm a real gangster in some old black-and-white Cagney flick.

She releases the pistol. It drops to the floor, dangerously close to her toes, which would have made the trek through the woods even worse. Okay, impossibly worse.

"Alrighty then," she says, her face suddenly taking on a scowl, like I've just broken up with her over dinner at some fancy restaurant. She makes her way to the open door. But before she walks out, she turns to me once more. "I truly hope you get your daughter back, Mr. O'Keefe. I truly do. But if you don't," she adds, "you'll have your wife to thank for it."

She might as well have shot me in the stomach after all.

"Just . . . go," I say.

She issues me a smart-ass smile, then exits the cabin, begins the long walk back through the forest to Lake Placid.

* * *

That leaves my wife.

Good old Penny. The beautiful apparition I married not long before doing one last job for Rabuffo. The woman who bore my one and only child. The woman whom I thought about incessantly inside the joint. The woman I'd do anything for. The woman I dreamt about. The woman for whom I kept my mouth shut, for fear that Rabuffo would kill her and our daughter.

Now, here we are, all alone inside a cabin filled with dead people and their respective pools of crimson DNA. Her coconspirators, who concocted an operation designed initially to get me out of prison, but inevitably to reap riches like she, or her cohorts, have never before known.

Penny looks over one shoulder, then the other.

"You're not going to kill me, are you, Doc?" She forces a grin. "I mean, you let Giselle go."

I laugh sadly, sit myself down onto the wood stool.

"Would you do me a favor, darling?" I ask. "Bring me a knife . . . pretty please?"

After hesitating for a long beat or two, she goes into the kitchen. What's left of the kitchen, that is. She comes back out with a steak knife. I make sure to hold the shotgun on her while she hands me the blade. I snatch it from her hand, cut the tape that surrounds my ankles. My legs freed, I stand, feel the circulation reenter into my lower legs and feet.

I toss the knife to the side.

"Your face," she says. "It looks . . . terrible."

"Things you gotta do in the name of what's right, Pen," I say, heading back over to the gun rack, pulling some shells from one of the three boxes that's stored there, reloading the shotgun. "I've had worse in prison."

Cocking a live round into the chamber, I bend down over Singh, rip the t-shirt off his torso, wipe my face with it, toss it onto his dead face. I then dig through his pockets, find a wad of bills. I stuff them into my pocket. Shifting myself over to Walton's body, I retrieve his wallet, pull out his license, stuff that in my pocket. I pick up his semi-automatic, thumb the magazine release, toss the pistol across the room and into the fire. I don't bother with checking him for money. Heading over to Giselle's piece, I grab it up off the floor, release the mag, and toss the gun into the fire along with Walton's.

Then, coming from out of the near distance, the sound of rotors slicing through the air. Penny and I lock eyes.

"The chopper's back," I say. "Walton's people know we're here. Rabuffo's people . . ."

I go to the bunk bed, grab the bag with the water, food, and extra shotgun shells.

"We still have the rifle," Penny says, cocking her head in the direction of the .30-30 leaning up against the far corner, near the spot where Burt Stevens is still bleeding out.

"You've lost your right to carry a firearm," I say.

I grab the roll of duct tape that's set on the top bunk. I take hold of her left wrist, yank her into me. She shrieks like I'm hurting her, but at this point I don't give a shit.

"Give me your other wrist," I order.

She just looks at me.

"Do it," I say. "Or I'll break it."

The chopper is closing in.

She gives me her other wrist. I wrap six layers of tape around both wrists, cut the tape off with my teeth, then place the roll into the daypack.

"Let's move," I say, "before this place is surrounded by assholes who want us dead."

* * *

Outside, most of the clouds have cleared, and I can make out the chopper coming at us from out of the west, where the afternoon sun is shining bright now that the clouds are gone. This time the Lake Placid Village Police Department chopper is not bothering to circle the property. There are no amplified calls for me to stand down. Instead, I see the side door opening, and another riot gear clad officer pointing an automatic rifle in my direction. The rifle is equipped with a grenade launcher, just like the first time around.

"They're just not gonna let up," I whisper to myself.

Grabbing hold of Penny's taped wrists, I drag her across the lawn to the road, toss her down into the ditch that runs the length of the logging road. The first grenade is launched, shrieks across the sky, strikes the Jeep. The vehicle explodes in a fireball of white-hot heat.

"Why are they doing that?!" Penny shouts.

"They want to pen me in. Destroy my mobility." I'm watching the Huey make a one-hundred-eighty-degree turn, coming back at us. "These assholes have to be working for Walton. And I don't mean in the capacity of serving and protecting Lake Placid."

A second grenade launched.

"Get down!" I shout, throwing my torso over Penny.

It hits Walton's SUV. The chopper makes a third pass, and yet another grenade launched, this one taking out Burt's truck. Then a fourth pass. The explosive smashes into the cabin, detonates. The entire building front explodes, the wood, stone, and glass debris raining like hellfire. The chopper makes another turn. This time it heads back in the direction it came from due west. After a few more seconds, it simply disappears.

*   *   *

When the debris has settled, I slip myself off of Penny, stand. She, too, stands.

"Why don't they just kill us?" she says. "They're destroying everything else."

"So long as there's breath in my lungs, I've got the codes they want. They kill you, or Chloe, then I don't want to live."

"So they make sure we don't die, but they do everything they can to torture us."

"Something like that," I say. "They're your friends, after all."

She gives me a look that stabs at my gut.

"That's not even remotely fair," she says. Then, inhaling and exhaling a deep breath, "So what'll we do now? How the hell do we get out of this jungle without a vehicle?"

"Good question, Pen." Looking her up and down. At her muddy jeans and formerly white pullover tank top. At her mussed-up hair, tired and frightened eyes. "Your phone still work?"

Wrists still bound, she manages to pat her pockets. But then shakes her head.

"It's still in the cabin," she reveals.

"Guess that answers that."

"So what do we do then?" she repeats. "Am I your hostage, Sidney? Is that what I am now?"

My eyes catch the lifeless body of Claudia Stevens lying facedown in the mud. A buzzing in my pocket. My phone, on vibrate. I pull it out, flip it open. I count twelve text messages left for me over the course of a three-hour period. Messages that I never noticed until now, not with my having been passed out and the subject of a prolonged beating.

All twelve texts say the same thing.

HELP ME . . . HELP US

The name attached to the messages is one that is very dear to my heart.

The name is Chloe.

CHAPTER 37

ONCE MORE, I take hold of Penny's wrists, help her up and out of the ditch.

"You don't have to hang onto me like that," she says. "I'm not an invalid."

"No," I say, releasing her. "You're just a cheater. And that's a hell of a lot worse."

I keep walking.

"Stop right there, you bastard!" she shouts.

I stop on a dime. Set before me, the smoldering and in some cases, burning remnants of the cabin and the three vehicles. Some of the burning cabin embers have settled onto Claudia Stevens's back. Some in her hair.

I turn, face my wife.

There's an intensity burning inside her. An anger so intense I can feel it without touching her.

She says, "Do you have any clue what it was like for me and Chloe over these past ten years? Knowing you'd never be coming home? That my daughter's father was a convicted murderer? Do you have any clue what it was like for Chloe to suffer through a single day of school? All those kids who made fun of her, who caused her to cry floods of tears night in and night out. Did you know I almost pulled her out of school altogether?"

"Why didn't you?" I ask. "You could have homeschooled her."

"And who was going to put food on the table, Sid? Who was going to pay for our lives?" She pounds her chest with her fist. "I have a college degree. I even have my teacher's certificate. I could have made a nice life for Chloe and me. But after your arrest, no one would employ me. I'd get a nice smile, a 'We're happy to keep your CV on file,' but I could see beyond their smiles. I could see their contempt. Their hatred." She wipes tears from her eyes with the backs of her hands. "Four people . . . four *innocent* people were killed in that house, Sid, and I know you were only the driver, and I've always trusted you on that. But it totally screwed up our lives. I was lucky to pick up what hours I could at the supermarket as a cashier. And even then, it was because the manager would stop at nothing to get his hands in my pants. So yeah, when Joel made a pass, I allowed it. When he told me he had a way of finally making some money, not for me, but for Chloe, and that it would mean your release, I jumped at it. I didn't give a damn how illegal the plan was or how dangerous, or what creeps it involved. I was desperate and at the end of my rope. I just wanted a future for our daughter, and . . ."

Her voice trails off.

"And what, Pen?" I beg.

"And I wanted her father to be there for her."

*   *   *

My eyes take in the destroyed cabin and the bodies now covered in smoldering rubble. Whatever fire has started is quickly burning out from the heavy rains that soaked everything earlier on, including the grass and the greenery surrounding the place. There's the acrid smell of burning oil and plastic from the destroyed vehicles. My face and head hurt. But my heart hurts more.

Oh Christ, should I forgive Penny, just like that? Allow her to walk right back into my heart and head, like she never sold me out, never slept with Joel behind my back? Like she's had nothing to do with Chloe's disappearance?

Maybe she's right.

Maybe I made my own bed when I decided to take on that last job with Rabuffo. Maybe I'm just as guilty as Singh and Wemps in the murder of that Chinese family. Maybe I've been fooling myself all this time by insisting that I was only the driver. Just because I didn't pull a trigger didn't mean I hadn't had a hand in killing them.

Can I blame Penny for wanting a life for Chloe? For wanting her to have a future where she didn't have to beg and scrounge for every single dime? A future without her father? Maybe in the end, Penny did the right thing for me. At least, that might have been her intention. How was she to know it would all go so wrong? That Chloe would suffer?

Once more, I flip the phone open. I type.

I'M COMING FOR YOU, CHLOE

I wait for a response. When it doesn't come, I close the phone, place it back inside my pocket.

"We need to go," I say.

"Go *where*?" Penny says.

Then, in my pocket, the phone vibrating. Pulling it out, I flip the top.

COME QUICK

"We're going to get Chloe back," I say, heart in my throat.

Penny shakes her head, hard.

"But that's just it, Sid," she says. "I don't know *where* they took her. I mean, I never knew they were going to take her in the first place. You have to believe me."

I reach into my pocket, pull out Walton's driver's license. My gut speaks to me and I feel ice cold shoot into my veins.

"Whether I believe you or not doesn't matter anymore," I say. "What matters now is I think I know where we'll find her."

Together, we start walking the logging road in the direction of Lake Placid.

CHAPTER 38

IT'S GETTING DARK by the time we reach the road.

"Do you really have to keep me tied up like this, Sid?" Penny asks. "I can barely walk as it is. It's easier when I can swing my arms."

She's breathing hard, perspiring. She's dead on her feet. She's my wife. For now, anyway. But then, she will always be the mother of my daughter, no matter what. Right now, we both want the same thing. To get our daughter back. Maybe, once that's done, we can turn ourselves in to the Albany police, or the FBI or who knows what, and put this thing behind us. Maybe, just maybe, I won't have to go back to prison if all goes well. That is, if we both tell the truth and nothing but the whole damned truth.

I pat my jeans pockets. I don't have a knife. Taking hold of her hands, I bend at the knees. Teeth still aching from Singh's beating, I bite into the tape, then tear it in two. I rip the tape away from her wrists as fast as possible to minimize the pain.

Tossing the tape to the grass, I check my phone again. No new text messages from Chloe. I nibble at my still swelled bottom lip, taste the dried blood. In all the confusion and violence back at the cabin, it never dawned on me to check the number she's calling from. But it's one that I don't recognize, and why would I? More than likely it's a phone she stole from her captor or captors. But how did she know my number? It's possible I've told her the cell phone's number since I've been back, or it's possible she snooped. Nothing unusual for a curious girl her age. What matters now is that she's in contact with me and I have every intention of locating her.

"We need a ride, Pen," I say. "Otherwise it will take us all night to get back to Lake Placid."

She looks over each of her shoulders.

"I don't think we have much choice but to start walking," she comments. "At least it's not winter."

"The glass half full girl," I say. "There's the Penny I used to know."

She smiles. But then she rears back quick.

"Oh God," she says. "What the hell was that?"

A rustling in the brush a few feet ahead of us. What looks like a coy dog, or even a wolf, racing off, something in its mouth.

"Easy, Pen," I say, pressing the shotgun stock against my shoulder.

But the animal is gone now. Something's not right. Animals like that are nocturnal. They hunt in the darkness, and even if nightfall is coming, it's still too early for them to be out and about. Unless, that is, there's game to be had.

"Stay right there, Pen. Don't move."

"Where are you going, Sid? Let's just keep moving."

"I need to check something."

What I don't tell her is that my gut is speaking to me. My gut and my head. I slowly make my way into the brush. I only make it a few steps when I see the blood. It soaks the ground, smears the thick brush. Fresh blood. A few more steps in I see her. Giselle. A portion of her jaw is gone, as is her left eye and the tip of her nose. Her neck has been bitten through; her carotid artery punctured. She died within a couple of minutes of the wolf's bite.

I swallow something bitter and give her entire body a cursory examination. Her left ankle is broken badly, a jagged piece of white bone protruding through the skin. The high heel on her shoe is broken, and the sole of the foot is facing outwards at an unnatural ninety-degree angle.

"What's happening, Sid?" Penny begs. "What do you see?"

"Don't come in here," I demand. "Stay where you are."

The wolves must have sniffed her out after she broke her ankle, and come after her. I raise up my head, attempt to gaze through the thick brush. Those same wolves are out there. They're watching us. They move in packs, and it won't take much for them to come after Penny and me once it's full dark. They'll also go after the bodies back at the destroyed cabin, I suspect.

"So long, Giselle."

I turn, head back out onto the logging road.

"We need to move, Pen," I say.

Her face goes tight as a tick.

"It was Giselle, wasn't it?" she says. "She's dead."

"Let's just go," I say.

As we move on, I feel the eyes of the wild animals watching our every move.

*   *   *

We begin our trek along the roadside, secretly hoping that no cops are cruising the area. At least, that's my hope. But my guess is the cops are combing the place for us. If it weren't dark out, we'd have no choice but to hike it through the woods, which would take forever. Naturally, after spotting Giselle and her—let's call it bad luck—the woods would never be an option at this point. In the end, we have only one choice, and that's to hijack a car. Sure, it's a crime, but what the hell does it matter at this point?

A couple more minutes go by until I make out a pair of halogen headlamps cutting through the night sky. Judging by the look of the vehicle's grill, it's not one of the police SUVs, but, in fact, a pickup truck.

"Penny," I say, handing her the daypack, but hanging onto the shotgun. "Head into the brush. Just step in far enough to hide yourself, until I tell you to come back out."

"What are you gonna do?" she asks.

"I'm gonna rent us a truck."

Hiding the shotgun by setting it vertically beside my left leg, I step out into the road and wave my free hand over my head like it's an emergency. The truck must be doing about fifty along the narrow mountain road, which tells me whoever is driving knows the road like the veins on the back of his hand. The lights make contact with my good eye, and for a half second, I'm blinded. Lowering my hand, I shield my eye by using it like a visor.

The driver hits the brakes, and I can hear the tires leaving burn marks on the pavement. The truck sways across the meridian into the oncoming traffic, but the driver quickly regains control and shifts it back into its rightful lane. When he comes to a stop, he's already rolling down his window on the 1980s-era Ford F-150 pickup.

"What hell are you doing, son?" he says. "You trying to get yourself killed?" He says *get* like *git*, and *killed* like *killt*. A real country boy. The kind of man who refers to fishing as *fishin'* and hunting as *huntin'*.

I try to work up a smile with my swelled lips.

"I'm nobody's son," I say.

He's an older man. Maybe seventy, but chesty in his hunter green t-shirt, his arms thick, not like a weightlifter, but a man who knows the meaning of working with his hands for a living. He's got a gray goatee and thick gray hair to match. His blue eyes focus in on the shotgun, which I'm not concealing very well.

"I hope the other guy looks worse," he says.

"Excuse me?"

"Your face, son. It might be dark, but I can see the pain on your face plain enough. And that twelve gauge." He pauses for a beat while the truck idles. "You can tell your wife to come out of the bushes. I'm not gonna say anything. I'm not gonna say anything 'bout you neither. You wanna ride into town, you best hop on up before someone comes along. Someone like the Lake Placid Village PD, if you catch my drift."

Turning toward the woods, the wolf pack comes to mind. The sooner she emerges from the bush, the better.

"Penny," I say. "Come on, we gotta move."

She reveals herself, and together we go around the front of the truck. Opening the door for her, I help her up inside while I follow, closing the door behind me, the shotgun in between my knees. I'm not aiming the gun at the driver necessarily, but then I'm not keeping it away from him either. I'm keeping it at the ready. Just in case.

Gray Goatee throws the truck back in drive, gives it the gas.

"I'm Lou," he says. "Lou Garrity. But my friends call me Gary, for obvious reasons."

"Thanks for helping us, Gary," Penny says.

He nods, negotiating the winding road as we pass through the mountain gaps, some of which are surrounded by pristine narrow lakes while others support bases of thick pine forest. On my right, the moonlight is lighting up a waterfall that's mostly dried up this time of year. If I weren't in search of my daughter and on the run at the same time, I'd be tempted to pitch a tent and stay awhile, for this is truly God's country.

"When was the last time you two had a good meal or some sleep?" Gary asks.

I find myself looking at Penny.

"I can't remember," I say. "We have some pizza in the pack. Old pizza, I guess."

"You should eat," he says.

"We don't have time," I say. "Or the appetite. Who would?"

He drives for a minute. Then, "I understand what you're doing."

"You do?" Penny jumps.

"I do," he affirms. "I had a daughter once. I know what it feels like to lose her."

This stranger picks us up off the road and he is suddenly in tune with our most personal details. But then, our faces must be broadcast all over the news by now. My face has been broadcast all week long.

"You know who we are," I say, like a question.

"Yup," he says. "They say you took your own daughter. That you were the one who caused her to go missing. That you probably got mad at her and flipped out, maybe even killed her. But I don't believe that crap. They keep showing a CCTV clip of you inside the hotel, grabbing your wife, snapping at her. Like it's supposed to be proof that you're as volatile as a powder keg. They list the violent crimes you allegedly committed in prison."

"My husband has been nothing but good to me since he's been back," Penny interjects. "It's me who's the criminal."

"In prison," I say, "I defended myself against men who wanted me dead. That's not a crime. That's survival. Do you understand me, Gary?"

"I get it. Here's what I also get. Men do desperate things during desperate times. I believe you are one of those men." He turns to me. "The condition of your face is proof enough of that."

We drive for a while in a silence so heavy, I feel like it's pressing against my sternum. Slowly, I turn my head, peer over my shoulder beyond Penny to Gary. The lights from the dash illuminate his eyes. Big, blue, sad eyes. Eyes that know loss. The loss of a child. The worst kind of loss there is.

"Your daughter," I say, filling the quiet. "Did you ever find her?"

He presses his lips together, nods slowly.

"Oh, yah," he says, "we found her all right. When the detectives uncovered her in the village dump two weeks after she'd gone missing, she was mostly decomposed. She'd been stripped of everything but her underclothes. She'd been raped and beaten and left to die on a pile of garbage." He shoots me a glance. "Yes, we found her all right and it was quite the find. But that was the day I lost my soul."

My entire being feels like it's crashing. The emotions that swim though my veins are a toxic mixture of sadness, desperation, and outright anger. How utterly strange that this man would have picked us up out of the blue. What are the chances that we would have a tragedy like this in common? Or has my situation not yet reached tragedy status? The answer to that one is too crippling to ponder.

Of course, that's when the realization punches me in the gut.

"Gary," I say, after a beat, "how long did it take for you to find us?"

He cocks his head over his shoulder.

"I wasn't sure I would *ever* find you," he answers. "There's over six million acres of wilderness out there. But then, I sensed you wouldn't go far, not even after having stolen that Jeep. You'd stay relatively close to Lake Placid because that's where your daughter went missing. But you still needed to get out of town, now that the police were wrongly fingering you. So where's the next logical place to go? Into Keene Valley. I knew, or hoped, that if I cruised Highway 73, I'd eventually find you. It was either that or the cops were gonna pick you up. I saw the helo making passes over the forest, heard the explosions. Brought back flashbacks of Nam, let me tell you."

Penny puts her hand on my thigh, presses it. It feels good, but I'm still not entirely sure how I should feel about her after what she's done. I guess it's a matter of trusting her. Believing she was committing a big wrong in order to do something that was right. Insuring a bright future for our daughter.

"I need to find my daughter, Gary," I say. "And I think I know where she is. All I need you to do is drop us off in the village."

"In a dark corner, preferably," Penny adds.

"We can take it from there," I add.

I tell him about Walton, what he's done. That he's dead now and that it's his own fault. Gary doesn't respond for a long beat or two as we begin the long climb up the mountain road that will take us past the 1980 Olympic ski jump facility, past the airport, past the row of cheap motels and eateries, past the village police HQ, and finally into the village itself. It's like he's trying to digest everything I've revealed to him and it's not going down so easy.

"I'm not about to drop you off," he says, after a weighted beat. "You won't last ten minutes in that village without getting caught or shot at by a cop, or at the very least, spotted on the street by someone fixated on their Facebook or Twitter accounts. You're famous, Mr. O'Keefe. Or infamous, anyhow."

"For all the wrong reasons," I say.

"Here's the deal," Gary goes on as the village begins to take shape. "I intend to take you all the way."

"All the way?" I ask. "What's that mean?"

"I intend to take you to your daughter."

CHAPTER 39

I DIG WALTON's driver's license out of my pocket. Recite the address to Gary.

"That's a high-end trailer park outside of town," he comments. "On the way to Whiteface Mountain."

"Isn't that kind of a contradiction?" Penny says. "A high-end trailer park."

"They exist," Gary says. "All over the Adirondacks. In high-end places like Lake George and Schroon Lake, too. A piece of property in a high-end trailer park can cost three hundred grand. The trailer you put on it is more like a big prefabricated house than a trailer."

"What kind of postage stamp you get for three hundred Gs?" I inquire.

"That's the point," Gary goes on. "You don't get a postage stamp. You get an acre or more. It will usually be surrounded by trees and vegetation, very private. I've been inside Walton's trailer park community before. It's got maybe one hundred fifty one-acre parcels that are nice and secluded, with plenty of trees and privacy fences. But in the center of all that is a private town with its own general store, its own post office, a coffeehouse, a nondenominational church, a fire department, you name it."

"Sounds like Walton never had to leave the place if he didn't want," I comment. "Everything he needed was right at his beck and call."

Penny squeezes my leg again. I can't help but wonder if this place is familiar to her. But then, my insides are telling me that not only has she never been anywhere near Walton's home, she never had much contact with the man before yesterday when Giselle sent us to his village PD office. My guess is she was kept separate from the major players in this charade, kept in the dark as to their true plans. No wonder she was so shocked and hurt over Chloe's disappearance. Her tears and her despair were all too real.

"Sort of like the perfect place to keep someone against their will," she adds. "Secluded, but then you never have to go very far to keep them alive."

Pulling my cell phone from my pocket, I check the texts again. Nothing new. It dawns on me that I haven't tried the number in a while. I press SEND, and the last incoming number automatically dials for me. An automated message comes on. "The number you've reached is temporarily disconnected or out of service. Please check the number and try again."

I close the phone, glance at Penny.

"Nothing," I say.

Her body is pressed up against mine. I feel her shivering.

"This is all my fault," she says.

"Listen, Pen," I say. "We're going to get Chloe back. Right now. And then this will all be behind us."

"There's all those dead bodies back there at the cabin. The police are searching for us. They're going to lock us up forever, Doc."

"Not if we go to the police with the truth," I say. "Surrender ourselves at the first opportunity. But not until we get Chloe back."

"He's right, ma'am," Gary says. "All you got to do is tell the truth. I don't always trust in the system, but sounds to me like you're gonna have no choice in the matter."

"So what are you saying?" Penny begs.

"I'm saying the law is the law, and no matter what side of right you are on, you are always gonna lose."

We drive on in the darkness. In the moonlit distance, White-face Mountain looms large. In the winter, it would be veined with white ski trails running top to bottom. Soon we come to a piece of road running perpendicular to Route 73. There's a large sign made of logs and rough wood planks that bears the name "Adiron-dack Acres." Gary slows the truck, flicks on his directional.

"Now's as good a time as any," he says. "The Lake Placid cops will be swarming on this place within the half hour to be sure."

"Let's go," I say.

"I want my daughter back," Penny says.

"So do I," Gary says. "So . . . do . . . I."

*　　*　　*

The road into Adirondack Acres is long and winding, flanked on both sides with tall, thick pine trees, making the night even darker since the tree cover blocks most of the full moon's glow. Gary takes it slow. Could be he wants to avoid any unwanted attention by anyone who might be watching, even if the only living things out here are deer, coy dogs, snakes, moose, and wolves.

After about a mile, we come upon a road that forces us to either turn right or left. Gary goes left and proceeds past a trailer that's set back on a flat piece of ground. It's a double-wide by the looks of it, with a porch built onto the front facade. He continues, passing three more trailers, until he comes to another property accessed by a stone and gravel driveway that, at present, is blocked by a chain-link fence gate that is secured with a padlock and chain.

"This is it," Gary says, a little under his breath. "Chief Walton's property."

"Looks like we'll have to climb the fence," I point out.

Gary opens his door.

"No, we won't," he says.

Slipping out, he reaches into the metal toolbox setup in the pickup's cargo bay.

"What's he doing?" Penny asks.

"He's grabbing some bolt cutters," I answer. "Big ones."

Gary comes around the front of the vehicle, goes to the gate, his body awash in the bright white halogen headlamp light. Opening up the cutters, he places the blades on one of the chain links, then quickly and forcefully pulls the handles together. The chain link snaps in two. Grabbing hold of the chain, he pulls it out of the tubular aluminum gate posts, and swings open the gates.

Turning, he returns the cutters to his toolbox and gets back in the truck.

"We're in," he says, with a satisfied smile. "Let's go get your daughter, Mr. O'Keefe, Mrs. O'Keefe."

The pit in my stomach is growing bigger and bigger, pressing against all my organs like a grade-four tumor. Pulse pumps over-oxygenated blood fast enough to take my breath away. But for the first time since this thing started, I feel like Chloe is already back in our arms.

We drive for maybe three hundred feet over uneven road, two-sided by heavy brush and second-growth trees. When we come to the trailer situated at the end of the drive, I feel the pit in my stomach shift north. It becomes more like a rock that lodges itself in my sternum. My heart beats so fast and loud I can't believe no one can hear it. Penny takes hold of my hand, squeezes it.

"Oh, dear God," she says, "please let Chloe be inside there. Please let her be all right."

The trailer is a double-wide, just like all the others. There's also a porch attached to the front of it. This porch has a roof on it and wall panels fashioned from screens to keep the bugs and black flies out. The place is dark. Darker than dark. Pitch black. It doesn't look like a place where anyone lives, much less survives.

I open the door, slide out, the shotgun gripped in both hands. Penny slips out behind me, staying close to me. Gary gets out, comes around the front of the truck. He's got a gun in his hand. A revolver. A Colt .45 1871 Army issue by the looks of it. Something a cowboy would carry.

"Let me go first," he says. "I've been here before. I know where he hides the key."

I'm going with my gut here. My built-in-bad-guy-detector. Thus far, Gary has given us no reason to doubt his sincerity, and his story about the daughter he lost to some psycho killers. But he never revealed until now that he knew the exact location of Walton's property. I guess it's possible he looked at the numbers on some of the mailboxes, but I didn't notice a number on any mailbox belonging to the now dead chief.

Penny and I are out of our element here. Or, that's not right. It's like we're suddenly not in control of our every move, right or wrong. So what should we do? How should we proceed from this point forward? Stay close to Gary, but not too close. If he wants to take the lead, let him. But keep the shotgun at the ready.

We make our way slowly to the stairs leading up to the porch. Gary takes hold of the opener. It's locked. But without hesitating, he punches through the screen, unlocks the screen door from the inside. Opening the door, he walks on through. Penny and I follow, a few paces behind.

The place smells bad.

It's a kind of sweet, but sour smell. Sickening. Like Walton lost power and all the meat in the freezer and refrigerator has now gone bad. The smell doesn't seem to faze Gary, as he makes his way across the rough wood porch floor to the front door of the double-wide trailer.

He goes to open the door. This time, the door is unlocked. He glances over his shoulder at us, his revolver pointed out front of him at the ready.

"Stay close, folks," he whispers. "And watch it with that shotgun, Mr. O'Keefe. I wouldn't want an accident to happen."

He opens the door wide, enters. We enter right behind him. Terror is there to greet us.

CHAPTER 40

CONFUSION.

I'm blind in the darkness. But I can feel the shotgun being ripped from my grip and then I feel myself falling. It happens not like two distinct actions, but instead, one quick, swift, well-planned maneuver. The drop isn't far, but far enough that the wind is knocked out of me when I land flat on my belly. Penny drops on top of me, which I'm glad for, since I'm able to break her fall.

"What the hell just happened?" she cries. "What did we fall into?"

. . . You just fell into your worst nightmare . . .

I can't speak. I'm trying to get my air back, trying to work up the breath in my lungs, get my diaphragm back under control. Then, a bright round beam of halogen Maglite blinds me.

"Bet you didn't see that comin," Gary says, pleasantly. "He's standing over the hole, looking down at us, the Maglite gripped in one hand, his cowboy pistol in the other. "I'm a little surprised at you, Mr. O'Keefe. I'd a thought your instincts would be sharper than that. But then, maybe you're tired. You probably haven't had a good night's sleep in forever. Now ain't that right?"

I pull myself up onto my knees. Penny grabs hold of my arm, holds herself tightly against me.

"You sick son of a bitch," I spit. "Where the hell are we?"

"You're right where you're supposed to be," he says. "Inside Chief Walton's trailer." He pauses for a moment, as if to think about what he's just said. "Well, that's not entirely right, since the chief is dead, last I heard, thanks to you. So I guess that makes this place my trailer now."

"You broke in here," I say. "You used bolt cutters to access the place. It doesn't make sense."

He giggles, not like a barrel-chested late-middle-aged man, but like a little boy.

"I've got some serious acting skills, now don't I? Maybe I missed my calling."

The anger boiling inside me creates a fury that's as palpable as the sweat pouring off my body. I try and leap out of the hole, but it's too deep, the exposed clay soil moist and slippery.

"Don't even bother," Gary informs. "You'd have to be Jesus to climb out of that pit. And even he'd have a devil of a time."

My eyes are locked on him. But in my head, I'm seeing the silhouette of a big man standing on the moonlit beach behind the Golden Arrow Hotel, his hand gripping Chloe's.

"Is our daughter here?" I beg. "Is Chloe here?" Then, cupping my hands around my mouth, I scream, "Chloe! Chloe!"

I listen for a response, but I get nothing.

Turning, Gary walks away from the pit's edge and out of our line of sight, such as it is in the pitch darkness. Then, the lights come on inside the trailer. Bright, industrial, overhead lights. Not like this place is used as a home, but more like a factory or warehouse.

When he returns to the pit's edge, his revolver is stored in a brown leather holster on his hip, his Maglite nowhere to be seen. He's running his hands over his white beard, smoothing it out.

"What are you going to do with us?" Penny begs, her voice trembling.

"What am I going to do with you, little lady?" he says, running his long pink tongue over his lips. "I haven't really figured that out yet. But I'll know it when it comes to me." He giggles, like a little kid. "And oh boy, is it gonna hurt or what?"

CHAPTER 41

GARY WALKS AWAY again.

A second or two later, I make out the trailer door opening and closing.

Penny is crying so hard, she can't speak. She drops down onto the clay floor on her bottom, slams her knees into her chest, and sobs uncontrollably. That's when I smell the onions. The floor is littered with them—and rotting, putrid potatoes.

"She's dead," she cries. "Chloe is dead. Don't you see what's happening, Sidney? Chloe is dead, and it's all because of me, of my horrible decisions. Soon we'll be dead, too, and on our way to hell."

Something goes snap inside my head then. Like when you break a pencil in half. You sense the tension of it bending in your fisted hands, and then, just like that, it goes snap. Reaching down, I grab hold of her arm, yank her back onto her feet, pull her into me, her face so close to mine we're swapping sweat.

"Now you listen to me," I utter, my words forced, coming from deep inside me. "You are *not* going to do die. Chloe is *not* dead. And we are *not* fucking going anywhere, let alone hell. This hole we're trapped in . . . this onion cellar or whatever it is . . . this *is* hell on earth. That creep up there, he's the devil." I feel a smile growing on my face. "And guess what, Penny? I'm going to kill the devil tonight. I'm going to make the son of a bitch pay."

Penny stares into my eyes. She's not making a sound, not making a move, her eyes unblinking and startled.

"All right, Sid," she whispers. "I believe you."

I let go of her arm. She takes a couple of steps in reverse, pressing her back up against the clay wall.

"Now if only we can figure a way out of this pit," I say, staring up at the bright, ceiling-mounted trailer lights.

Then, a voice that belongs neither to me, or Penny, or Gary comes to me from out of nowhere. A faint voice. A child's voice.

"Daddy," the voice says. "Daddy, is that you?"

CHAPTER 42

"CHLOE?!" I SHOUT. "Chloe, is that you?!"

"Oh, sweet Jesus," Penny cries. "It's Chloe. Oh, my sweet Jesus."

She separates herself from the wall, plants herself foursquare in the center of the pit.

"Chloe, sweetheart?" she goes on. "Can you hear me?"

"Daddy!" Chloe says. "Mommy? Is that really you?"

"Yes, Chloe," I say. "It's us. We've come for you, sweetheart. Where are you?"

"I'm in a hole," she says. "It smells in here, like they use it for storing meat. Susan is with me."

A pit for storing venison, I imagine. For smoking fish, maybe.

Turning to Penny. "Susan. Who is Susan?"

Her eyes grow wide. "My God, that's the Stevenses' daughter. The little girl Chloe was playing with when she disappeared." Hesitating. "Could it be . . . ?" her thought drifts off.

"Either Walton and this creep Gary stole her from the Stevenses, or she was never theirs to begin with," I point out. "But that's not what's important at the moment. Right now, we gotta figure a way out of here. A way out for *everybody*. Do it now."

"Daddy?" Chloe says. "Can we go home now?"

I can tell by the sound of her voice that she's shivering. It's maybe seventy-five degrees in here, but if she's been wet for far too long, and dehydrated, she could be experiencing the effects of hypothermia. Shivering, slow, shallow breathing, confusion. I've got to get her out of here now.

I about-face, make a three-hundred-sixty-degree scan of the pit, like a ladder or even a rope is suddenly going to emerge from out of the clay walls. I look up. I'm guessing the pit is about twelve feet deep. I'm five feet nine inches. Penny is about five feet four inches. If I put her up on my shoulders, it's possible she can reach over the side, shimmy herself up and over the top. She can then find something like a rope or an electrical cord, which she can tie off onto something sturdy like a structural bearing beam. I can use the rope or cord to climb my way to freedom. From inside the depths of this pit, it sounds like a bit of a bridge too far, but it's our only hope. Gary will be back soon, or so I can only assume, and who the hell knows what he's got planned for us.

I tell Penny I'm going to put her on my shoulders.

She nods in agreement. No need to explain the plan. She already knows what to do. Bending at the knees, she climbs up onto my back. Then pressing my body up against the moist clay wall, she slowly, carefully, climbs up onto my shoulders. Penny can't weigh more than a buck twenty wet, but I feel my knees wobbling a bit, unsteady. It's not the lack of strength so much as the exhaustion. It tells me we need to succeed at this, or we're doomed.

"How are you doing, Pen?" I say through grinding teeth, through the strain.

"I can get my hands over the edge," she explains. Then, tiptoeing on my shoulders, reaching, extending herself, "If I . . . can manage . . . to get ahold of something . . . something to give me more leverage. Something on the floor maybe."

I feel my load lighten a little.

"You able to catch hold of something?" I beg.

"There's nothing . . . to grab," she says, voice stressing, straining. "But if I can manage to press my palms flat on the floor, I can then lift myself up, if you help me." She braces herself. "Give me a jump, Doc."

"Here we go," I say. "Get ready."

Bending at the knees, I then spring up, sending her off my shoulder and farther up onto the pit's edge. From there she shimmies herself out of the pit, rolls over onto her side on the floor. My heart fills with absolute sunlight.

Then the trailer door opens.

CHAPTER 43

"WELL, WHAT DO you know?" Gary says. "I assumed the onion cellar was a foolproof trap. Never underestimate the power of a mare. You are something special, let me tell you, Mrs. O'Keefe."

I'm trying to get a clear and unobstructed look at Gary. But all I can make out are his legs.

"Here," he says, crouching, "let me help you up, little lady."

"Don't you touch me," Penny spits.

She's crabbing away from him, or so I assume. But he's chasing after her, and when he gets his hands on her, he will be too strong for her. Too heavy. Too psychotic.

"You don't come near me!" Penny barks. "You hear me?"

"Now, now, Mrs. O'Keefe," he says, his voice steady and even. "I'm only trying to help."

"Mommy!" Chloe shouts from down in her hole. "Don't go near that man! He's a monster! He killed his friend just a little while ago. He stabbed his friend, Mr. Bertram. They had a fight over money. The money that only Daddy can get down in Albany."

Tom Bertram. The man who followed us home from the police station. The man who coldcocked me with his .38 snub-nose revolver. The man I nearly beat to death.

"Penny," I bark, "just do as he says. He has a gun."

"That's right, little lady. Listen to your husband. He knows what you have to do to survive in this cruel world. He must be smart. I hear he was gonna be a doctor. Be he's a killer, too. Take his advice."

"Get the hell away from me," Penny repeats.

That's when I hear it. Something solid coming into contact with something covered in flesh. I can see it happening in my brain. Penny raising up her booted foot, kicking him in the face.

I see Gary's broad back as he raises himself up on his knees.

"Why, you vicious little bitch," he snorts. "You are going to pay for that."

But she kicks him again, and again. She's so quick and swift with her kicks, he falls onto his side, rolls over onto his back. He doesn't have a chance to go for his gun. I make out the sound of her crabbing forward. No longer backing away. No longer afraid. I hear her breaths, her short inhales and exhales.

I can feel her fury.

Then another swift kick into Gary's most sensitive of places. I know this because the big mountain of a man screams like a little girl. Right now, rapid-fire electronic signals are being sent to his brain via synapses at some 265 MPH. Substance P, a neurotransmitter, is being released by the damaged testicles, telling the brain to *Please, for God's sake, send some fucking endorphins into the blood stream to ease this pain!* Only that's gonna take a while, pal. In the meantime, the pain will be accompanied by severe nausea, migraine headache, and gross tearing of the eyes.

As expected, Gary curls up into himself on the edge of the pit. He's so close to the edge that, for a split second, I'm convinced he's about to fall in, and I'd better not be on the receiving end of his massive deadweight.

But something else happens instead. Penny jumps back up onto her feet.

"Sid," she says, "send up your belt."

I don't argue. I pull off my thick brown leather belt, toss it up to her. She does something then that I never thought her capable of. She wraps my belt around Gary's thick neck, pulling the leather belt back through its metal buckle. She proceeds to yank on the belt with all her strength, so that it chokes him like a noose. He's in terrible pain from the kick in the groin, but he begins to clutch at the belt now that his airway is cut off. It's his survival mechanism kicking in at high gear. Pulling with both her hands, like reining in a runaway horse, Penny rears backward, throwing all her body weight into it.

I see Gary's round face go from pink to red, his eyes bulging out of their sockets, his fleshy tongue protruding from his mouth, purple and veiny. He spits and snorts like a gut-shot pig. Until just like that, his head drops face-first onto the floor.

Penny exhales, drops to her knees.

She removes my belt from Gary's neck, tosses it back down to me. For a split second I think about using it like a rope, with her hanging onto one end while I use the other to climb out of the pit. But the pit is too deep and no way is Penny supporting my weight.

"Just let me catch my breath," she exhales, panting. "Then, I'm going to find something to help you climb out of that hellhole."

I slip my belt back through the pant loops, buckle it.

"Watch your back," I say, still not quite believing what I just witnessed. "The monster is down, but that doesn't mean the beast is dead. Could be he's passed out from hyper-asphyxiation."

She gets up.

"Wait there," she says.

"Is that supposed to be a joke?"

She doesn't laugh.

While she's searching the trailer, I hear the words she's speaking to Chloe.

"Don't worry, sweetheart," she says. "We're going to get you out of there in a minute. I need to get Daddy out first since I'll need his help."

"Hurry, Mommy," Chloe says.

I'm still standing down here, looking up at Gary's fat face. His dead—God willing—fat face, I should say. I make out footsteps coming from overhead. Then I see Penny standing very close to the edge of the pit.

"These creeps were into their rope," she reveals. "There's spools and spools of it in a back room. I thought they might have a step-ladder for accessing the cellars, but no such luck." Shaking her head disgusted, disturbed. "There's something in the bathtub. I didn't look at it too closely, but there's blood on the floor. Bloody foot-prints. What if it's that man who attacked you behind the hotel?" She can hardly get the words out.

. . . Bertram . . .

"Don't look at it, Pen," I insist. "Let's just get out of here as fast as we can."

Chloe's face flashes in my head. If I find out Gary or Walton or Tom Bertram laid a hand on her, I will kill them. Doesn't matter that they are all dead. I will kill them again, and again, and then I will cut them up and feed them to the wolves.

. . . Okay, don't get ahead of yourself, Sid. Could be Gary and Walton and Tom didn't have time to do anything other than lock Chloe and Susan up inside the trailer while they focused on getting at Rabuffo's stash. Just get yourself out of the hole, grab the girls, and get the hell away from there . . .

"Just let me get this tied up to something," Penny adds.

She disappears from view. I do my best to be patient while she ties the rope off, my eyes glued to Gary's face. How I could have been so wrong about him I'll never know. Maybe my instincts are off, after all. Maybe I shouldn't trust my gut the way I do. But then, maybe I should look at it another way. Gary led us directly to our daughter. That was his mistake. But in the end, if he hadn't picked us up on that mountain road in Keene Valley, we might not have found Chloe. Rather, we would have found her. I had Walton's address in my pocket after all. But by then, it might have been too late.

The opposite end of the rope drops down into the pit.

"Hope you know how to use this thing," Penny says, peeking down into the hole.

"I'm a quick study," I say, grabbing the rope with both hands, yanking it tight, and pulling myself, hand over hand style, up the entire vertical length of the pit.

When I get to the top, I reach out for Penny. She takes hold of my hand with both her hands, pulls me over the side with all her strength. I roll onto my back, my beat-up face only inches from Gary's gray-haired head.

Bounding up onto my feet. "Let's get Chloe."

That's when I get my first real look at the mostly wide-open trailer. On one end of the structure is the kitchen. There's a wood kitchen table with matching chairs pulled up to it. A stainless-steel gas stove and a large modern refrigerator/freezer, plus a microwave and even a glass wine cooler unit are also included in the kitchen appliance lineup. Walton must have loved to cook and drink. What he didn't love is cleaning up after himself. The place stinks. But then it dawns on me that the trailer more than likely doesn't have access to a sewer system but, instead, to a septic tank.

Those two open holes in the floor are only going to help transmit the foul odor.

The living room contains two easy chairs and a leather couch that has been pushed aside to accommodate entry to the cellar where Chloe and Susan reside. A flat-screen television hangs on the opposite wall. A short hallway accesses the bedrooms, bathroom, and storage closets. The removable floor panels that access both cellars are leaning up against the counter that separates the kitchen from the general living space.

"Help me, Penny," I say, grabbing hold of the rope, transferring it to the pit that holds Chloe and Susan. "I'm gonna climb down inside, part way. That way the girls can take hold of my hand and I can physically lift them up to you at the pit's edge. Understand?"

Her eyes wide and intent, she is focused entirely on the task that awaits her.

The rope in hand, I get my first look at my daughter since she disappeared. What I see brings tears to my eyes. But they are tears of joy. She's dressed in an adult-sized t-shirt that fits her like a dress. It's covered in dirt and mud stains. Her long hair is matted to her head from the filth. But her eyes are bright and wet, and she's smiling at me like I'm an angel sent from heaven. But it's really she who's the angel.

Susan is also covered in the cellar's filth, but she too is smiling, so happy to see Penny and me. So happy to know that she's going to survive this hell. I have to wonder if she looks like the daughter Gary lost. If she's a substitute for her. Or maybe Gary never lost a daughter in the first place. Maybe by describing a little girl who was raped and left for dead on a trash heap, he was confessing to one of his own horrible crimes. The truth is just too horrific to ponder.

"Here's comes the rope, girls," I say.

Then, grabbing hold of the rope, making it taut, I sit myself on the edge of the pit wall. I climb down inside, stopping when I know the girls can easily reach me with their hands.

"Who wants to go first?" I say, straining from supporting my entire body weight with one hand.

"You go first, Sue," Chloe says. "You've been living here a lot longer than me."

Good old Chloe. Thinking not of herself, but the poor soul that has been living this hell for God knows how long. It's becoming more and more obvious to me that Burt and Claudia Stevens weren't her parents after all. But two evil jerks acting the role of her parents in order to lure Chloe into their trap. A trap Penny helped set, whether she knew it or not. I recalled Susan arguing with her mother about an iPhone. An argument that sounded similar to the one Chloe was waging with Penny yesterday morning. Maybe too similar. Had Penny helped script the argument for the Stevenses? Maybe they had no clue how to interact with a girl Susan's age, and Penny helped them out. I could ask her directly, but what would be the point at this stage of the game?

"Okay, Susan," I say, my left hand held out for her. "Grab hold of my hand and let's do this."

At first, she hesitates. Like I'm not really going to save her life at all, but instead, take it. And who can blame her? She's been held captive by the sons of bitches who lived here for God knows how long. The last man's hand she touched was no doubt one of theirs.

"Do it, Sue," Chloe encourages. "He's my dad. He's a very nice man. He's going to save us. Just do it."

I'm straining to hold myself, the pain in my forearm, biceps, and shoulder, searing. But I'm not about to let go of the rope. Not until these girls are free of the pit.

Susan slowly raises her hand. It's trembling. The pale skin is stained with dirt and pink clay, the nails scraped down to nothing, as if on several occasions, she tried to dig her way out of this trap.

I snatch the hand, grip it tightly. She shrieks, but I try not to pay attention to it. Emotions like fear don't matter at this point.

"Okay, get ready," I say. "You're going for a ride, Susan." Looking up at Penny who is reaching down into the cellar with her right hand. "Here she comes, Pen!"

Using all my available strength, I swing the girl up and over my head. Penny grabs hold of Susan's free hand and pulls her up onto the edge of the floor and finally to safety.

Peering back down into the hole, I now focus on my daughter.

"Let's do this, Chloe," I say, holding out my hand for her.

More of that smile I've come to cherish. She takes hold of my hand.

"Okay, babe," I say. "On three. One, two . . ."

"Three!" she shouts, leaping while I pull her up and over my head to Penny's waiting arms. When Chloe has made it over the pit's edge, I can make out Penny's cries of relief. I know she is not just hugging our daughter right now, she is holding her so tight she's liable to break her bones. It is a sight and a sound to behold.

Climbing back up the rope, I crawl over the edge and for the first time in what seems forever, breathe.

But I don't take a whole lot of time to catch my breath. We need to get the hell out of here. Soon the police will arrive at this trailer. I'm wanted for the abduction of my daughter. I've been accused of her probable murder by the chief of police. Penny is just as wanted. We need to get to Albany, to police officers who are not loyal to Walton. Who knows how many cops were working with him? Judging by that chopper that attacked us on two separate occasions, this whole thing could run pretty deep. Who knows how many cops knew about this trailer and the horrible things going down here? How long was Susan being kept here against her will? Was Walton holding her hostage with the intent to release her only when her parents came up with the right amount of blood money? That would be my guess.

But there's another reason I want to get to Albany as quickly as possible and without the Lake Placid police being aware. Rabuffo's fortune is in Albany. If I'm to take Penny at her word—and God knows how much I want to—she intended to take some of that fortune to ensure a future for our daughter. The plan was not without its risks, it turns out. Not without its dangers. Not without its selling of one's soul to many devils. But now that we have our daughter back—now that I am no longer paying for four homicides I did not commit by rotting away inside a prison cell—it's time we got what's ours. Rather, it's time our daughter got what's hers.

Here's what we're going to do: we're going after Rabuffo's fortune, and we're going to get it before any of those other motherfuckers do.

CHAPTER 44

WE'RE CAREFUL TO step over Gary's body on our way to the trailer door. We're also careful to avoid the onion cellar that abuts up against the entire doorframe, as if it were originally designed as a trap for whoever might stumble into this place unexpectedly or unwanted. Opening the door, I swing my leg around and over the deep hole, plant my foot on the porch floor, and step out onto it. I extend my hand out through the now open doorframe.

"Chloe," I say. "You first. No arguments."

She grips my hand and I safely pull her through the door. Then I repeat the process with Susan. Finally, Penny takes hold of my hand and, with my guidance, she safely makes it onto the porch.

"Let's go," I say. "Outside."

We head across the bare wood porch floor and out the busted screen door onto the gravel footpath that leads to the driveway and Gary's truck.

"The truck, girls," I direct. "There's room enough for us all to pile in the front."

"The little sheep are scattering," comes a voice from out of nowhere. A man's voice. "Stop right where you are . . . sheep."

An electric shock runs up and down my spine—an ancient animal response to danger and/or sudden surprise. There's trouble afoot.

I turn.

He's standing at the top of the drive, his big body bathed in the light of the moon. The man I fired upon point-blank. The man whose body was inside the cabin when the police officer's grenade blew it all to hell.

Chief Joseph Walton.

He's bleeding from the shoulder. What's left of it. Half his face and neck has been burned and blackened by fire. He's got one hand pressed against the wound on his stomach. Gripped in his shooting hand is a short-barreled semi-automatic that he must have had hidden on his person. Probably in an ankle holster. Son of a bitch must have crawled out of the woods, or maybe his chopper boys picked him up once they figured out he'd survived somehow.

"Surprise, surprise," he says, half his round face ghost white in the moonlight. "You can't get rid of me that fast." He focuses on Penny. "We made a deal, sweetheart. A cut of Rabuffo's money in exchange for your man's freedom."

"That deal didn't include the kidnapping of my daughter," she insists.

He bears gray teeth, which he's grinding to fight back the pain that must consume his body.

"See, now that's where you're wrong, Penny," he says. "Did you really think you were coming to Lake Placid on a vacation? You were coming here to get rid of your husband. He knows too much. And as for your daughter, well, for our plan to work out, she suddenly had to become the girl who wasn't there."

"What are you talking about, Walton?" I jump in.

"Your wife made a deal with the devil."

"My wife was thinking of our daughter," I insist, glancing at Penny.

I see her face. It's tight and tense. She's not afraid of Walton, so much as she's angry with him. Furious.

Shifting my focus to the girls.

"You girls get in the truck," I demand. "Do it now."

"But, Daddy," Chloe says. "What about Mommy?"

"Just do it, Chloe."

I could approach this situation by using my intellect. By attempting to talk Walton out of holding that gun on us, by promising him immediate health care to cauterize his wounds. 911 is only a phone call away, after all.

I could lie, assure him I won't press charges, if only he'll drop the gun. I can attempt to stay one step ahead of him by reasoning with him, lying to him, calming him down, stalling him.

But let's face it. The man is shot to shit. He's desperate. He's out of his mind, and he wants only one thing. The code to Walton's vault. Once he's forced that from my lips, he'll kill me, and more than likely, kill my entire family. He'll also kill Susan.

So here's the deal. I know in my head that I have no choice but to bull-rush Walton. In the process I might get shot. If that happens, everyone I love and care about is as good as dead. But without rushing him, they're as good as dead anyway. He's got to be put down. If I were still back inside prison walls, this is exactly how I would handle it. How I trained myself to handle kill-or-be-killed situations like this. The would-be doctor . . . the *healer* . . . become the *killer*.

"You have a sickness, Walton," Penny says. "It's called greed. You killed your partner, Tom. You killed your friend. You did it for money."

"Money sings and I love music," he says. "But I'm not sick. I'm just a little beat up. Isn't that right, *Doctor* O'Keefe? And as for Tom Bertram, he talked too much. He royally screwed himself when he started mouthing off to the press. It was too risky. It got on Gary's nerves and Gary did something about it." He works up a smile. "You've no doubt met Gary by now."

"No one told me about you," Penny says, her tears having returned, along with her guilt, her self-loathing. "Not Joel, not anybody. No one warned me about what I was getting into. That you would steal a child in exchange for a payday. You are greedy bastards, all of you. Criminal greedy sons-a-bitches."

Walton laughs. But he's also in agonizing pain. I can see it painted on his black and pale white face, see it throbbing in his mutilated shoulder, see it bleeding from his punctured gut.

He says, "What you knew—or didn't know—about me is beside the point right now. You and Joel needed me and my men. That's all that matters."

"Why'd you do it, Pen?" I plead. "Why did you need this psycho for anything? Rabuffo's money is down in Albany."

She looks at me, crosses her arms over her chest, holding herself so tight it's like she's trying to prevent her heart from spilling out.

"Joel has a summer house up here on Lake Placid," she explains. "He got to know Walton over the years. The two developed a trust. Joel knew that getting at Mickey Rabuffo's money could be very hard. But Mickey had set up shop up here. Expanding operations north inside the tourist village. A new cheap Chinese take-out joint on Main Street, smack in the middle of two five-star restaurants. Only Mickey could get away with that depending upon who he paid off. Plus, a tailor shop just outside of town. He has some serious friends up here now. Walton and quite a few of his support staff cozied right up to them. Isn't that right, Chief?

The men still loyal to Rabuffo would prevent us from getting anywhere close to the major stash down in Albany. So Walton would be the hired muscle. The go-to man, you could say."

"In exchange for a cut," I surmise.

She nods.

"We would all get major cuts," she adds. "But I did it not for me. Not even for you, Doc. But for Chloe. She could escape this life, go to overnight prep school, and from there, a great college and from there med school. Just like you once wanted for yourself, Doc."

My eyes glued to Walton. "But what you didn't tell Penny was that you planned on having Chloe kidnapped, make it look like she was killed. And it would look like I did it. Because I'm a crazy killer now. A monster. A kidnapped Chloe was your ultimate leverage."

"I never dreamed anything would happen to Chloe," Penny cries. "That she would end up here, Sid. You have to believe me."

Even if she has said this same thing to me more times than I can count, I don't ever quite believe her. It's unsettling to hear her say it, no matter how much I want to believe it. The ground beneath me spins out of control. Nausea settles in. Vertigo. I see the blood hemorrhaging from Walton's abdomen, and I know there's no better time to do what I've got to do.

The time for talking is over. Survival instinct kicks in once again. Maximum-security Darwinism.

I bull-rush the bastard, hope for the best.

CHAPTER 45

Shots fired.

Two, maybe three.

But bullets don't stop me from burying my shoulder directly into Walton's wounded belly. I hear and feel a guttural wince as his breath escapes what's left of his damaged torso.

My body is not my own anymore. It belongs to someone else entirely. Some sort of demon. Some sort of monster that was introduced to me inside the prison. It has never left me, just like my own shadow.

Before I know it, I've knocked the pistol out of his grip, and both my hands are wrapped around his badly injured neck. I'm digging both my thumbs into his carotid artery. So hard I'm not only stopping the blood flood flow between the heart and the brain, I feel like they're about to pop through the charred skin. He's choking, gagging, his black and white face filling with blood, his eyes popping, bulging out of their sockets. His mouth is agape, his tongue blue and thick and sticking out of his mouth like a snake. He's spitting, snarling, struggling for the air that won't come. He is the devil. He is my worst nightmare.

Until just like that, his body turns off, like the plug being pulled on a lamp—a pathologist once described the moment of death to me in those exact terms. The air that's left in his lungs escapes, and the devil deflates, his soul no doubt heading directly for hell. God knows, I hope it exists. For heaven's sake.

I hear it then, while I'm trying my best to catch my breath.

Chloe, screaming, crying.

"Mommy! Mommy what has he done to you?!"

Her words break me out of my trance. I pull myself off of Walton, stand, turn. I see Penny lying on her back in the driveway. A pool of blood is forming under her. The blood is dark red, nearly black in the moonlight. Chloe has gotten out of the truck. She's standing over her, crying, screaming.

My own blood feels like it's spilling out the bottoms of my feet, my shredded heart along with it. I go to her, drop to my knees, stare down at her blood-spattered face. My vision is clouded by tears.

She tries to raise up her hand, but she doesn't have the strength. That's when I take hold of it, clasp it between both my hands. It's as cold as ice. Her eyes close. Her breathing ceases.

Instinct kicks in. Not the instinct to kill, but to heal.

I bring my mouth to hers, blow air inside it. I press my hands together, apply pressure to her sternum, pressing down upon it in five second intervals. She's been shot in the chest and abdomen so while I'm trying to jump-start her heart, it's just as likely I'm doing damage to her internal injuries. Causing more internal bleeding. But what choice do I have?

"Come on, Pen!" I shout. "Live!"

She coughs, her eyes opening and closing. I remove my hands from her chest, only to see the blood that's exiting the sides of her mouth, streaming down the sides of her face.

"I'm calling 911," I insist, reaching for my phone.

"It's over, Doc," she says, trying her hardest to work up a smile. The blood is oozing like a small fountain out of the entry wounds in her chest and stomach. The blood is all over my hands. "Over for me, for us. Over before it begins again."

"Don't talk, babe," I say, my soul shattering. "Save your strength. We're gonna get you out of here. Get you to a doctor. A real doctor."

"Stop it, Doc. You of all people know I'm not making it out of this." Then, trying to lean up, "Looks like you caught a bullet, too, Doc. You'd better dress it before it gets infected."

I nod, the tears streaming down my face. I haven't been shot. At least, I don't think I've been shot. The blood that soaks my shirt. It's Penny's blood. It's Walton's blood, too.

"I'll take care of it," I whisper, knowing there's no point in explaining the truth.

She looks beyond me, at Chloe.

"We finally found you, sweetheart," she says, her voice weakening, barely audible now. "You had us so worried."

"I'm okay, Mom," Chloe says, voice trembling, tears falling. "I love you."

"I wanted something better for you, Chloe," Penny whispers. "I thought I was doing the right thing. But it turned out to be so wrong. I'm so, so, so sorry. Will you forgive me? Will you both find it in your hearts to forgive me?"

"Shhhh, Pen," I say. "It's all going to be okay. Your heart was in the right place."

"Come here," she says. I can barely hear her now. "Come . . . here."

I bring my face down toward her, position my ear over her lips.

"I always loved you, Doc," she says. "I always will."

I feel her warm breath against the side of my face. I make out a final profound exhalation. It is the sweet breath of her soul. And then she's gone.

"Mom?" Chloe, begs. "Mom, Mom?"

My little girl drops to her knees, starts clawing at her mother.

"It's okay, Chloe. It's okay." I grab hold of her, stand, lift her up in my arms, clutch her tightly. "It's okay. She's in a good place now. Mommy's in heaven."

"Mom!" Chloe screams. So loud the birds light from the trees and fly away like lost souls into the moon glow.

My body is shaking. Trembling. No choice but to hold it all together. I set Chloe back into the truck. Then, I search the truck bed for a cloth or a tarp. But there's nothing to be had. I do however find a rag stored behind the seat, with which I wipe the blood from my hands. I also find a navy blue windbreaker. It bears the words "Lake Placid Fire Department" on its back. I carry it to Penny, drape it over her face. As soon as we're out of here, I'll dial 911, and report the shooting. It's possible the police will already be on their way, but I don't want to take any chances on Penny being left to the elements, or the wolves that surely live among the trees that surround this place.

I love her too damned much for that.

CHAPTER 46

Driving.

Sick to my stomach now that I have no choice but to leave Penny behind. Her body behind. How the hell did it all come to this? How did I finally get my family back only to lose my true love? My Penny from heaven?

. . . You've done some bad things, Sid. Karma. It can be a real bitch . . .

When we come to the highway, I head south for Albany. Immediately following my 911 call to the local authorities under condition of anonymity, I dial the one person on God's earth who can possibly help me at this point. My parole officer, Drew Lochte.

"Tell me I'm not waking you," I say when he answers.

"I can't believe it," Lochte says, his somewhat muffled voice telling me, *Yeah, I woke him up.* "Sidney, what the hell have you done? There's state and fed BOLOs out on you. Every cop from Albany, New York to Albany, Georgia, wants to put a cap in you, pal."

"I didn't do it," I say, my mouth dry, my eyes still filled with tears.

"You didn't just say that."

"I did not kidnap or hurt my daughter. And I did not beat and/ or kill anyone." Then, thinking about it for a brief beat. "Well, scratch that last part, but trust me when I say they had it coming, and the law will see it that way."

"How do I know I can trust you?"

"Hang on," I insist.

Then, I hand the phone to Chloe, who's seated directly beside me.

"Speak into the phone, Chloe," I say. "Tell the man on the other end your name."

I give her the phone and she presses it to her ear.

"Hello?" she says, her voice sounding hollow and distant over the shock of her mother's death. "My name is Chloe O'Keefe. My daddy rescued me and another girl. Her name is Susan. They kept us inside an old cellar under a trailer in the woods. It was really, really horrible." Her voice shaking, the tears coming again. "They did something really bad to my mom."

"That's enough now, Chloe," I say, holding out my hand.

She places the phone on my palm, then wipes her eyes. Susan takes her hand, holds it tightly.

The phone once more pressed against my ear.

"That satisfy you, Lochte?"

"What happens now?" he asks. "How do I know you're not still in the process of abducting your own daughter, and from the sound of it, another kid also?"

"Because I'm contacting you of my own free will and because I'm dropping them off at your house."

"My . . . *house*?"

"Either I hear an echo or I have a great signal all the way up here in the mountains."

"Listen, Sidney," he goes on. "The best thing for you to do is turn yourself over to the authorities—"

"—Drew, if I do that, they'll lock me up for good, and Chloe will be out on the street. You know how the system works. Close the cage door on him now, ask questions later."

"I *am* the system, Sidney."

"Then I'm asking you to help me out for just an hour. That's all I'm asking. Let me drop off the girls to you. No cops, no feds, no press, nothing. Understand? After that, just give me one hour. I don't find what I'm looking for in that time, I'll turn myself in. Fair enough?"

Breathing on the other end of the line.

"Not exactly the most fair and balanced deal I've ever heard in my life. But if you're willing to turn your daughter over to me, I guess that's saying something. You know where I live?"

"I know it. I found it on Google earlier this week."

"I should have known."

"And, Drew?" I add. "Remember, no cops. I don't want things getting more ugly than they've already gotten. That happens, I'll have nothing more to lose. And there's no telling what I'll do."

The parole officer is smart enough to read between the lines. He knows exactly what I mean by "ugly." By "no telling what I'll do." That, should he betray me, things could get ugly for him. No doubt he can feel my desperation over the phone.

"I read you, Sid," he says. "I'll see you when I see you."

"Not if I see you first."

"Oh, and Sid? What is it you're looking for?"

"I'm not sure exactly," I say. "But I think I'll know it when I find it."

I cut the connection.

* * *

We drive.

The truck is filled with a silence so heavy and thick, it's like we're caught up in a different dimension altogether, where gravity is twice as heavy and the oxygen twice as difficult to breathe. I'm trying to rationalize this whole thing in my head. One question looms large. I understand Penny's desire to see Chloe get a fair shot at life, even if it entails stealing Rabuffo's money. But was it worth pursuing if it meant she'd become beholden to people like Walton, House Detective Giselle Fontaine, and the Stevenses? These were some bad people, and in the end, they wouldn't have hesitated to cut Penny out of what she was owed.

That is, had they lived.

No matter how I try to navigate the logic on this whole thing, I keep coming back to the same starting place. And that is my lawyer, Joel Harwood. For the longest time, Joel was my hero. The man who counseled me, fought for me, believed in me. He got me out of prison at a time when I'd lost all hope.

But then, the freedom wasn't really free since it came at one hell of a price. I'd have to expose Rabuffo for what he was. And in doing so, place my life at risk or, more importantly, the lives of my wife and child. But I'd still have my freedom, and not just some half-assed freedom where I'd be required to live in a halfway house, wear an ankle bracelet, report in to my employer at the supermarket where the best job I could ever hope for would be to stock some shelves and bag groceries.

The kind of freedom I was ultimately bargaining for was absolute and came with no conditions other than reporting in to a parole officer. That was one rule that I could not get around. But I didn't mind, so long as I was out of prison and back with my family.

My girls.

* * *

I drive, my eyes fixed on the open road, the halogen lamp light reflecting the white line stripes speeding under the truck like tracer bullets. But in my head, I see Joel. The big, thick-chested man, always impeccably dressed in his dark blue suit and red and white Albany Law School rep tie forwarded to him by his alma mater as a thank-you for his generous donation. The little matching pocket hanky over his heart, the perfect salt and pepper hair slicked back against his round skull with product, the expensive white Oxford, the gold Rolex, the wad of money-clipped cash in his pocket, the shark skin, gold credit card carrying wallet stored in the interior of his jacket pocket. The gold ring on his pinky finger.

I picture the whole package.

I also see him with Penny. See him wining and dining her. See him luring her into bed. I try not to see what happens next, but that doesn't prevent me from knowing precisely what happened. But what I want to know is when he finally worked up the courage to propose his idea to Penny. When he finally felt confident enough to bring her in on the plan. To have Rabuffo arrested, to have him out of the way for good. How he must have convinced her that she had no choice but to work with him on finding out the combination to Rabuffo's vault. To find a way to coerce it out of me. Or else, Chloe wouldn't have a chance in the world at a future.

I've seen him live and in action in a court of law. If there was one thing Joel could do it was litigate and manipulate. He could convince a jury that the sky was falling if he wanted to. It was a gift Joel had, and no doubt, he used it on my wife.

Chloe is asleep, her head resting on my shoulder. I can't tell you how good it is to feel her pressing against me. Susan, however, is not sleeping. She's staring at her phone, which seems to be dead.

"You doing okay, Susan?"

She nods, her eyes still glued to the dark phone screen.

"I'm okay," she says.

Like my daughter, she's in shock. I'm also wondering if she's requiring an insulin shot. God knows I have no way of getting my hands on any, anytime soon.

"Susan," I say, "you don't have to talk if you don't want. But can you tell me how long you've been living inside that trailer?"

Slowly, she peels her eyes away from the useless blank screen and shifts her focus to me.

"I'm not really sure," she confesses. "It's hard for me to remember anything else but that smelly, awful hole in the ground."

"But you were on the beach yesterday morning. You seemed so . . . normal. Unaffected by anything."

She smiles. "Did I? Was I nice? Did Chloe have fun with me?"

It hits me then. "You don't remember, do you?"

"What?"

"You don't remember being on the beach with Chloe. With two older people who claimed to be your parents. You don't remember any of it."

She shakes her head. "They would do things to me sometimes. Mr. Walton and that other big man with the gray beard, Gary. Plus, that man they killed today. Mr. Bertram. They put needles in me. Drugged me. They said I had diabetes, so they would inject me. The drugs made me sleepy. Made me forget things."

In my head, I'm going over the many mind control drugs that might have been utilized in Susan's case. Sodium amytal, which has been around since World War II. Pipradrol. Chlorpromazine or what's also known as Thorazine. Even good old LSD laced with Ritalin has been known to control people's minds, when administered in the right doses. In a way, I'm relieved. She doesn't require insulin after all.

"Gary," I interject. "Walton. Tom. They all injected you, or held you down while you were injected."

"Yeah, they would stick big long needles in me. They'd make it hurt. I'd fight them, but they were so big and strong. Yesterday morning, they lifted me out of the hole, washed me up, injected me with something bad. They said it was because I was having a sugar attack. That I would have a seizure. I remember riding in the truck into the village, and I sort of remember touching the water with my toes, and I remember laughing. I remember saying the things they wanted me to say. Something about wanting an iPhone. Stuff parents and kids talk about." Shrugging her shoulders. "But other than that, I don't remember much of anything. But . . ."

"But what, Susan?" I say, giving her a quick look.

"I do remember taking this cell phone. The man who was acting like my father."

"Burt," I say. "Burt Stevens."

"Whatever his name was. He left it out on the beach chair. I just took it, put it inside my bathing suit. Then Gary and Tom came and took us away, dropped us in the cellar."

"You're starting to remember more of it," I suggest, recalling Burt complaining that he'd lost his cell phone on the beach when he arrived at the cabin in the forest with Singh. It all made sense now.

"I guess if I try real hard, I can remember some things."

In my head, I'm seeing Tom Bertram. I see myself beating him. I see him standing before a whole bunch of media darling microphones, lying, telling the entire world that I attacked him for no good reason, other than I'm a monster who should have remained in prison. In my mind, I see him lying in a bathtub soaking in his own blood.

"You did the right thing, Susan. If Chloe hadn't sent me those texts, I might not have gotten to you two in time."

I also realize how lucky it was that Burt must have been too lazy to install an access code on his phone. I give Chloe another glance. She smiles at me.

"Thanks," she says. "And I'm terribly sorry about Chloe's mom."

My stomach sinking, once more. I'm choking up, but I don't want her to know it.

"It's okay," I say. "What about your folks? They must be awfully worried."

"My dad left a long time ago," she says. "My mom didn't have the money Mr. Walton thought she had. She never came for me."

So that explains it then. Susan was a permanent hostage in the Walton trailer. A prisoner not only of that cellar and evil men, but of fate. What horrible ordeal she's truly gone through, I'll never have any idea. But she's young and she seems unharmed, physically speaking that is. But I know that the real emotional damage she must have endured will take years to heal. Years and time.

"I'm going to go to sleep now. If that's all right with you, Mister . . ."

"Call me Doc," I say. "All my friends do."

"Okay, Doc," she says. "Good night."

"'Night, Susan. Have a good sleep. You're gonna need your strength come daylight."

CHAPTER 47

IT'S THE MIDDLE of the night by the time we reach the Albany city limits. One of the first things I did upon my discharge from prison was look into my parole officer. His age and experience, his marital status—divorced—no kids, his record on returning parolees to prison and, of course, where he resided. In this case, Albany's Pine Hills district. Pine Hills is a popular area for city, state, and federal workers who rely on public transport to take them to and from their downtown office buildings, day in and day out.

Turning onto the Fairlawn Avenue, I don't pull up to the small, yellow bungalow right away. I take a moment or two to scope the place out, make sure Lochte was being true to his word when I told him no cops. Thus far anyway, it looks like he's keeping his word. That's one of the things I liked about his profile. Word around town was that many of the parolees who'd been assigned to him made it through the parolee period unscathed, telling me Lochte was a man of his word. Something he prided himself on.

For an ex-con, I lucked out, you could say.

I pull up to the yellow bungalow, open the door, get out.

He's already up on the porch waiting for my arrival. He descends the porch stairs onto the concrete landing, and then a second set of steps down to sidewalk level.

"I didn't want to turn on the porch light," he whispers, "attract unwanted attention."

He's not a tall man, but he's not short either. His face is clean shaven, his hair closely cropped and curly. His skin is the color of coffee with lots of milk. He is wiry and thin. Like a bicyclist maybe, or a cross trainer. He's wearing a plain white cotton t-shirt, and black Levis over brown work boots.

"They're both asleep," I say, opening up the passenger-side door.

He grabs hold of Susan, cradles her in his arms, carries her up the steps. I do the same with Chloe, cradling her in both my arms like she's a little baby. He manages to open the screen door and together we enter into the humble home with the girls. I must admit, I half expect a team of police to be waiting for us. But the place is empty. He sets Susan on the far end of a sectional couch, near the fireplace. I set Chloe on the end closer to the front door.

He goes to a closet that's located between the kitchen and living room, pulls out two blankets, which he lays out over each girl.

"My guess is they'll sleep for a while," I say.

"What about you, Sid?" he asks. "What happens now? With each second that passes, I feel my state pension going bye-bye."

In my head, a vision of Joel Harwood. He's not fast asleep, like most of the people in Albany who spend their precious time working long days running law firms. My gut tells me he is instead where I expect him to be. Question is, will he be expecting me when I get there?

"If I'm not back in an hour," I say, "call in the APD. Don't let any harm come to my little girl or to Susan."

"Where are you going, Sidney?"

"You know where I'm going."

"I was afraid of that," he says.

* * *

The Rabuffo estate.

You can't see the main house from the road. It's set back a half mile inside some of the lushest, greenest, unspoiled acreage left-over in north Albany's wealthy hamlet of Loudonville. The gate outside is controlled electronically. There's always a man or two stationed outside guarding it. But now that Rabuffo's been busted by both the locals and the Feds, the gate is unmanned, whatever support staff he had leftover scattering into the woodwork like cockroaches. As I pull up to it, the round headlamps on the truck shining on it, I can see that it has also been left wide open. By who and by what, I have no idea.

No, scratch that. I do indeed have an idea or two.

The police are one of those thoughts that pass through my head. The yellow Do Not Enter crime scene ribbon wrapped around the gate every which way, is one dead giveaway. If the FBI haven't al-ready been here to tear the place apart, they will be soon. Maybe even Department of Homeland Security will join them, given Rabuffo's penchant for smuggling undocumented Chinese in and out of New York City.

But here's what I think. It's the middle of the night. The gate's been left wide open. It's dark, and seeing that Walton and all his partners are now dead, including my wife, there's only one soul left on God's good earth who would take a chance on disturbing that yellow ribbon and crossing over that police line.

That would be my lawyer, Joel Harwood.

I drive on through the open gate, some of the ribbon ripping away when the truck plows through it. I take it slow, careful not to rev the engine for fear of giving myself away. I pass by one of the outlying buildings that Rabuffo's men would use as a lunch room, or just a place to get warm in the winter. Then I approach the main house, which is situated at the apex of a cobblestoned turnaround. The white, four-story, red brick and white clapboard Colonial never ceases to impress me. It's bigger than a Radisson, and the attached garage can house more cars, full-sized Suburbans, and pickup trucks than your average used car dealership. Or so it seems.

There's a car parked at the top of the turnaround.

Caught in the pickup's headlamps, I can see that it's an old-model Mercedes convertible. Baby blue, with tan leather seats, and a matching leather-covered steering column. Its license plate isn't entirely anonymous, but instead bears the epitaph "Esquire III" in white on New York State–blue lettering.

I park the pickup behind it. But before I get out, I can't help but notice that the shotgun I stole from the cabin is set on the floor in the passenger-side foot well. Gary must have stored it there after he ripped it out of my hands inside Walton's trailer. That's my good luck, and Joel's bad luck. Grabbing the shotgun, I exit the truck, and shut the door as gently and quietly as possible.

Showdown time has arrived.

More yellow crime scene ribbon is taped to the front door. Some of it has been pulled away to make way for a man. A big man like Joel. I place my free hand on the door, depress the opener. The latch releases. Pushing the door open, I enter into the great vestibule. The floor is black and white marble, and the cathedral ceiling is white stucco, with a massive chandelier hanging down from it. A wraparound Scarlet O'Hara staircase begins on my right-hand side and accesses the second floor of the big house.

The shotgun gripped in both my hands, I make my way across the vestibule floor and into the narrow hallway that leads to both a large living room where Rabuffo would host his NFL football parties, and beside it, a large kitchen boasting only the best stainless-steel and glass appliances known to man.

To my left is a door that goes down into a basement that long ago was converted into a game room for some of Rabuffo's never-ending poker games. I make my way down the carpeted staircase, my pulse throbbing in my temples, but my ears wide open. The overhead cans have been turned on already so there's no need for me to be feeling and fumbling my way around in the dark.

When I come to the landing, I take notice of the half dozen round wood card tables that occupy the floor, and the full bar that takes up one entire wall. The opposite wall sports three side-by-side 64-inch flat-screened HDTVs. The TVs have been turned on. A video is playing. Rather, not a video, but a home movie shot with an old-fashioned Super 8 camera.

I recognize myself in the full color movie. Recognize all the people I'm hanging out with. We're standing around the pool out back. Me, Rabuffo, Wemps, Singh, and one other man, Joel Harwood. We're drinking cocktails from long-stem glasses and laughing for the camera. We're speaking at whoever is shooting the film, but there's no sound, so I can't really make it out. About a dozen, very attractive women are swimming in the pool, or lounging around it on chaise lounges, their eyes masked with expensive sunglasses.

One of these women turns onto her side, waves for the camera. She is beautiful, with her long dark hair, big teardrop eyes, a perfect build, and peppy smile. I have just begun dating her when this home movie was shot. She is Penny, and seeing her right now rips my heart to shreds.

Men and women dressed in black and white serve us hors d' oeuvres on silver platters. They're all Chinese. In the film, I pull one of them into the camera shot with me. His tray is empty so he nervously tucks it under his arm. I must be telling him to smile for the camera because his face goes from anxious to suddenly bright and shiny. I recognize this man. He is Chen, one of the four who were executed by Wemps and Singh so many years ago now.

*   *   *

My already broken heart begins to disintegrate.

"None of us are without guilt," says the voice from behind me. "Isn't that right, Sidney? Or should I call you killer, just like Rabuffo so affectionately did way back when."

I feel the cold hard barrel pressed against the back of my skull.

"Guess I walked right into this one," I say, while exhaling a profound sigh.

"That's not like you, Sidney," he says. "I will give you that. But now that I have the upper hand, I'll ask that you lose the shotgun."

Survival instinct kicks in, and for a brief moment I consider spinning around and blasting him in the belly. But then it will only take him a half second to pull the trigger on the semi-automatic and the effort will have been for nothing. Penny might be gone now, but my daughter is alive. She needs me to stay alive. Maybe for once, I can deal with this situation without having to resort to brute force. Maybe for once, I can simply outsmart my enemy. The enemy whom I'd assumed was my friend.

I drop the shotgun to the floor.

"Kick it away," he orders.

I press the tip of my boot against the weapon, push it away . . . out of reach.

"You can turn around now," he says.

I turn. My eyes lock on the big, salt-and-pepper-haired man. He's dressed casually in tan slacks, black loafers, no socks, a white Izod polo shirt under a blue blazer, both its pockets stuffed with something I can't identify. As usual, his gold Rolex is attached to his left wrist.

He blinks rapidly, as if startled by what he sees.

"Where'd you get that face, Sid? A car wreck?"

If only he'd seen it before the swelling abated.

"She's dead, you know," I say.

"Who's dead, Sidney?" he says. "Communications accuracy is of paramount importance in these matters. Especially when you planned on sneaking in here and killing me in cold blood."

"And what kind of fruit has your *plan* to steel the Rabuffo stash born thus far?" I beg. "Or is the metaphor not accurate enough?"

The corner of my eye once more catches the film. Joel, jumping into the pool, surrounding himself with the ladies swimming around the deep end like beautiful mermaids.

He says, "It got you out of the nasty ole' penitentiary, now didn't it?"

"Penny told me all about your plan. You had every intention of sending me right back once you were done with me. That's what you had in mind when you stole my daughter and made it look like I was the perp. Because, naturally, I was already convicted of murder. And ten years in a max security joint like Green Haven would have turned me into a monster. Isn't that right? It would make the healer become the killer."

"Something like that, Sidney," he admits. "Of course, Penny wasn't aware of the full plan."

It comes as a relief to hear him say that, as I notice his eyes glancing at the televisions.

"We had some good times back then," he says. "We made some money. But you were unhinged. You, Wemps, Singh. Killers, all of you. You three high school amigos were walking time bombs. Rabuffo had no choice but to get rid of you."

His words slap me upside the head.

"Hell you talking about, Joel? I was just the driver and bag man. I was planning on going back to med school as soon as possible."

He smiles, shakes his head a little. Like he doesn't believe the words coming out of my mouth.

"You were indeed the driver and the bag man," he says, smiling. "You were also the executioner. The killer." He laughs out loud. "If you were my doctor, I'd be running for the hills."

"I did not shoot that family." My voice, getting louder. More tense.

"Didn't say you did, Sid. You'll see what I'm talking about in a few short moments."

"I'll take your word for it, Counselor."

Joel giggles. "You did how many years in the pen, Sidney? Ten? Tell me something, how much of that ten years did you spend down in the hole?"

It's the strangest sensation, but it feels like my brain is beginning to spin. Slowly at first, but speeding up faster and faster with each second that passes. My equilibrium is totally devastated. It's dizzying, my stomach doing flips. I almost feel like I'm caught up in a bad dream. A vivid dream.

"Jesus, you don't recall a whole lot, do you, Sid?" he goes on. "I'm told solitary will do that to a man. You talk to yourself inside that steel cage. Convince yourself of things. Your subconscious becomes your bitch. You dream the dreams you *want* to dream. How did Tennyson so eloquently put it? Do we not live in dreams?"

I'm hearing his words, but I suddenly feel like it's not me standing before him, but an imposter. It's like I've gone out of body and now I'm watching the scene from a distance. From somewhere else inside the room.

"Tell me," Joel goes on. "Did you dream about spending sultry nights in bed with Penny? Did you dream about walking sandy beaches together? White, sun-baked beaches in Cuba? Did you dream about making love to her in the moonlight?"

He's right, of course, because those are the precise dreams I experienced. I sent her letter after letter detailing my dreams. She must have told him back when they were together. She must have revealed my private letters to him. But whether I trained myself to have those particular dreams or not, they were the dreams I looked forward to when I lay my head down at night. Sleep is the only thing you come to look forward to inside prison walls. It is your only escape from the hard reality of the iron house. It is your safety and your refuge.

You make up your own reality.

"I'm guessing you did not dream about the men and women you killed," he intuits. "That would have been too painful. You, the man who wanted to cure people, not execute them, even if they did have it coming."

Now on the televisions, the Super 8 switches over to digital video. Something shot from a smartphone maybe. One of the men being videotaped is myself. I'm holding a gun over a man who is down on his knees. Several men are standing around me. Wemps, Singh, and Rabuffo.

The man on his knees is dressed in black. He's got a goatee, and tattoos covering his face. A swastika is tattooed to his forehead, just like Charlie Manson.

"Fuck you!" he's shouting. "Fuck you and your children."

"You know what to do, Doc," Rabuffo says, glancing at the camera. "You know how we handle organization traitors."

I see myself smiling as I pull the trigger. The gunshot feels like a punch to the gut.

"How can that be?" I whisper, more to myself than Joel. "It's got to be faked. A faked videotape. Faked history."

"It's no fake and you know it, Sidney. There's a dozen more films just like this one out there."

As if to add credibility to what he's revealing, another videotape begins. This time, I'm standing outside the passenger-side door of a black BMW sedan. Once more, Rabuffo is standing close by. Also, Wemps and Singh are standing in the video backdrop, which is the parking lot to a restaurant or bar.

"The money!" I'm shouting. "What . . . happened . . . to the money?!"

Gunshots follow, the brilliant flashes lighting up the night sky.

"Memory can be a stubborn whore, now can't it, Sid?" Joel adds. "And how about this one? Now this one was an absolute beauty. A real George Bailey moment."

This next video is grainy black and white, shot from the closed-circuit cop cruiser dash cam. I see a small, ratty bungalow. It's night. Two men are emerging from the house, guns in hand. It's Wemps and Singh. Wemps, tall with thick blond hair. Singh, shorter, stockier, with short dark hair. The police are shouting at them to drop their guns, to get down on the ground. To surrender themselves. But my old high school buddies decide to shoot it out with the cops.

It's exactly how I remember it.

Or is it?

That's when I see myself enter into the frame. I've got a semi-automatic gripped in my right hand. I'm firing at will, shooting Wemps in the gut, point-blank. I nail Singh in the left hand from a distance of a couple feet, the hand exploding in a haze of blood, bone, and shredded skin. I unload an entire magazine into my two best friends. Then, a team of cops tackling me, throwing me down on the ground. Joel was right after all. I was driver *and* executioner. The killer.

The televisions turn off automatically.

My brain is spinning so hot, I feel like it's about to turn to liquid. Like it's about to spill out of my ears. I see the men I killed in prison in self-defense. All of them. The one in the laundry, the one in the yard, the one I nearly killed in the kitchen . . . I see them all like they are alive again.

"I am a killer," I say, swallowing something bitter and dry. "A natural born killer. Is that what you're trying to tell me, Joel?"

"If it smells like a killer, tastes like a killer, looks like a killer, guess what, Sidney? It's a fucking killer."

"But you arranged for my parole."

"I'll give you this much, Doc. You are indeed a killer. But your selection of victims was beyond reproach. You have a conscience, and you maintain high moral standards, much like most would-be, could-be doctors of medicine. Those blood teardrops tattooed to your arm are trophies, but they had it coming. Just like Wemps and Singh had it coming for what they did to Chen and his family. You did the cops a favor when you put those two madmen down. On more than one occasion Rabuffo asked you to kill some of his deadbeat Chinese tenants, but you refused. Once he even asked you to kill a woman. But you *married* her instead."

He lets loose with a belly laugh. It's like a shot to the heart.

"Penny," I whisper. I bite down on my swelled lip, taste the blood on my tongue.

"Penny owed the boss," he goes on. "She kept getting deeper and deeper and deeper. But you stepped in, covered her debt, just like

Rabuffo had done for you years before. You even married her, had a kid with her."

"Now she's dead," I say, my voice a hoarse whisper. "Your friend Chief Walton shot her."

I'm not certain he knows about Penny's murder. How could he? The news seems to drain the color from his face. He and Penny were lovers when I was away. Maybe he truly loved her. Maybe he knew full well the danger she faced when she agreed to this operation. Maybe one of his worst fears is now realized.

He clears the dismay from his throat. "Let me tell you something, Sidney. Take it from your lawyer. If Penny is dead because of Walton, then it's not your fault."

Am I supposed to thank him for that? Is the logic intended to comfort me?

I gaze into his blue eyes, breathe in and out. I'm trying to regain my equilibrium. Trying to set the newly regained memories aside for the moment. Concentrate on the here and now. The present.

"I'm not going back to prison, Joel," I say. "I have a daughter who needs me now."

He pulls the hammer back on the semi-automatic.

"Right now, I need you for something else," he says. "I think you know what that something else is."

I nod and I drown in a cesspool of defeat.

"Walk," he says.

He doesn't have to tell me where to go. I just do it. I step past the televisions to an area of wall that looks like all the rest. Using the tip of my left boot, I press it against a piece of base molding. A four-by-eight piece of wall panel slides open, revealing a glass elevator door. I punch in a code I memorized a long time ago, and the elevator door opens. Like Penny said, Rabuffo never bothered to change it.

I step inside, Joel following.

The door closes.

"I have to admit," he says, as the elevator begins its rapid descent. "You're being a good boy. A smart boy."

"I want to live," I say.

"Good to know, Sid. Looks like your communications skills have already improved one hundred percent."

CHAPTER 48

THE ELEVATOR COMES to a stop.

The door opens onto a brightly lit corridor. Numerous unidentified rooms occupy both sides of the long space, each of them protected by a solid metal door. But I know from personal experience these rooms are meant to house smuggled Chinese looking to be placed in any one of numerous Chinese restaurants between Albany and New York City—and now Lake Placid; all of them owned and operated by Rabuffo; all of them sweatshops.

Other spaces are for the production of crystal meth. And yet others for storage of the product. There are offices, conference rooms, a kitchen, a safe room made of metal and a special glass that's impervious even to the most sophisticated of listening devices. It's where we would hold our most sensitive meetings.

One more room, too.

The vault.

*   *   *

I stop when I come to the room.

It's covered not with the usual solid metal door, but instead, a safety glass–paneled door not unlike the one located outside the elevator up top. Once more I punch in a long-ago-memorized code, and the door unlocks with a burst of released air and solid gunmetal tubing. The door automatically slides into the wall, exposing a massive solid stainless-steel walk-in vault.

I step into the vault's narrow vestibule, feeling the weight of the gun behind me, even if the barrel is no longer touching me. Embedded into the solid steel vault wall beside the door is a retinal eye scanner, and below that, an eight-digit keypad.

"I think you know how to handle things from here, Doc," Joel comments. "You're doing great so far. As your lawyer, I advise you to keep it going."

I'm guessing that's supposed to be funny. Like I'm finding anything funny at this point. Like I don't have a gun pointed at my back by a man whose hell bent on seeing me head back to prison as soon as he gets what he feels he has coming. If it weren't for Chloe, I'd rather he shoot me dead.

Something dawns on me then. Yet another cold realization.

"You knew everyone would die, didn't you, Joel?"

"What are you talking about, Doc?"

"You knew that by orchestrating the abduction of my daughter, I'd stop at nothing to get her back. Even if I had to dispose of a few people along the way. Who were your partners in all this? The major partners, I mean. Detective Giselle Fontaine, Chief Joe Walton, and my wife, Penny. All of them, dead. There were more minor players like Singh, Burt and Claudia Stevens, even Tom Bertram and Gary and who knows how many Lake Placid police. They all played a part, but they were more like tools. You didn't really care whether they lived or died because you had every intention of stiffing them anyway."

He smiles, like he's proud of his handiwork.

"So how am I doing, Counselor?" I ask.

"Let me tell you something, Sid," he says. "One of the reasons I like you, and that Rabuffo liked you, is you're smart *and* ruthless. But then, smart and ruthless is a dangerous combination. Hitler was smart and ruthless. So was Dr. Joseph Mengele, but you gotta add crazy to that mix. Better that you were on our side than our sworn enemy."

"And how would you describe our relationship now, Joel?"

"It's complicated," he says. "Now why don't you be a good pal and open that vault."

Exhaling a bitter breath, I turn to the eye scanner, and position my no longer swelled left eye over the device. A bright but painless beam connects with my retina. It rapidly shuffles side to side several times until an electronic "APRROVED" message appears on the readout directly below the scanner. I then punch in the eight-digit code that will open the vault door, which happens to be my birthday in reverse of all things.

The room fills with the mechanical noise of numerous locks releasing inside the vault. When the door slowly opens, the brightly lit interior is revealed. That's when I make out the gunshot, and I feel the solid baseball bat–like connection to my lower abdomen. My knees buckle and a curtain of darkness falls.

CHAPTER 49

MY EYES OPEN.

Half-mast.

I'm shot. But I'm somehow still alive. Still breathing. It's like I'm looking through a thick fog. But I can see Joel Harwood systematically filling one plastic supermarket shopping bag after the other with cash. As soon as one bag is filled, he ties off the handles, sets it down onto the floor. He then pulls another one out of his jacket pocket, starts filling that one. I don't recall the denominations Rabuffo had on hand, but I do recall they were large and that there were lots of them.

Millions of dollars' worth of them.

I feel wet.

It's my own blood pool. I'm not sure where I've been hit, but I can feel my toes and I can move my limbs, telling me the bullet has avoided my spine.

That's the good news.

The bad news is this: if I don't get to a hospital soon, Harwood will realize his wish, and each and every person in the way of his being the sole recipient of Rabuffo's mother lode will be dead. What this means, of course, is that I'm not done killing.

The killer has one more enemy to euthanize.

He's got his back to me while he works quickly but steadily, emptying out the cubbies of my former boss's precious cash. I pull myself up onto my knees, and like a bleeding bull that's been speared nearly to death, I inhale one last deep breath, and charge the son of a bitch.

I hit him solidly in the lower spine with my forehead and shoulders. The hit is so violently delivered, I feel the air exit his body like a suddenly punctured tire. I hear and feel his ribs snap. He drops on the spot, his bag of cash spilling all over the floor. He's convulsing, trying to get his wind back. But he's also panicked. He's not used to going without his lungs.

I can't make out where he hid the pistol, so I'm hitting him square on the jaw with one foot and searching his pockets with the other hand. Until I feel the bottom of his boot connect with my chest, and just like that I'm being heaved across the vault floor.

I land on my back, the electric pain shooting from my abdomen, up and down my spine. For a beat, I'm sure I won't be able to make it back up onto my feet, and he's going to shoot me dead once and for all, the coup-de-grace bullet only seconds away from entering into my brain pan. But then I see Chloe's face in my mind. I see her pretty face as clear as day and I know I have no choice but to get up.

Breathing in, I jump back up to my feet, just as he finds his semi-automatic. He points the gun at me. Shoots. I thrust myself against the wall to my right. The bullet ricochets against the heavy vault door, sending sparks flying. The bullet bounces off the opposite wall. Harwood cries out. When I focus on him, I can see the bullet has traveled full circle and found a home in his left thigh.

"You stupid son of a bitch!" he spits. "Why won't you die already?"

I go after him again, this time my head ramming his belly. He screams again, grabs hold of both my ears with his hands, twists them so hard I feel like they're ripping off my skull. I send my knee up into his groin. He screams, releasing my ears. He triggers the pistol, three times. Three rounds bounce and ricochet against the vault's interior like the metal ball inside a pinball game.

"Die, killer!" he screams. "Die now! Just die!"

That's when I snatch the pistol out of his hand, press the barrel against his temple.

"You first," I say.

He looks up at me, wide eyed and disbelieving, breathing hard.

"Sidney, think about what you're doing," he says, smiling. "You're a healer. Not a murderer."

I pull the trigger.

Pushing myself away from him, I drop onto my backside, press my back up against the wall. I feel the dull, but throbbing pain in my lower abdomen, and I feel the blood slowly but steadily draining from it. But for some reason I'll never understand, I begin to laugh.

The laughter originates from deep inside my gut, almost like I'm puking up my dinner. But I haven't eaten anything in days and I don't feel sick. The pain from my internal injuries hasn't yet arrived. The adrenaline is pouring into my bloodstream and the shock of the bullet wounds is blocking the pain receptors in my brain. For now, anyway, I feel good, satisfied, relieved, and ... how do the snowflakes put it?

At one with myself.

My hand pressed against my exit wound, the other still gripping the semi-automatic, I manage to get back up onto my feet. I'm still laughing so hard, tears are pouring out of my eyes, down my face.

How absurd is all this? I'm standing all alone inside a vault that contains millions upon millions of dollars with my lawyer, whom I just shot dead, and I can't think of anything else to do but laugh.

Gazing down at Joel, his wide blue eyes looking back at me, his smooth-shaven face sprinkled with fresh blood. I know he can't see through the eyes anymore, but I sense them following my every move. I go to him, set myself down on one knee.

Pulling the hanky from his jacket pocket, I wipe the semi-automatic clean of prints, then I place it in his left hand, wrap his fingers around it. I maneuver his index finger so that it rests on the trigger. Returning the hanky to his jacket pocket, I stand, careful not to step in any of the blood that's pooled on the floor, including my own.

Reaching into his lower jacket pocket, I pull out two more garbage bags, and place them over my boots, tying off the handles around my ankles. I tiptoe my way across the floor and out into the corridor to the bathroom, where I pull a bunch of paper towels from the dispenser. Peeling four or five of them from the thick stack in my hand, I place them on the exit wound and pull my t-shirt back over them.

In the closet behind the door, I find a bottle of Lysol disinfectant, and I carry everything back into the vault. Dropping to my knees over the small puddle of blood I've left behind, I proceed to clean it up. It will be impossible to get everything. But if the forensics team that will surly descend on this place is convinced that what they are viewing is a corrupt lawyer who could no longer live with himself, then they will feel no need to vacuum the floor and walls for signs of secondary blood spatter.

. . . Hey, Doc, you never know. It's as good a plan as any . . .

When the vault is cleaned to my satisfaction, I peel two more bags from Joel's jacket pocket. In the first, I place all the blood-soaked paper towels, tying off the handles. I set the bag on the floor by the door so I won't forget it on my way out. Then, the second bag in hand, I make my way to the vault wall that has been untouched by Joel or anyone else since Rabuffo was tossed in jail. I fill the bag with cash until it can hold no more. Then I grab another bag and fill it, and another, and another.

Fill a bag with cash, rinse, repeat . . .

I have to laugh, because it's the most fun I've had in ten years. Or maybe I'm just giddy because of blood loss. Because death is circling me, like vultures around a gut-shot dog.

In my head, I see a sun-soaked beach.

Cuba.

Chloe and I are headed to Cuba.

CHAPTER 50

By the time I get back behind the wheel of the pickup truck, the morning sun has risen bright red/orange over the Blue Mountains to the east. Already the day is warm.

"Gonna be a scorcher," I comment to myself.

A vibration coming from inside my jeans pocket. I dig into the pocket, pull out my cell phone. A new text has arrived. This time from a number I most definitely recognize.

Drew Lochte.

But the message isn't from him.

It reads: Hi daddy, when are you coming back? I'm hungry.

My heart melts, but in a good way. A great way. In a way I have been dreaming about for ten solid years. I type,

On my way XOX

Setting the phone onto the seat beside me, I feel the throbbing of the exit wound, and I sense more of the warm blood slowly oozing out of me. I lift up my t-shirt, press some fresh paper towels against it, and try my hardest to avoid the dizziness that's filling my head.

. . . *Stay awake, Doc. Stay alert. Chloe needs you now . . .*

I peer at all those plastic shopping bags full of money on the truck floor, and I smile. I picture the ones I've stored behind the seat, and even the ones that are stored in the back cargo bed.

"Cuba, here we come, Chloe," I whisper aloud.

I'm in pain, but it feels good to say it.

Turning the engine over, I pull around Joel Harwood's Mercedes, and drive around the cobblestoned circle. I hook a right onto the private road that will lead me onto the main road. I pass the trees and the manicured lawn. I pass by the Olympic pool where I first met Penny and partied with my friends. I leave it all behind me, knowing I will never set eyes on this place again. And why in God's name would I want to?

I'm a different man now. I'm no longer a killer. The violence is all behind me. I've become a healer. I cure. I make things better.

Penny's gone, but somehow, I have everything I've ever wanted in the world. She's waiting for me. My daughter is waiting for me. We're going to have a beautiful life together. I'm going to watch her grow up. Grow up in peace. No more killing, no more struggles, no more lies, no more deception. No more blood tears tattooed to my arm. No more fury.

Just peace, love, and understanding.

Then comes the pain. The real pain. The receptors are no longer blocked. It throbs in my guts telling me my spleen and perhaps my liver are punctured. But I feel a smile growing on my face. It's a broad smile. I can live through this if I receive medical attention right away. I see the light at the end of the long ten-year tunnel. It's as bright as hell and it's warm and fuzzy. If only Penny could have lived to see this moment. If only she could have lived.

*   *   *

I drive on, the road two-sided by the old trees, shading me from the bright summer sun. I see them parked at the front gate. Five or six Albany PD blue and whites. Behind them, a black armored van. It bears the letters "SWAT" on its side panels in big white block letters.

I stop the pickup maybe twenty feet away from them, throw the transmission into park, allow the engine to idle. There's a big man dressed in black tactical gear standing in the center of the open gates. He's got a megaphone positioned against his lips.

"Sidney O'Keefe!" the man barks. "Come out of the truck with your hands up! Do it now!"

I roll down the window, my heart beating a mile a minute, my gut bleeding out.

"There must be some mistake!" I shout, weakly, breathlessly. "I'm going . . . to see . . . my daughter!"

"Get out of the truck, O'Keefe, and get down on the ground! Face . . . Down! Do it now! Or we will fire on you!"

"You're making a mistake . . . Please . . ."

Why don't they listen? Why can't they hear me? They have to hear me. That's how close I am. I peer down at my lap. I'm sitting in a puddle of my own blood. Not much time left. I need to contact my parole officer. He can talk them down. Talk some sense into them. Drew Lochte will take care of everything. He'll work it out so I can drive on, like nothing happened.

"Sidney O'Keefe!" the bullhorn voice blares. "Exit the truck now or we will have no choice but to fire on you!"

My eyes take in all the guns aimed directly at me. Semi-automatic and fully automatic short and long guns.

What the hell have I done to these people to make them so angry with me?

I make a quick search for the cell phone. It's slid down to the edge of the long seat during the drive out here. No choice but to reach for it, despite the pain in my gut.

"He's going for a gun!" a man shouts. "He's got a gun!"

I sit up straight, flip the phone open. I text,

CHLOE, DADDY LOVES YOU

Tears drop onto the phone while I text. Blood smears the screen.

"He's got a weapon!"

The front man drops the bullhorn to the pavement, draws his sidearm. Fires. They all fire. The truck shakes and trembles from the massive onslaught of lead, my body growing rapidly cold, my head spinning, the light growing brighter.

Using my left hand, I open the truck door. I try to step out, but fall flat onto the surface of the drive on my chest and face. The bullets rake the pavement. I feel the little bee stings, from the chewed-up bits of pavement colliding with my face. Until I can't feel them anymore. Until I can no longer see or speak or feel anything.

Have any rounds connected with my body?

I have no way of telling. It's most certainly possible, if not probable.

But in my mind, I see Chloe. I see Penny. I see us together, playing in the sand on a bright, sunny beach.

I see us happy forever . . .

. . . But wait.

Stop everything.

I need to clarify something here. Tennyson comes to mind again. Do we not live in dreams? After spending ten years in prison, we also learn to live in our imagination. We learn to control it.

So now . . . right now . . . I'm shutting down my mind, reining in my thought processes, putting an end to my fear of being killed by cops. What was I doing before my imagination sidetracked me? Before the dream went south?

Of course, I remember.

Rewind, then press play . . .

. . . I'm driving, the road two-sided by the old trees, shading me from the bright summer sun. Soon, the open front gates appear for me. The torn yellow crime scene ribbon is blowing in the summer breeze, along with the leaves on the trees. No police officers surround the gates. No SWAT team having assumed combat position with their automatic rifles and handguns. The coast is perfectly clear.

I drive through the gates, head south on the main road in the direction of downtown Albany. When, ten minutes later, I come to Fairlawn Avenue, the bleeding in my gut has all but stopped. It tells me the wound is mostly superficial. My luck is getting better all the time. Our luck. Chloe's and my luck.

I head up into the house, money bags in hand.

"One of these is yours, Lochte," I say, "if you help me . . . help us out."

He takes the bags from me, sets them on the floor.

"There's more in the truck," I inform. "If you wouldn't mind, I've got a wound to take care of."

My parole officer heads outside while I go to Chloe, who is still lying on the couch. Bending over, I kiss her face. She opens her eyes. Smiles.

"Guess I must have fallen back to sleep," she says, softly.

I glance at Susan, lying on her back, sound asleep, breathing in and out steadily.

"If I were you two, I'd sleep for years," I say. "But not yet. I need you to get up, Chloe. We're taking a trip."

"Where to, Daddy?" she says.

"Somewhere where the ocean water is crystal blue and the beach goes forever."

Her eyes light up. "I can make a huge sandcastle."

"Of course," I say. "I can help."

She looks at my side.

"You've been hurt, Daddy."

"Oh, it's nothing, Chloe. Looks worse than it is. I'm gonna go in the bathroom and clean it up while you get ready."

*   *   *

When I come back out of the bathroom, I feel like a new man. I've cleaned off most of the blood, washed my face, combed my hair. Turns out the bullet from Joel's pistol passed right through some loose flesh, avoiding the major organs altogether.

How lucky am I?

Chloe looks rested and fresh. Even the sadness of losing her mom seems to have disappeared.

Lochte has set all the cash bags on the dining room table.

"Can I trust you with all this?" I say, shoving a dozen cash stacks away in the old daypack. "When it's time, I'll send for more."

He nods.

"No worries, Sid," he assures. "I want you to know that Susan can stay with me. She has a home with me if she wants."

I smile. "You're a good man, Drew. She needs a solid father figure like you."

"Listen," he goes on. "While you were in the bathroom, I went online and purchased bus tickets for Florida. From there you'll charter a fishing boat my friend captains to Havana. No one will bother you there. Besides, you're an innocent man in my eyes. You will be in the eyes of the law, too, once the truth comes out."

He hands me the newly printed tickets. I stare at them resting in the palm of my hand.

"There's three," I say, perplexed.

Lochte smiles.

"That's where the surprise comes in, Sid."

A knock on the front door.

"Why don't you answer that," he goes on.

I go to the door, open it. She's standing there, a beaming smile painted on her face. Penny.

"Oh, my Lord," I say, my throat closing up on itself, my heart pumping against my ribs. "You are alive, and so beautiful."

I take her in my arms, squeeze.

"Don't squeeze too hard, Doc," she says. "Those bullets only caused flesh wounds, but they're still pretty tender. I've been in the emergency room all night. If you hadn't called 911 when you did, I might have been a goner."

I loosen my hold and back away.

"Sorry, baby," I say, tears in my eyes. "It's just that I thought I lost you for good. We both did." Then, my heart pulsing in my sternum, I turn. "Penny, there's someone here I think you'd love to see."

Penny approaches the door.

"Mommy! Oh my God, it's Mommy!"

Penny steps inside and takes her little girl in her arms and I swear she will never let her go again. They cry happy, sweet tears and they run their hands through one another's hair and they can't believe that any of this is for real. That is has to be some kind of vivid dream come true.

. . . It's all working out, Doc. It's working out the way it's supposed to . . .

"Okay, family," I say, throwing my arms around them. "We have a bus to catch."

*   *   *

The bus takes us south to Florida. It takes two full days, but eventually we end up in Key West, where we quickly head to the docks and board a large white fishing boat. The white-bearded captain is jovial and friendly. I call him Captain Hemingway and he seems to love it. We drink six cold beers apiece on the trip from Key West to Havana. After we pull into the docks, I hand him a full stack of Rabuffo's money, and tell him to "keep the change."

"Keep the change?" he bellows. "How's about I buy another boat!"

We all have a good laugh as he pulls away from the dock and disappears into the bright blue horizon.

* * *

It doesn't take us long to find a hotel right on the water and suddenly, just like that, we're back where we started. With Chloe down by the water's edge, digging a big hole in the sand. She's wearing a brand-new yellow polka-dot bikini, and she's found a friend to play with. A girl about her own age with long brunette hair and a blue one-piece bathing suit. They laugh and play, and it's a delight to watch them. Innocent kids with not a care in the world.

I'm seated on a chaise lounge, a cold bottle of Dos Equis set on a table by my side. When I look over my shoulder, I see Penny approaching me. She's wearing a black bikini, and she's holding her own bottle of beer in her hand.

She sets herself on the edge of the lounge, leans in for a kiss. Our lips lock for what seems a long time. But never long enough.

"Nice life you have there, Dr. O'Keefe," she says. "How about a little fishing tomorrow?"

"Life is but a dream, Pen," I say. "Yes, tomorrow we can fish in the morning, do a little house hunting in the afternoon. Man, the homes are cheap down here."

"Cuba is once more up and coming," she says. "Whatever we find will be one hell of an investment."

"Don't worry, we're never going to sell. Why leave paradise?"

She raises her beer to make a toast.

"To paradise," she says.

We touch bottlenecks with our eyes locked together or else break the spell of the toast.

We drink.

Coming up for air, Penny says, "Hey, Doc, now that things have calmed down, what say we take a little break and, ah, you know, get better acquainted?"

I sit up.

"Are you kidding?" I say, not without a smile.

"Chloe's got a friend and we'll only be gone a few minutes."

"Not a chance, my love. I've learned my lesson."

She purses her lips, nods.

"You know what?" she says, the brilliant sun glistening off her metal ring. "Silly idea. You're right. We both should know better." She places her hand gently on my leg. "Tell you what, we'll find a little time in the shower later, when Chloe is fast asleep."

"Now you're cooking with gas, Pen."

She looks up at me then. Her face has taken on a patina of seriousness and intensity. I feel the bright sun on my own face. It makes me feel young and healthy.

"I love you, Doc," she says. "I never stopped loving you. I'm glad you've come back to us."

I feel my eyes filling. Tears and bright light blur my vision. Happy tears.

"And I'm glad you came back to us," I say. "You are everything to me, Penny."

She leans into me entirely, resting her head on my chest. She holds my hand tight, and I feel her against my beating heart, and I breathe in her flowery fragrance, and I see our daughter happily playing in the sand. When she tosses me a wave, it's like my heart can't possibly fit all the love that's filling it. Raising my hand, I wave back, close my eyes, and say a silent prayer of thanks to my maker . . .

*   *   *

The bright overhead lights sting my eyes when I open them. This isn't sunlight. It is, instead, the light that pours down on me from a series of halogen lamps mounted to the ceiling in a post-operative/post-anesthesia care unit. The sweet, almost fragrant smell is the translucent oxygen mask that's been placed over my nose and mouth. An abundance of tubes, hoses, and electrodes have been connected to me and it's nearly impossible to move without pulling one of them out. But I manage to turn my head just enough to spot Chloe. She's holding my right hand with both her hands. She smiles now that she sees I'm awake.

"You did it, Dad," she whispers directly into my ear. "You're going to make it. The police, they know everything. And, boy oh boy, did they make a mistake when they shot at you. But you're okay now. You're free, Dad. We're together, Mommy is in heaven, and Susan is with your friend Mr. Lochte."

How I've managed to live through this ordeal is anybody's guess, but maybe it's the way the good Lord intended. Maybe I'm one of the lucky ones, the blessed ones. Maybe the former killer is being offered a second chance at life. An opportunity to raise his daughter in peace. Because that's what it's all about in the end. Living a full life in peace. It's all any of us can ask for.

Chloe is crying, her tears streaming down her face. I try my best to squeeze her hands as tightly as I can. I never want to let her go. Not ever. She is my reason for living.

Once more looking into the light.

I see Penny. See her big brown eyes, her smooth skin, her thick dark hair parted neatly over her left eye. She's throwing me a kiss from heaven. I can't exactly return the kiss. Not in my condition. But I sense she knows I'm kissing her back. My love, Penny. My Penny from heaven.

Chloe leans in once more, kisses my cheek. I've never really noticed before until now, how she has her mother's eyes. My hand gripped in her gentle hands, I feel in my heart that she is my home now. She is my sandy beach, my big blue ocean, my bright sunlight, my castle in the sand. She is why I've made it through the darkness to the other side. Made it back to the light.

I could ask her about the money bags I took from Rabuffo's vault, but she has no idea about them, and they are almost certainly in the hands of the police by now. They'll use it as evidence when they prosecute Mickey to the fullest extent of the law. It's possible I will be charged with something, too. I'll need a good lawyer once I'm healthy. Or even before I'm healthy. Of course, in the end, I'm still dead broke. But I have my daughter back and that's all any man can ask. Just being with her makes me the richest man in the world.

"Love you, Chloe," I whisper into the mask. "Always have. Always will."

Sidney "Doc" O'Keefe is back.

It's good to be home again. And let me tell you something else. I'm so, so damned lucky to be alive.